THEIR ISLAND HOME ✤ ✤

And when the elephants lifted their trunks and waved them about and started trumpeting, there was a general stampede.

(*Page 268*)

THEIR ISLAND HOME

THE LATER ADVENTURES OF THE SWISS FAMILY ROBINSON

By

JULES VERNE

**AUTHOR OF
TWENTY THOUSAND LEAGUES UNDER
THE SEA, THE MYSTERIOUS ISLAND,
THE LIGHTHOUSE AT THE END OF
THE WORLD, Etc.**

GROSSET & DUNLAP
Publishers - - New York

Printed in the United States of America

PREFACE

IN a long preface to the original French edition of this story—too long to be given in full here— M. Jules Verne tells how the stories of "Robinson Crusoe" and "The Swiss Family Robinson" were the books of his childhood, and of the imperishable impression they made upon his mind.

They influenced his bent in literature to a very marked extent—not only the two books named, but imitations such as "The Twelve-Year-old Robinson," "The Robinson of the Desert," and "The Adventures of Robert Robert," half-forgotten, perhaps now completely forgotten, French stories for young readers, and an island story of Fenimore Cooper's, "The Crater," which it is safe to say has not been read by one person for every hundred who have rejoiced in the great Leatherstocking series.

To this influence we owe "The Mysterious Island" and "Godfrey Morgan." There were also "The Robinsons at School" and "Two Years' Holidays," which have not yet appeared in English form. The author does not mention "Godfrey Morgan," by the way, but that book must surely be classed with these.

Jules Verne found the part of "Robinson Crusoe" which deals with the island "a masterpiece which is merely an episode in a long and tedious tale." But he drew delight from every page of "The Swiss Family Robinson." He came to believe, he says, that New Switzerland was a real island and he felt that the story did not really end with the arrival of the *Unicorn*. The surface of the island had not been fully explored.

PREFACE

Fritz, Frank, and Jenny Montrose had gone to Europe. They must have had adventures, and those adventures ought to be told. So he felt that he positively must write about them.

One can guess that the romancer of Amiens got out of his work upon this book—"Their Island Home" —and its sequel—"The Castaways of the *Flag*"—a pleasure at least equal to that he derived from the writing of any of the numerous volumes which have enchanted generations of boys. All his stories were very real to him; but one doubts whether any other was quite so real as these two, whether even Captain Nemo or Dick Sands were quite as dear to him as the Wolstons and the Zermatts.

The author of the original work was Rudolph Wyss, who was born at Berne in 1781, and died in 1860. The book which made him a popular author was not his only one, but the others seem to have been more the product of his mind as a professor than of his imaginative faculties, and they do not matter here. "The Swiss Family Robinson" was published (in German) at Zurich in 1812, and a first French translation appeared in 1813. The English version could not have been very long after this, and the book has maintained its popularity in England as in France and Switzerland, doubtless as in a dozen other countries.

"THEIR ISLAND HOME"

TRANSLATOR'S NOTE

It is a commonplace of criticism that sequels are unsatisfactory. For the most part they are, and the reason is fairly obvious. If the original story has been properly planned and written it should be a complete and completed thing with which the author has finished. If, yielding to public clamour for "more," he then professes to have regarded it merely as a "first part" of a larger thing and grafts something else on to it the probabilities are that his "second part" will prove to be but a mechanical invention mothered not by the necessity of inspiration but by some less noble emotion such as vanity or desire for further gain. Sir Walter Scott made no such blunder. He was not lured by the prodigious success of "Waverly" into putting forth any "farther adventures" of that somewhat precious young man but directed his creative powers upon a wholly new subject and while thereby satisfying the public desire for further romance set fresh laurels on his own brow and put more money in his purse.

Inspiration, in truth, is not to be captured. It comes from an outside source. And if sequels are to be written—and one must admit that sometimes they seem to be required—they should be written by another hand

TRANSLATOR'S NOTE

irresistibly compelled by the inspiration derived from the first originating genius. Robert Louis Stevenson could have written a better "second part" to "Robinson Crusoe" than was accomplished by Daniel Defoe and —to come to the particular—Jules Verne achieved a triumph when, his imagination fired by the one great work of Rudolph Wyss, he was impelled to carry it a further stage in "Their Island Home" and to its final stage in "The Castaways of the Flag."

Of the genius manifested by Rudolph Wyss, Jules Verne had much more than a double portion. An Island was ever his spiritual home and no one, not even Robert Louis Stevenson, was ever happier upon one. "Their Island Home" is a satisfactory sequel to "The Swiss Family Robinson" because it is essentially the spontaneous production of an original genius set in activity by something outside itself. Wherever "The Swiss Family Robinson" is read—and that is everywhere— "Their Island Home" and "The Castaways of the Flag" should be read. In French they are already established classics. I hope that in this English translation they will prove equally enduring.

CRANSTOUN METCALFE.

CONTENTS

[The sequel to this story is "The Castaways of the *Flag*,"
which is on sale at the same time and the same price.]

THEIR ISLAND
HOME ❧ ❧

THEIR ISLAND HOME

CHAPTER I

SHOTS ASHORE AND SHOTS AT SEA!

THE dry season set in at the beginning of the second week of October. This is the first spring month in the Southern zone. The winter in this nineteenth degree of latitude between the Equator and the tropic of Capricorn had not been very severe. The inhabitants of New Switzerland would soon be able to resume their wonted labours.

After eleven years spent upon this land it was none too soon to attempt to ascertain whether it was a part of one of the continents laved by the Indian Ocean or whether it must be included by geographers among the islands of those seas.

Since the rescue by Fritz of the young English girl upon Burning Rock, M. Zermatt and his wife, his four sons and Jenny Montrose had been happy on the whole. Of course they had at times fears of the future and of the great improbability of deliverance reaching them from outside, and they had, too, of memories of home and a longing to get into touch again with mankind.

To-day, then, at a very early hour, M. Zermatt passed through the orchard of Rock Castle and walked along the bank of Jackal River. Fritz and Jack were there before him, equipped with their fishing tackle. As for Ernest, always bad at getting up, yearning for five minutes longer between the sheets, he had not yet left his bed.

Mme. Zermatt and Jenny were busy within doors.

"Papa," said Jack, "it is going to be a fine day."

"I think it is, my boy," M. Zermatt replied. "And I hope that it will be followed by many more as fine, since we are at the beginning of spring."

"What are you going to do to-day?" Frank asked.

"We are going fishing," Fritz answered, showing his net and lines.

"In the bay?" M. Zermatt enquired.

"No," Fritz answered; "if we go up Jackal River as far as the dam, we shall catch more fish than we shall require for breakfast."

"And then?" said Jack, addressing his father.

"Then, my boy," M. Zermatt replied, "we shall not be at a loss for a job. In the afternoon, for example, I am thinking of going to Falconhurst to see if our summer dwelling requires any repairs. Besides, we shall take advantage of the first fine days to visit our other farms, Wood Grange, Sugar-cane Grove, the hermitage at Eberfurt and the villa at Prospect Hill. And then there will be the animals to attend to and the plantations to get into order."

"That, of course, papa," Fritz rejoined. "But since we can have an hour or two this morning, come along, Jack; come along, Frank."

"We are quite ready," cried Jack, "and I can feel

a fine trout at the end of my line already. Houp-la!
Houp-la!"

Jack pretended to gaff the imaginary fish caught
on his hook while calling in glad and ringing tones:
"Off we go!"

Perhaps Frank would have preferred to remain at
Rock Castle, where his mornings were generally
devoted to study. However, his brother pressed him
so eagerly that he made up his mind to follow him.

The three young men were going towards the right
bank of Jackal River when M. Zermatt stopped them.

"My children," he said, "your eagerness to go fishing
has made you forget——"

"Forget what?" Jack asked.

"What we have made a practice of doing every
year, at the beginning of the dry season."

Fritz came back to his father.

"What can that be?" he said, scratching his head.

"What—do you not remember, Fritz—or you,
Jack?" M. Zermatt persisted.

"Is it that we have not given you an embrace in
honour of the spring?" Jack replied.

"No, no!" Ernest answered, who had just come
out from the paddock, rubbing his eyes and stretching
his limbs.

"Then it is because we are going off without having
had breakfast, isn't it, Ernest, you young glutton?"
said Jack.

"No," Ernest replied, "it has nothing to do with
that. Papa only wants to remind you of our custom

of firing the two guns of Shark's Island battery every
year at this time."

"Precisely," M. Zermatt answered.

As a matter of fact, it had been the custom of
Fritz and Jack, on one of the days in the second
fortnight of October, at the end of the rainy season,
to go to the island at the entrance to Deliverance
Bay and rehoist the New Switzerland flag, then to
salute it with two guns whose report could be heard
quite distinctly at Rock Castle. After this, without
much hope, they took a survey of the whole sea and
shore. Perhaps some ship passing through those waters
would catch the sound of the two reports. Perhaps it
would soon arrive within sight of the bay. Perhaps
some shipwrecked people had even been cast upon
some point of this land, which they must suppose
to be uninhabited, and these discharges of ordnance
would give them warning.

"It is quite true," said Fritz, "we were about to
forget our duty. Go and get the canoe ready, Jack,
and we shall be back in less than an hour."

But Ernest objected.

"What is the good of this artillery racket? Think
of all the years we have fired our guns, only to wake
the echoes of Falcon's Nest and Rock Castle! Why
waste these charges of powder?"

"That is you all over, Ernest!" Jack exclaimed.
"If a cannon shot costs so much it must bring back
so much, or else be silent!"

"You are wrong to talk like that," said M. Zermatt
to his second son, "and I do not regard the cost as

wasted. To fly a flag over Shark's Island cannot be sufficient, for it would not be seen from far out at sea, while our cannon shots can be heard a good two and a half miles. It would be foolish to neglect this chance of making our presence known to any ship passing by."

"In that case," said Frank, "we ought to fire every morning and every evening."

"Certainly; just as they do in the navy," Jack declared.

"In the navy there is no danger of running short of ammunition," remarked Ernest, who was by far the most obstinate of the four brothers.

"Make your mind easy, my boy; we are not nearly out of powder," M. Zermatt assured him. "Two cannon shots, twice a year, at the beginning and the end of winter, only cost a trifle. It is my opinion that we should not discontinue this custom."

"Papa is right," said Jack. "If the echoes of Falcon-hurst and Rock Castle object to being disturbed from their sleep, well and good! Ernest will make an apology to them in verse, and they will be delighted. Come along, Fritz!"

"We must go and let Mamma know first" said Frank.

"And Jenny too," Fritz added.

"I will attend to that," M. Zermatt replied, "for the reports might cause them some surprise, and even lead them to imagine that some ship was coming into Deliverance Bay."

Just at this moment Mme. Zermatt and Jenny

Montrose, who were coming out of the verandah, stopped at the gate of the orchard.

After having embraced his mother Fritz gave his hand to the young girl, who smiled upon him. .And as she saw Jack moving towards the creek where the long boat and the pinnace were moored, she asked:

"Are you going to sea this morning?"

"Yes, Jenny," answered Jack, returning. "Fritz and I are making our preparations for a long voyage."

"A long voyage?" Mme. Zermatt repeated, ever uneasy about absences of this kind, however great her confidence might be in the skill of her sons in managing the canoe.

"Make your mind easy, my dear Betsy, and you, too, Jenny," M. Zermatt said. "Jack is only joking. It is only a matter of going to Shark's Island and firing the two regulation guns when the flag is hoisted, and of coming back after seeing that everything is in order."

"That is all right," Jenny replied, "and while Fritz and Jack are going to the island Ernest and Frank and I will go and fish—that is, of course, if Mme. Betsy does not want me."

"No, my dear child," said Mme. Zermatt, "and meanwhile I will go and get the washing ready."

After going down to the mouth of Jackal River, whither Jack brought the canoe, Fritz and he embarked. All wished them a good voyage and the light boat shot quickly out of the little creek.

The weather was fine, the sea calm, the tide favourable. Sitting one in front of the other, each in the narrow opening allotted to him, the two brothers plied their paddles alternately and rapidly drew away from Rock Castle. As the current bore a little towards the east, the canoe was obliged to approach the opposite shore, crossing the inlet which connected Deliverance Bay with the open sea.

At this time Fritz was twenty-five years of age. Vigorous and skilful, well trained in every physical exercise, a tireless walker and an intrepid hunter, this eldest son was a credit to the Zermatt family. His temper, in his boyhood rather bad, had become better. His brothers never suffered now, as they used to do, from those fits of anger of his which had often brought upon him remonstrances from his father and mother. Something had changed him materially.

He could not forget the young girl whom he had taken off Burning Rock, and Jenny Montrose could not forget that she owed her deliverance to him. Jenny was charming, with her fair hair falling in silky ringlets, her graceful figure, her pretty hands, and the fresh complexion which was not spoiled by the sunburn on her face. When she came into this family she brought into it what it had lacked till then, gladness of the home, and she was the good genius of the hearth.

Ernest, Jack, and Frank saw no more than a sister in this charming girl. But was it quite the same with Fritz? Was it the self-same emotion that made his heart beat so? Was it only friendship that Jenny felt for the brave young fellow who had come to her rescue? Already nearly two years had passed since that poignant incident upon Burning Rock. Fritz had not been able to live by Jenny's side without falling in love with her. And many a time did the father and mother talk of what the future held for these two.

If Jack's character had undergone any modification it was in the development of his natural inclination for all exercises which called for strength, courage and skill, and on this score he now had nothing to envy Fritz. His age was now one and twenty, his stature medium, his figure strapping, and he was still the same gallant, merry, pleasant, impulsive, and also good fellow as ever. He had not given up teasing his brothers, but they were always ready to forgive him. Was he not the best pal in the world?

The canoe sped like an arrow over the surface of the water. Fritz had not hoisted the little sail which it carried when the wind was favourable, because the breeze was blowing off the sea. On the return journey the mast would be stepped, and it would not be necessary to use the paddles to make the mouth of Jackal River.

Nothing happened to catch the attention of the two brothers during their short voyage of a couple of miles. To the east, the arid, desert shore showed only a long succession of yellowish dunes. To the west, the verdant coast extended from the mouth of Jackal River to the mouth of Flamingo River and beyond that to False Hope Point.

"There is no doubt," said Fritz, "that our New Switzerland does not lie in the course of any ships, and this Indian Ocean is pretty well deserted."

"Well," said Jack, "I am not so very keen upon their discovering our New Switzerland! A ship which touched at it would not lose any time in taking possession of it. And if it planted its flag here, what would become of ours? You may be quite sure it would not be a Swiss flag, seeing that it isn't exactly over the seas that Switzerland carries her flag, so we should run a considerable risk of not feeling ourselves at home any more."

"And the future, Jack: what about the future?" Fritz replied.

"The future?" Jack made answer; "the future will be a continuation of the present, and if you are not satisfied——"

"All of us are, perhaps," said Fritz. "But you forget Jenny; and her father who believes that she was lost in the wreck of the *Dorcas*. Must she not be longing to be restored to him? She knows that he is over there, in England, and how is she ever to join him there unless a ship arrives some day?"

"Quite so," said Jack with a smile, for he guessed what was going on within his brother's heart.

In about three quarters of an hour the canoe reached the low-lying rocks of Shark's Island.

Fritz and Jack's first business was to visit the interior and then to make a circuit of the island. It was important to ascertain the condition of the plantations made some years ago round the battery hill.

These plantations were much exposed to the winds from the north and north-east, which lashed the island with their full force before rushing down the funnel-like entrance into Deliverance Bay. At this point there were actually atmospheric backwaters, or eddies, of dangerous strength, which more than once already had torn the roofing off the hangar under which the two guns were placed.

Fortunately the plantations had not suffered excessively. A few trees were lying on the beach on the north side of the island, and these would be sawn up to be stored at Rock Castle.

The enclosures in which the antelopes were penned had been so solidly constructed that Fritz and Jack detected no damage done to them. The animals had abundant pasture there throughout the year. The herd now numbered fifty head, and was bound to go on increasing.

"What shall we do with all these animals?" Fritz asked, as he watched them frolicking between the quickset hedges of the enclosures.

"Sell them," was Jack's answer.

"Then you do admit that some day or another ships will come to which it will be possible to sell them?" Fritz enquired.

"Not a bit of it," Jack replied; "when we sell them it will be in open market in New Switzerland."

"Open market, Jack! From the way you talk one would suppose it won't be very long before New Switzerland has open markets."

"No doubt about it, Fritz; or that it will have villages and little towns, cities, and even a capital, which, naturally, will be Rock Castle."

"And when will that be?"

"When the provinces of New Switzerland have several thousand inhabitants."

"Foreigners?"

"No, no, Fritz," Jack declared; "Swiss: none but Swiss. Our native land has enough people to be able to send us a few hundred families."

"But it never has had any colonies, and I don't suppose it ever will, Jack."

"Well, it will have one, at any rate, Fritz."

"But our countrymen don't seem to show any inclination to emigrate."

"What about ourselves?" Jack exclaimed. "Didn't we develop the liking for colonisation—and not without some advantage?"

"Because we were obliged to," Fritz answered. "No, if ever New Switzerland is to be populated, I am very much afraid she won't continue to justify her name, and that the large majority of her inhabitants will be Anglo-Saxon."

Fritz was right, and Jack knew it so well that he could not refrain from making a grimace.

For at this period Great Britain was still frequently acquiring new possessions. Bit by bit, the Indian Ocean was always giving her fresh domains. So the great probability was that if a ship ever did come in sight, the British flag would be flying at her peak and her captain would take possession of New Switzerland and hoist the British flag on the summit of Prospect Hill.

When they had finished their inspection of the

island the two brothers climbed the hill and went to
the hangar where the battery stood.

Standing upon the edge of the upper terrace they
swept with their telescopes the whole vast segment
of sea contained between False Hope Point and the
cape which shut in Deliverance Bay to the east.

Nothing but a desert waste of water! Right out
to the extreme horizon, where sky and ocean met,
nothing was to be seen except, three or four miles
away to the north-east, the reef on which the *Landlord*
had run aground.

Turning their eyes towards False Hope Point, Fritz
and Jack perceived between the trees upon the hill the
belvidere of the villa at Prospect Hill. The summer
dwelling was still standing—which would be a satisfaction to M. Zermatt, who was constantly afraid that
it might be destroyed by some of the sudden squalls
of the rainy season.

The two brothers went into the hangar, which the
storms had spared, although there had been more
than enough thunderstorms and squalls during the
two and a half months that the winter had lasted.

Their next business was to run up to the head of
the mast near the hangar the red and white flag which
would wave there until the end of autumn, and to
honour it with the annual salute of two guns.

While Jack was busy taking the flag out of its
case and fastening it by the corners to the halyard,
Fritz examined the two carronades that were pointed
towards the open sea. They were both in good condition, and only required to be loaded. In order to

economise powder, Fritz was careful to use a wad of damped sod, as it was his practice to do, which increased the intensity of the discharge. Then he fixed in the touch-hole the quick match which would fire the gun the instant the flag reached the top of the mast.

It was then half past seven in the morning. The sky, cleared now of the mists of early dawn, was absolutely serene. Only towards the west a few wisps of cloud rose in delicate spirals. The breeze seemed dying down. The bay, glittering beneath the streaming rays of the sun, was almost dead calm.

As soon as he had finished, Fritz asked his brother if he was ready.

"When you like, Fritz," Jack answered, satisfying himself that the halyard would run without catching on the roof of the hangar.

"Number one, fire! Number two, fire!" cried Fritz, who took himself very seriously as artilleryman.

The two shots rang out one after the other while the red and white bunting fluttered out in the breeze.

Fritz busied himself reloading the two guns. But he had hardly put the cartridge in the second cannon when he jumped upright.

A distant detonation had just struck upon his ear.

At once Jack and he rushed out of the hangar.

"A gun!" cried Jack.

"No!" said Fritz. "It isn't possible. We are mistaken."

"Listen!" answered Jack, scarcely breathing.

A second detonation rang through the air, and then after an interval of a minute a third resounded.

"Yes, yes!" Jack insisted. "Those are cannon shots all right."

"And they came from the east," Fritz added.

Was it really a ship, passing within sight of New Switzerland, that had replied to the double discharge from Shark's Island, and would that ship steer her course for Deliverance Bay?

CHAPTER II

DIRECTLY the double report rang out from the battery on Shark's Island the echoes of Rock Castle repeated it from cliff to cliff. M. Zermatt and his wife, Jenny, Ernest, and Frank, running down at once to the beach, could see the whitish smoke of the two guns drifting slowly in the direction of Falconhurst. Waving their handkerchiefs, they answered with a cheer.

Then all were preparing to resume their several occupations when Jenny, who was looking towards the island through her telescope, exclaimed:

"Fritz and Jack are coming back."

"Already?" said Ernest. "Why, they have barely had time to reload the guns. Why are they in such a hurry to get back to us?"

"They certainly do seem to be in a hurry," M. Zermatt replied.

There could be no doubt that the moving speck revealed by the telescope a little to the right of the island was the frail boat being lifted swiftly along by the paddles.

"It is certainly odd," said Mme. Zermatt. "Can they have any news for us—important news?"

"I think they have," Jenny answered.

15

Would the news be good or bad? That was the question each one asked himself without attempting to answer it.

All eyes were fastened on the canoe which was growing larger to the sight. In a quarter of an hour it was halfway between Shark's Island and the mouth of Jackal River. Fritz had not hoisted his little sail, for the breeze was dropping, and by paddling the two brothers travelled faster than the wind over the almost unruffled waters of Deliverance Bay.

It occurred to M. Zermatt's mind that this hurried return might be a flight, and he wondered whether there would appear in chase some canoe full of savages, or even a pirate vessel from the open sea. But he did not communicate this highly alarming idea to anyone else. Followed by Betsy, Jenny, Ernest and Frank, he hurried to the far end of the creek, in haste to question Fritz and Jack.

A quarter of an hour later the canoe stopped by the nearest rocks, which served as landing stage, at the end of the creek.

"What is the matter?" M. Zermatt cried.

Fritz and Jack jumped out onto the beach. Quite out of breath, their faces bathed in perspiration and their arms worn out with exertion, they could only answer with gestures at first, pointing to the coast east of Deliverance Bay.

"What is the matter?" Frank repeated, grasping Fritz's arm.

"Didn't you hear?" Fritz asked at last when he had recovered his breath.

"Yes: you mean the two guns you fired from the Shark's battery?" said Ernest.

"No," Jack answered; "not ours; those that answered!"

"What?" M. Zermatt exclaimed. "Reports?"

"It isn't possible! It isn't possible!" Mme. Zermatt repeated.

Jenny had drawn near Fritz, and, pale with excitement, she asked in her turn:

"Did you hear reports near here?"

"Yes, Jenny," Fritz answered; "three guns fired at regular intervals."

Fritz spoke so positively that it was impossible to believe he had made a mistake. Besides, Jack confirmed what his brother said, adding:

"There can't be any doubt a ship is off New Switzerland and that her attention has been caught by the discharge of our two cannon."

"A ship! A ship!" whispered Jenny.

"And you are sure it was to the eastward?" M. Zermatt insisted.

"Yes, to the eastward," Fritz declared; "and I am sure now that Deliverance Bay can only be a few miles from the main sea."

This was very likely the case; but no one knew, as no exploration had yet ben carried out along that coast.

Great was the emotion of the inhabitants of New Switzerland after the first moment of surprise, almost of stupefaction.

A ship—there really was a ship within sight, a ship,

the report of whose guns had been borne by the breeze to Shark's Island! It was a connecting link by which this unknown land, where for eleven years the survivors of the wreck of the *Landlord* had lived, was united once more to the rest of the inhabited world! The cannon is the deep voice of ships that make long voyages, and that voice had just been heard for the first time since the battery on Shark's Island welcomed the returning dry season! It was almost as if this happening, on which they had ceased to count, took M. Zermatt and his people unprepared, as if this ship spoke a tongue which they had forgotten.

However, they pulled themselves together and only thought of the bright side of this new situation. This distant sound which had reached them was not one of those sounds of nature to which they had been so long accustomed, the snapping of trees by the violence of the gale, the roar of the sea broken by the tempest, the crash of the thunder in the mighty storms of this intertropical zone. No! This sound was caused by the hand of man! The captain and the crew of the ship which was passing by at sea could no longer suppose that this land was uninhabited. If they should come to anchor in the bay their flag would salute the flag of New Switzerland!

There was none of them but saw there the certainty of an impending deliverance. Mme. Zermatt felt herself freed from fears of the future; Jenny thought of her father, whom she had despaired of ever seeing again; M. Zermatt and his sons found themselves once more among their kind.

So the first emotion felt by this family was that caused by the realisation of their dearest wishes. Thinking only of the happy side of this great event, they were all full of hope and of gratitude to heaven.

"It is right that we should first give thanks to God, Whose protection has never failed us," said Frank. "It is to Him that our thanks ought to ascend and to Him that our prayers should be given."

It was natural for Frank to express himself so. His religious feelings had always been deep, and had become even deeper as he grew older. His was an upright, tranquil character, full of affection for his people, that is to say for what had been all human kind to him hitherto. Although the youngest of the brothers, he was yet their counsellor in the very few disputes that arose between the members of this most united family.

What would his vocation have been if he had lived in his native land? No doubt he would have sought in medicine, or the law, or the priesthood to satisfy the devotional need which was the basis of his being, as physical activity was in the case of Fritz and Jack, and intellectual activity in the case of Ernest. And so he sent up a fervent prayer to Providence, in which he was joined by his father and mother, his brothers, and Jenny.

It was necessary to act without delay. The ship, of whose presence no one would any longer admit a doubt, was probably anchored in one of the little bays along the coast, and was not passing by off New Switzerland. Would the sound of the guns to which it had replied induce it to set about the exploration of this land? Would it even try, perhaps, to make its entry into Deliverance Bay, after doubling the cape which closed it in to the east?

That was what Fritz maintained, and he wound up his argument by saying:

"The only thing we have to do is to go and meet this ship, following along the eastern coast, which must run from north to south."

"Perhaps we have waited too long as it is," said Jenny.

"I don't think so," Ernest answered. "It is out of the question that the captain of this ship, whatever it is, won't try to find out all about it."

"What is the good of all this talk, talk!" cried Jack. "Let us go!"

"Give us time to get the launch ready," said M. Zermatt.

"It would take too long," Fritz declared, "and the canoe will serve."

"Very well," said M. Zermatt. Then he added: "The important point is to behave with the utmost caution. I do not think it likely that any Malay or Australian savages have landed on the eastern coast, but the Indian Ocean is infested by pirates, and we should have everything to fear from them."

"Yes," said Mme. Zermatt, "and it would be better for this ship to go away if——"

"I will go myself," M. Zermatt declared. "Before we get into communication with these strangers we must know with whom we have to deal."

This decision was a wise one. It only remained to put it into execution. But as ill luck would have it, the weather had changed since the early morning. After having dropped, the wind had now veered to the west and was freshening perceptibly. The canoe could not have ventured into the bay, even if it had only been a matter of getting to Shark's Island. The sky was covered with clouds which were rising out of the west, squall clouds of which a sailor is always mistrustful.

But, failing the canoe, and although it might involve a delay of an hour or two in getting her ready, was it not possible to use the launch, heavy as the swell might be outside the mouth of the bay?

Hugely to his disappointment, M. Zermatt was obliged to abandon the idea. Before midday a veritable tempest was tossing the waters of Deliverance Bay, rendering them unnavigable. Even if this sudden change of weather could not last at this time of the year, at least it thwarted all their plans, and if the storm endured only twenty-four hours it might still be too late for them to find the ship. Besides, if its anchorage did not offer it absolute protection, it would almost certainly leave, and, with this wind blowing from the west, it would speedily be out of sight of New Switzerland.

Ernest, on the other hand, argued that the vessel would perhaps try to take refuge in Deliverance Bay if it happened to double the cape to the east.

"That is possible, it is true," M. Zermatt replied.

"and is even very much to be wished, provided it is not pirates we have to deal with."

"Well, we will keep watch, Papa," said Frank. "We will keep watch all day, and all night, too."

"If we could get to Prospect Hill, or even only to Falconhurst," Jack added, "we should be in a better position still to keep watch over the sea."

Obviously, but it was idle to think of that. During the afternoon the weather became worse. The fury of the squalls was twice as violent. The rain fell in such torrents that Jackal River overflowed its banks, and Family Bridge was within an ace of being swept away. M. Zermatt and his sons kept an unceasing vigil, and it was all they could do to prevent the flood from invading the enclosure of Rock Castle. Betsy and Jenny were unable to set foot outside. Never did day pass more heavily, and if the ship went away was it not only too certain that it would not return to these same waters?

When night came, the violence of the storm increased further. On the advice of M. Zermatt, who was compelled by his children to take some rest, Fritz, Jack, and Frank took it in turns to watch until day. From the gallery, which they did not leave, they had a view of the sea as far as Shark's Island. If any ship's light had appeared at the mouth of the bay they would have seen it; if any gun had rung out they would have heard it, in spite of the tumult of the waves which were breaking upon the rocks with an appalling din. When the squall abated, somewhat, all four wrapped themselves in their oilskins and went as far as the mouth of Jackal River, to satisfy themselves that the launch and the pinnace had not dragged their anchors.

The storm lasted for forty-eight hours. During the whole of that time M. Zermatt and his sons were barely able to get as far as halfway to Falconhurst in order to survey a wider sweep of horizon. The sea, white with the foam of rolling waves, was absolutely deserted. Indeed, no ship would have dared to venture close to shore during a storm like this.

M. Zermatt and his wife had already given up their hopes. Ernest, Jack, and Frank, who had been accustomed to their present existence since childhood, did not very greatly regret the loss of this opportunity. But Fritz regretted it for their sake, or rather for Jenny's sake.

If the ship had gone away and were never to return to these waters, what a disappointment it would be for Colonel Montrose's daughter! The chance of being restored to her father was slipping away. How long a time would elapse before this opportunity of returning to Europe would present itself again! Would it ever do so, indeed?

"Don't give up hope! Don't give up hope!" Fritz said over and over again, overwhelmed by Jenny's distress. "This ship will come back, or some other must come, since New Switzerland is now known!"

During the night of the 11th of October the wind veered back to the north and the spell of bad weather came to an end. Inside Deliverance Bay the sea

dropped quickly, and with daybreak the rollers ceased
to sweep onto Rock Castle beach.

The whole family left the enclosure and turned their
eyes out to the open sea.

"Let us go to Shark's Island," was Fritz's immediate suggestion. "There is no risk for the
canoe."

"What will you do there?" Mme. Zermatt asked.

"Perhaps the ship is still lying up under shelter of
the coast; and even supposing it was compelled by
the storm to stand out to sea, may it not have come
back again? Let us fire a few guns, and if they are
answered——"

"Yes, Fritz, yes!" cried Jenny eagerly.

"Fritz is right," said M. Zermatt. "We must not
neglect any chance. If the ship is there she will hear
us and make herself heard."

The canoe was ready in a few minutes. But as
Fritz was about to take his seat in it M. Zermatt
advised him to remain at Rock Castle with his mother,
his brothers, and Jenny. Jack would accompany
his father. They would take a flag in order to indicate whether there was any good news or whether
any danger threatened them. In the latter case M.
Zermatt would wave the flag three times and then
throw it into the sea, and Fritz was at once to take
the whole family to Falconhurst. M. Zermatt and
Jack would join them there as speedily as possible,
and if necessary they would then take refuge at Wood
Grange or Sugar-cane Grove, or even at the hermitage
at Eberfurt. On the other hand, if M. Zermatt waved

his flag twice and then planted it near the battery, that would signify that there was no ground for anxiety, and Fritz would await his return at Rock Castle.

Jack had brought the canoe to the foot of the rocks. He and his father stepped into it. A few cables' length outside the creek the heavy swell had given place to a slightly choppy sea. Driven by its paddles the boat sped rapidly towards Shark's Island.

M. Zermatt's heart beat fast when he drew alongside the end of the island; and it was at the top of their speed that he and Jack climbed the little hill.

Outside the hangar they stopped. From that point their eyes swept the wide horizon between the eastern cape and False Hope Point.

Not a sail was to be seen upon the sea, which was still rolling heavily far out.

Just as they were about to go inside the hangar M. Zermatt said for the last time to Jack:

"You are quite sure you heard——"

"Absolutely positive," Jack answered. "They really were reports that came from the eastward."

"God grant it!" said M. Zermatt.

As the guns had been reloaded by Fritz they only needed to have the match applied.

"Jack," said M. Zermatt, "you are to fire two shots at an interval of two minutes, and then you will reload the first gun and fire a third time."

"Very well, papa," Jack replied; "and you?"

"I am going to station myself at the edge of the

plateau that faces east, and if a report comes from that side I shall be in a good place to hear it."

As the wind had changed to the north, although it was very faint, the conditions were favourable. Any reports of heavy runs coming either from the west or the east must be heard easily, provided the distance were not more than three or four miles.

M. Zermatt took up his position by the side of the hangar.

Jack fired three guns from the battery at the intervals arranged. Then he ran at once to his father's side, and both stayed motionless, their ears strained towards the east.

A first report came distinctly to Shark's Island.

"Papa!" cried Jack, "the ship is still there!"

"Listen!" M. Zermatt rejoined.

Six other reports, at regular intervals, followed the first. The ship was not only answering, but seeming to say that things must not remain as they were.

M. Zermatt waved his flag and planted it near the battery.

If the reports of the ship's guns had not reached Rock Castle, at all events the people there would know that there was no danger to be feared.

And half an hour later, when the canoe had reached the creek again, Jack called out:

"Seven guns! They fired seven guns!"

"May heaven be praised sevenfold!" was Frank's reply.

Deeply moved, Jenny seized Fritz's hand. Then

she flung herself into the arms of Mme. Zermatt, who wiped away her tears and kissed her.

There was no doubt now about the presence of the ship. For some reason or another it must be lying up in one of the bays along the eastern coast. Possibly it had not been obliged to leave the bay during the storm; now, it would not leave without having got into direct communication with the inhabitants of this unknown land, and perhaps the best course would be to wait until it came in sight of the bay.

"No, let us go, let us go!" Jack insisted. "Let us go at once!"

But the cautious Ernest suggested some considerations of which M. Zermatt expressed approval.

How were they to find out what the ship's nationality was? Was it not possible that she might be manned by pirates who, as every one knows, were very numerous in the waters of the Indian Ocean at this period?

"Well," Fritz declared, "they must be answered as quickly as possible."

"Yes, yes, they must!" Jenny repeated, unable to control her impatience.

"I am going to put off in the canoe," Fritz added, "and since the state of the sea now allows of it, I shall have no difficulty in getting round the eastern cape."

"Very well," M. Zermatt replied, "for we cannot remain in this state of uncertainty. Still, before boarding this vessel it is necessary to know all about it. I will come with you, Fritz."

Jack intervened.

"Papa," he said, "I am accustomed to paddling; it will take more than two hours merely to reach the cape, and it may be a long way then to where the ship is anchored. I must go with Fritz."

"That will be much better," Fritz added.

M. Zermatt hesitated. He felt that he ought to take part in an undertaking like this, which called for caution.

"Yes, let Fritz and Jack go," Mme. Zermatt put in. "We can leave it to them."

M. Zermatt yielded, and the most earnest injunctions were given to the two brothers. After rounding the cape they were to follow the shore, glide between the rocks that studded that part of the coast, see before being seen, only ascertain the position of the vessel, on no account go aboard, and come back at once to Rock Castle. M. Zermatt would then decide what course to pursue. If Fritz and Jack could avoid being seen at all it would be better.

Perhaps—too—as Ernest suggested—Fritz and Jack might manage to be taken for savages. Why should they not dress themselves up like savages and then blacken their faces and arms and hands, as Fritz had done once, when he brought Jenny back to Pearl Bay? The ship's crew would be less astonished to meet black men on this land in the Indian Ocean.

Ernest's suggestion was a good one. The two brothers disguised themselves as natives of the Nicobars, and then rubbed soot all over their faces and arms. Then they embarked in the canoe, and half an hour later it was past the mouth of the bay.

Those left behind followed the canoe with their eyes as long as it was visible, and only returned to Rock Castle after they had watched it go out of Deliverance Bay.

Off Shark's Island Fritz manœuvred so as to get near the opposite shore. If a boat put off from the ship and rounded the extreme point, the canoe would have time to hide behind the reefs and remain on watch.

It took quite two hours to reach the cape, for the distance was more than five miles. With the breeze blowing from the north it would have been useless to set the little sail. It is true, the ebb tide had been favourable to the progress of the cockleshell of a boat.

This cape was about to be rounded for the first time since the Zermatt family had found refuge in Deliverance Bay. What a contrast it offered to False Hope Point, which was outlined ten miles away to the north-west! What an arid front this eastern part of New Switzerland presented! The coast, covered with sand dunes and bristling with black rocks, was set with reefs that stretched out several hundred fathoms beyond the promontory against which the ocean swell, even in fine weather, broke with never flagging violence.

When the canoe had rounded the furthest rocks,

the eastern shore revealed itself before the eyes of
Fritz and Jack. It ran almost due north to south,
forming the boundary of New Switzerland on this
side.   Unless it was an island, therefore, it must
be on the south that this land was joined to a continent.

The canoe skirted the coastline in such a way as
to be indistinguishable from the rocks.

A couple of miles beyond, within a narrow bay, a
vessel appeared, a three-master, with top-gallant-sails
unstepped, undergoing repairs at this anchorage.
Upon the neighbouring beach several tents were
pitched.

The canoe approached within half a dozen cables'
length of the vessel.   The moment they were seen
neither Fritz nor Jack could fail to apprehend the signs
of friendship made to them from on board.   They
even heard a few sentences spoken in the English
language, and it was clear that they were being taken
for savages.

On their part they could be in no doubt as to the
nationality of this vessel.   The British flag was flying
from the mizzen.   She was an English corvette carrying
ten guns.

Thus, there would have been no objection to
opening communication with the captain of this
corvette.

Jack would have liked to, but Fritz would not
permit it.   He had promised to return to Rock Castle
the moment he had ascertained the position and the

nationality of the ship, and he meant to keep his promise. So the canoe resumed her northward course once more, and after a voyage lasting two and a half hours passed through the entrance into Deliverance Bay.

CHAPTER III

THE BRITISH CORVETTE "UNICORN"

T HE *Unicorn,* a small ten gun corvette, flying the British flag, was on her way from Sydney to the Cape of Good Hope. Her commander was Lieutenant Littlestone, and she had a crew of sixty men. Although ordinarily a war-ship carries no passengers the *Unicorn* had received official permission to take on board an English family, the head of which was compelled by considerations of health to return to Europe. This family consisted of Mr. Wolston, a mechanical engineer, his wife, Merry Wolston, and his two daughters Hannah and Dolly, aged seventeen and fourteen, respectively. Mr. and Mrs. Wolston also had a son, James, who at this time was living in Cape Town with his wife and young son.

The *Unicorn* had left Sydney harbour in July, 1816, and after skirting the southern coast of Australia had turned her course towards the northeast waters of the Indian Ocean.

Lieutenant Littlestone had been ordered by the Admiralty to cruise about these latitudes and endeavour to find, either upon the western coast of Australia or in the neighbouring islands, traces of the existence of any survivors of the *Dorcas,* of whom no news had been heard for two and a half years.

It was not known precisely where the wreck had occurred, although there was no doubt about the catastrophe, since the second mate and three men of the crew had been picked up at sea and taken to Sydney, only those four out of all who were in the ship's longboat. As for Captain Greenfield, the sailors and the passengers—the daughter of Colonel Montrose among them—it would have been difficult to cherish any hope of their recovery after the story told of the wreck by the second mate. However, the British Government had desired that further search should be made in this portion of the Indian Ocean as well as in the approaches to the Timor Sea. There are many islands there not much frequented by trading vessels, and it was desirable to pay a visit to those in the neighbourhood of the seas where the *Dorcas* had probably been lost.

So, after doubling Cape Leeuwin, at the southwest extremity of Australia, the *Unicorn* had borne northwards. She touched at a few of the Sunday Islands without result, and resumed her journey to the Cape. It was then that she met with a succession of violent storms against which she had to struggle for a whole week, sustaining serious damage, which compelled her to seek some anchorage for repairs.

On the 8th of October the lookout descried to the southward a land—in all probability an island—which was not marked in the latest charts. Lieutenant Littlestone steered for this land and found refuge in the heart of a bay on its eastern coast which was completely sheltered from adverse winds and offered an excellent anchorage.

The crew set to work at once. Tents were pitched on the beach at the foot of the cliff. A regular camp was arranged, and every precaution taken that prudence dictated. It was quite possible that this coast was inhabited or visited by savages, and as everybody knows the natives of the Indian Ocean have an evil reputation.

The *Unicorn* had been at her moorings for two days when, on the morning of the 10th of October, the attention of the commander and the crew was arrested by a double detonation coming from the west.

This double report was entitled to a reply, and the *Unicorn* answered with the discharge of three guns from her port side.

Lieutenant Littlestone could do nothing but wait. His ship, being still in dock undergoing repair, could not have got under way and rounded the cape on the north-east. Several days were required before she would be in a condition to put to sea. And in any case, he assumed that the corvette's guns had been heard, since the wind was blowing off the sea, and he quite expected to see some ship come within sight of the bay at any moment.

So lookout men were posted at the mast-head. Evening came yet no sail had appeared. The sea to the north was absolutely deserted, as was that portion of the coast bounded by the bend of the bay. As for landing a detachment of men and sending it to reconnoitre, Lieutenant Littlestone decided not to do this from prudential considerations. Besides, the circumstances did not appear to demand it imperatively. Directly the *Unicorn* was in a fit state to leave her moorings she would follow round the coastline of this land, whose precise position had now been definitely fixed as latitude 19°30', longitude 114°5' east of the meridian of Ferro Island which belongs to the Canary Islands group in the Atlantic Ocean.

Three days passed without anything fresh happening, except, indeed, a violent storm, which caused wide and profound disturbance but left the *Unicorn* unharmed under the protection of the coast.

On the 13th of October several reports of cannon were heard from the same direction as the former ones.

To this fire, each discharge of which was separated by an interval of two minutes, the *Unicorn* replied with seven guns fired at equal intervals. Inasmuch as the new reports did not seem to come from any nearer point than those which had preceded them, the commander concluded that the ship whence they proceeded could not have changed her position in the meantime.

On this same day, about four o'clock in the afternoon, Lieutenant Littlestone, while pacing the bridge with his spyglass in use, caught sight of a little boat. Manned by two men, it was gliding between the rocks, coming from the promontory. These men, who were black-skinned, could only be Malay or Australian aborigines. Their presence was proof that this portion of the coast was inhabited, and accordingly steps were taken to be prepared for an attack, an eventuality always to be feared in these waters of the Indian Ocean.

However, the canoe drew near, a craft resembling an Esquimau kayak. It was allowed to approach. But when it was within three cables' length of the corvette, the two savages spoke in a language which was absolutely unintelligible.

Lieutenant Littlestone and his officers waved their handkerchiefs and held up their hands to show that they were unarmed. But the canoe showed no disposition to draw nearer. A moment later it sped rapidly away, to disappear behind the promontory.

At nightfall Lieutenant Littlestone took counsel with his officers as to sending the ship's longboat to reconnoitre the northern coast. The situation was certainly one which required to be cleared up. It could not have been the aborigines who had fired the guns which had been heard in the morning. Beyond all question there must be a ship on the west of the island, and perhaps she was in distress and asking for assistance.

Accordingly it was decided that a reconnaissance should be made next morning in that direction and the ship's boat was on the point of being launched, at nine o'clock, when Lieutenant Littlestone stopped the proceedings.

There had just appeared at the extreme point of the cape, not a kayak, nor yet one of the canoes commonly in use among the aborigines, but a light vessel of modern construction, a pinnace of some fifteen tons. As soon as she had drawn near the *Unicorn* she hoisted a red and white flag.

The astonishment of the commander, officers, and crew of the corvette can be imagined when they saw a canoe put off from the pinnace, carrying a white flag at the stern in sign of friendship, and make straight for the corvette.

Two men came aboard the *Unicorn* and introduced themselves. They were Swiss, Jean Zermatt and his eldest son Fritz, survivors of the wrecked *Landlord*, of whom no news had ever been heard.

The Englishmen welcomed most heartily the father and son, and Lieutenant Littlestone responded with alacrity to the invitation they gave him to go on board their pinnace.

It was only natural that M. Zermatt should feel some pride when presenting the commander of the *Unicorn* first to his brave helpmate and then to his other three sons. It was impossible not to admire their resolute bearing, their intelligent faces, their splendid health. Every member of this family was good to look upon. Then Jenny was introduced to Lieutenant Littlestone.

"But what land is this, where you have been living for these twelve years past, M. Zermatt?" he enquired.

"We have named it New Switzerland," M. Zermatt replied, "a name which it will always keep, I hope."

"Is it an island, commander?" Fritz asked.

"Yes: an island in the Indian Ocean, which was not marked on the charts."

"We did not know that it was an island," Ernest observed, "for we have never left this part of the coast, fearing that we might meet with danger."

"You did right, for we have seen some aborigines," Lieutenant Littlestone replied.

"Aborigines?" echoed Fritz, unable to conceal his surprise.

"Sure," the commander declared. "Yesterday—in a kind of canoe, or rather a kayak."

"Those aborigines were only my brother and myself," Jack answered, laughing. "We blackened our faces and arms in order to be taken for savages."

"Why disguise yourselves?"

"Because we did not know whom we had to deal with, commander and your ship might have been a pirate ship!"

"Oh!" said Lieutenant Littlestone. "One of the ships of His Majesty King George III.!"

"I quite agree," Fritz replied, "but we thought it better to get back to our dwelling at Rock Castle so as to return all together."

"I must add," M. Zermatt put in, "that we should have done so at break of day. Fritz and Jack had observed that your corvette was undergoing repairs, and so we were sure of finding her in this bay."

Jenny's happiness was great when the commander told her that he knew Colonel Montrose by name. Further, before the *Unicorn* had sailed for the Indian Ocean the papers had reported the Colonel's arrival at Portsmouth, and later in London. But since, subsequently to this, the news had been published that the passengers and crew of the *Dorcas* had all perished, with the exception of the second mate and the three sailors landed at Sydney, one can imagine the despair that must have racked the unhappy father at the thought of his daughter's death. His grief could only be equalled by his joy when he should learn that Jenny had survived the wreck of the *Dorcas*.

Meanwhile the pinnace was getting ready to return to Deliverance Bay, where M. and Mme. Zermatt proposed to offer hospitality to Lieutenant Littlestone. The latter, however, wished to keep them until the end of the day. And then, as they agreed to spend the night in the bay, three tents were pitched at the foot of the rocks, one for the four sons, another for the father and mother, and the third for Jenny Montrose.

And then the history of the Zermatt family could be related in full detail, from the moment of their setting foot on this land of New Switzerland. It was only natural that the commander and his officers should express their keen desire to go and see the arrangements of the little colony and the comfortable accommodations they had made at Rock Castle and Falconhurst.

After an excellent repast served on board the *Unicorn,* M. and Mme. Zermatt with their four sons and Jenny took leave of Lieutenant Littlestone and sought the shelter of the tents within the bay.

When he was alone with his wife M. Zermatt spoke to her as follows:

"My dear Betsy, an opportunity is afforded us of returning to Europe, of seeing our fellow-countrymen and our friends once more. But it behooves us to think that our position is altered now. New Switzerland is no longer an unknown island. Other ships will be putting in here before long."

"Of what are you doubtful?" Mme. Zermatt asked.

"I am trying to decide whether or not we should take advantage of this opportunity."

"My dear," Betsy replied, "ever since yesterday I have been thinking earnestly, and this is the result. Why should we leave this land, where we are so happy? Why should we try to renew relations which time and absence must have broken altogether? Have we not come to an age when one longs too ardently for rest to face the risks of a long voyage?"

"Ah! my dear wife," cried M. Zermatt, embracing her, "you have understood me! Yes, it would be almost like ingratitude to Heaven to forsake our New Switzerland! But it is not we alone who are concerned. Our children——"

"Our children," Betsy rejoined. "I quite understand that they should long to return to their own country. They are young; they have the future before them; and although their absence must be a great grief to us, it is only right to leave them free."

"You are right, Betsy; I agree with you."

"Let our boys sail on the *Unicorn,* my dear.   If they go, they will come back."

"And we must think of Jenny, too," said M. Zermatt.   "We cannot forget that her father, Colonel Montrose, has been in England two years, has been mourning her for two years.   It is only natural that she should want to see her father again."

"It will be a great sorrow for us when we see her go," Betsy replied; "she has become a daughter to us.   Fritz has a deep affection for her, and the affection is returned.   But Jenny is not ours to dispose of."

M. and Mme. Zermatt talked long of all these things.   They quite realised the consequences involved by the alteration in their situation, and it was at a very late hour that night that sleep came to them.

The next day, after having left the bay, rounded Cape East, and gained Deliverance Bay, the pinnace landed Lieutenant Littlestone, two of his officers, the Zermatt family, and the Wolstons at the mouth of Jackal River.

The Englishmen were as full of admiration and surprise as Jenny Montrose had been when visiting Rock Castle for the first time.   M. Zermatt received his guests at his winter habitation before taking them to see the chateau of Falconhurst, the villa at Prospect Hill, the farms at Wood Grange and Sugar-cane Grove, and the hermitage at Eberfurt. Lieutenant Littlestone and his officers could not

fail to marvel at the prosperity of this Promised
Land, all due to the courage and intelligence of a
shipwrecked family during their eleven years' stay
on this island. At the end of the repast which was
served to them in the great hall of Rock Castle they
did not forget to drink a toast in honour of the colonists
of New Switzerland.

In the course of this day Mr. Wolston, with his
wife and his two daughters, had an opportunity of
becoming much more intimate with M. and Mme.
Zermatt. Before they separated for the night, Mr.
Wolston spoke thus:

"M. Zermatt, have I your permission to speak quite
frankly and confidentially?"

"Of course."

"The existence you lead upon this island delights
me," said Mr. Wolston. "I fancy I am better already
in the midst of all these beauties of nature, and I
should think myself fortunate to live in a corner of
your Promised Land, provided, of course, you would
be so kind as to give your consent."

"Rest assured of it, Mr. Wolston!" M. Zermatt
replied with enthusiasm. "My wife and I would be
enchanted to admit you a member of our little colony
and to share its happiness with you. Moreover, so
far as we two are concerned, we have made up our
minds to end our days in New Switzerland, which has
become our second fatherland, and our intention is
never to leave it."

"Three cheers for New Switzerland!" cried their
guests gaily.

And in honour of New Switzerland they emptied their glasses which had been filled with the Canary wine which Mme. Zermatt substituted for the native wine on great occasions.

"And three cheers for those who want to stay here whatever happens!" added Ernest and Jack.

Fritz had not said a word, and Jenny was silent and hung her head.

Afterwards, when the visitors had gone in the ship's boat sent from the *Unicorn* to fetch them, and Fritz was alone with his mother he embraced her without venturing to speak.

Then seeing her so affected by the idea that her eldest son was thinking of leaving her, he dropped upon his knees beside her and cried:

"No, mother, no; I will not go away!"

And Jenny, who had joined them, threw herself into Mme. Zermatt's arms and said over and over again:

"Forgive me! forgive me, if I am causing you pain; I who love you as if you were my own mother! But, over there . . . my father . . . have I any right to hesitate?"

Mme. Zermatt and Jenny remained together. And when their conversation was ended it seemed as if Betsy were almost resigned to a separation.

M. Zermatt and Fritz came back at this moment and Jenny returned to M. Zermatt.

"My father," she said—it was the first time that she had so addressed him—"bless me as my mother has just blessed me! Let me—let us— leave for Europe! Your children will come back to

you, and you need not fear that anything can ever
separate them from you. Colonel Montrose is a man
of feeling who will wish to pay his daughter's debt.
Let Fritz come to England to meet him. Trust us to
each other. Your son will answer for me as I will
answer for him!"

Finally, this was what was arranged, with the
consent of the commander of the *Unicorn*. The
landing of the Wolstons would set some berths on
the corvette free. Fritz, Frank, and Jenny were to
embark upon her accompanied by Dolly, the younger
of the Wolston girls. Dolly was to go to Cape Town
to join her brother whom she would then bring back
to New Switzerland with his wife and child. As
for Ernest and Jack, they would not hear of leaving
their parents.

Lieutenant Littlestone's mission was accomplished,
for he had found Jenny Montrose, the sole survivor
of the passengers on the *Dorcas,* and in this island
of New Switzerland had discovered an excellent
anchorage in the Indian Ocean. And since M. Zermatt,
who in his capacity of its first occupier was its owner,
desired to offer it to Great Britain, Lieutenant Littlestone promised to take the matter to a satisfactory
conclusion and to bring back the formal acceptance of
the British Government.

The presumption, therefore, was that the *Unicorn*
would return to take possession of the island. She
would bring back Fritz, Frank, and Jenny Montrose, and would also embark at Cape Town James
Wolston with his sister Dolly, and his wife and

child. Fritz would provide himself, with the consent of M. and Mme. Zermatt, with the papers necessary for his marriage—a marriage of which Colonel Montrose would be delighted to approve. Everybody took it for granted that the colonel would want to accompany the young couple to New Switzerland.

So everything was arranged. But still it would not be without much sorrow that the members of the Zermatt family would be separated for a time. Of course when Fritz came back, with Frank and Jenny, and Jenny's father, with perhaps other colonists who might ask leave to accompany them, there would be nothing but happiness—happiness that nothing would disturb thereafter, and a prosperous future for the colony!

Preparations were made at once for the start. A few days more and the *Unicorn* would be ready to leave the bay upon the coast to which her name had been given. Directly her rigging had been repaired and reset, the corvette would stand out to sea again and turn her course towards the Cape of Good Hope.

Jenny naturally wanted to take away, or, rather, take to Colonel Montrose, the few articles she had made with her own hands upon Burning Rock. Each one of them would be a reminder of the existence she had endured so bravely during more than two years of utter solitude. So Frank took charge of these things, which he would guard like priceless treasure.

M. Zermatt placed in the hands of his two sons
everything that had marketable value and could be
converted into money in England, the pearls, which
would produce a considerable sum, the coral picked
up along the islands in Nautilus Bay, the nutmegs
and vanilla pods, with which several sacks were filled.
With the cash realised by the sale of these various
products, Fritz was to buy the material and stores
necessary to the colony—stores which would be sent
out by the first ship on which the future colonists might
take passage with their own outfit. The whole would
form a cargo large and valuable enough to require a
vessel of several hundred tons.

M. Zermatt, on his part, made various exchanges
with Lieutenant Littlestone. He thus procured several
casks of brandy and of wine, clothes, linen, stores,
and a dozen barrels of powder, shot, lead and bullets.
Inasmuch as New Switzerland was able to supply the
needs of her inhabitants, it was of the first importance
to make sure of an adequate supply of fire-arms.
These were indispensable, not only for hunting but
also for purposes of self-defence in the event, possible
if unlikely, of the colonists being attacked by pirates
or even by aborigines.

At the same time the commander of the *Unicorn*
undertook to return to the families of the passengers
who had perished the valuable securities and the
jewelry that had been found on board the *Landlord*.
As for the journal of his life which M. Zermatt had
kept from day to day, Fritz was to arrange for its
publication in England in order to secure the place to

which New Switzerland was entitled in geographical nomenclature.[1]

All these preparations were completed the day before the departure. Every moment that Lieutenant Littlestone could spare from his work he spent in the bosom of the Zermatt family. All hoped that before a year should have passed, after touching at the Cape, and after having received in London the Admiralty's orders with respect to the colony, he would return to take official possession of it in the name of Great Britain. When the *Unicorn* returned the Zermatt family would be reunited for good and all.

At last the 19th of October arrived.

The day before the corvette had left Unicorn Bay and dropped anchor within a cable's length from Shark's Island.

It was a sad day for M. and Mme. Zermatt, and for Ernest and Jack, from whom Fritz and Frank and Jenny would be parting the next morning, and it was a sad day for Mr. and Mrs. Wolston, too, since their daughter Dolly was leaving also.

At daybreak the launch took the passengers to Shark's Island. M. and Mme. Zermatt, Ernest and Jack, Mr. and Mrs. Wolston, and Hannah accompanied them.

It was on that island at the entrance into Deliverance Bay that the last farewells were exchanged, while the launch took the baggage to the corvette.

[1] It was this journal which appeared under the title of "The Swiss Family Robinson."

There could be no question of writing, since no means of communication existed between England and New Switzerland. No; they only spoke of seeing each other once more, of returning as speedily as might be, and of resuming their life together again.

Then the ship's boat of the *Unicorn* came for Jenny Montrose, for Dolly Wolston entrusted to her care, and for Fritz and Frank, and took them on board.

Half an hour later the *Unicorn* weighed anchor, and with a fair north-east breeze behind her she stood out to the open sea, after having saluted the flag of New Switzerland with a discharge of three guns.

To this salute the guns from the battery on Shark's Island, fired by Ernest and Jack, replied.

An hour later the top sails of the corvette had disappeared behind the farthest rocks of False Hope Point.

CHAPTER IV

IT will now be proper to give the reader a summary of the first ten years spent in New Switzerland by the survivors of the wreck of the *Landlord*.

On the 7th of October, in the year 1803, a family was cast upon an unknown land situated in the east of the Indian Ocean.

The head of this family, of Swiss origin, was named Jean Zermatt, his wife was named Betsy. The former was thirty-five years of age, the latter thirty-three. They had four children, all sons, in the following order of birth: Fritz, then fifteen; Ernest, twelve; Jack, ten; and Frank, six.

It was on the seventh day of an appalling storm that the *Landlord*, on which they had embarked, was driven out of her course in the midst of the ocean. Blown southwards, far beyond Batavia, her port of destination, she struck a mass of rock about four miles from the coast.

M. Zermatt was an intelligent and well-informed man, his wife a brave and devoted woman. Their children presented varieties of character. Fritz was bold and active, Ernest the most serious and studious of the four, though inclined to be selfish, Jack thoughtless and full of fun, Frank still almost a baby. They were a most united family, quite capable of doing well even in the terrible conditions into which evil fortune had just plunged them. Moreover, all of them were animated by deep religious feeling.

M. Zermatt had realised his few effects and left the land of his birth to settle in one of those Dutch over-sea possessions which at that time were at the height of their prosperity, and offered so much promise to active and hardworking men. Now, after a fair voyage across the Atlantic and the Indian Oceans, the ship which carried him and his family had been cast away. He and his wife and children, alone of all the crew and passengers of the *Landlord,* had survived the wreck. But it was necessary to abandon without the least delay the ship, entangled among the rocks of the reef. Her hull rent, her masts broken off, her keel snapped in half, and exposed to all the waves of the open sea, the next gale would complete her destruction and scatter her fragments far and wide.

Fastening half a dozen tubs together by means of ropes and planks, M. Zermatt and his sons succeeded in making a sort of raft, on which all the family took their seats before the day drew to an end. The sea was calm, scarcely heaving with a slow swell, and the flowing tide ran towards the coast. After leaving a long promontory on the starboard side, the floating raft came ashore in a little bay where a river emptied itself.

As soon as the various articles brought from the ship had been set ashore a tent was pitched in this spot which afterwards received the name of Tent Home. The encampment was gradually completed with the ship's cargo which M. Zermatt and his sons went on the following days to take from the hold of the *Landlord,* utensils, furniture, bedding, tinned meats, grain of various kinds, plants, sporting guns, casks of wine and liqueurs, tins of biscuits, cheeses and hams, clothes, linen, everything, in short, which was carried in this four-hundred ton vessel freighted to supply the requirements of a new colony.

They found that game, both furred and feathered, swarmed upon this coast. Whole flocks and herds were seen, of agoutis, a kind of hare with head like that of a pig, ondatras, a species of musk rat, buffaloes, ducks, flamingoes, bustards, grouse, peccaries, and antelopes. In the waters of the bay which spread beyond the creek was abundance of salmon, sturgeon, herrings, and a score of other species of fish, as well as mussels, oysters, lobsters, crayfish, and crabs. In the surrounding country, where cassava and sweet potatoes flourished, cotton trees and cocoa trees were growing together with mangroves, palms and other tropical species.

Thus existence seemed to be assured to these ship-wrecked folk, upon this land of whose bearings they knew nothing at all.

It had been found possible to land a number of domestic animals—Turk, an English dog; Floss, a Danish bitch; two goats, six sheep, a sow in farrow, an ass, a cow, and a perfect poultry yard of cocks, hens, turkeys, geese, ducks, and pigeons, which soon acclimatised themselves to the surface of the ponds and marshes and the grass lands adjoining the coast.

The final trips to the ship had emptied it of everything valuable or useful that it contained. Several four-pounder cannons were conveyed to the shore for the defence of the encampment, and also a pinnace, a light vessel which, as all its pieces were numbered, could easily be put together, and to which the name *Elizabeth* was given in compliment to Betsy. M. Zermatt was then master of a ship, brigantine-rigged, fifteen tons burthen, with square stern and after deck. Thus he had every facility for exploring the seas either to the east or the west, and for rounding the neighbouring promontories, one of which broke away towards the north in a sharp point while the other stretched out opposite Tent Home.

The mouth of the river was framed within lofty rocks which rendered it difficult of access, and self-defence there would be easy, at any rate against wild beasts.

One question which arose was as to whether the Zermatts had reached the shore of an island or of a continent washed by the waters of the Indian Ocean. The only information they had on this point was derived from the bearings taken by the commander of the *Landlord* before the shipwreck.

The ship was approaching Batavia when she was struck by a storm which lasted for six days and threw her far out of her course, to the south-east. The day before the captain had fixed his position as being latitude 13° 40′ south, and longitude 114° 5′ east of the island of Ferro in the Canary Group. As the wind had blown constantly from the north, it was a fair assumption that the longitude had not varied appreciably. By keeping the meridian at about the hundred and fourteenth degree, M. Zermatt concluded from an observation of latitude, taken with a sextant, that the *Landlord* must have drifted approximately six degrees southward, and consequently, that the coast of Tent Home could be located between the nineteenth and the twentieth parallels.

It followed that this land must be, in round figures, between six and seven hundred miles west of Australia. And so, although he did possess the pinnace, M. Zermatt would never have dared, however ardent his desire to return to his native country, to trust his family to so fragile a vessel and expose them to the dangers of the violent cyclones and tornadoes common in these seas.

In the predicament in which they now found themselves, the shipwrecked family could only look to Providence for help. At this date, sailing vessels making for the Dutch colonies hardly touched this part of the Indian Ocean. The western coast of Australia was almost unknown, offered the greatest difficulties in the way of landing, and had no geographical or commercial importance.

At the outset the family were content to live under canvas at Tent Home, near the right bank of the water-course which they had named Jackal River, in commemoration of an attack made upon them by those carnivorous animals. But the heat, untempered by the sea-breeze, became stifling between these lofty rocks. So M. Zermatt resolved to settle upon the portion of the coast which ran south and north, a little beyond Deliverance Bay, as the place was significantly named.

In the course of an excursion to the end of a magnificent wood not far from the sea, M. Zermatt stopped before a huge mangrove, of the mountain variety, the lower branches of which spread out quite sixty feet above the ground. Upon these branches the father and his sons succeeded in building a platform made of planks taken from the ship. Thus they constructed an aerial dwelling, covered in with a solid roof and divided into several chambers. It was called Falconhurst, "The Falcon's Nest." What was more, like certain willows which only subsist through their bark, this mangrove had lost its inner core, which had been taken possession of by numerous swarms of bees, and it was possible to put in a winding staircase, to replace the rope ladder by which access to the Falcon's Nest had been gained originally.

Meanwhile exploring trips were extended to a distance of seven or eight miles as far as False Hope Point, as the cape was called after M. Zermatt had given up all hope of finding any passengers or members of the crew of the Landlord.

At the entrance to Deliverance Bay, opposite Falconhurst, lay an island about a mile and a quarter in circumference, and this was christened Shark's Island because one of those enormous creatures got stranded there the day the tub boat was taking the domestic animals to Tent Home.

Just as a shark was responsible for the naming of this island, so a whale, a few days later, gave its name to another island about three-quarters of a mile in circumference, situated in front of Flamingo Bay, to the north of Falconhurst. Communication between this aerial dwelling place and Tent Home, which was about two and a half miles distant, was facilitated by the construction of "Family Bridge," subsequently replaced by a swing bridge, thrown across Jackal River.

After passing the first few weeks under canvas, as the fine weather had not come to an end before Falconhurst was completed, M. Zermatt removed there with all the domestic animals. The enormous roots of the mangrove, covered with tarpaulins, served as cattlesheds. No traces of wild beasts had been found as yet.

However, it was necessary to think of preparing for the return of the winter season, which, if not cold, was at any rate disturbed by those torrential rains of the intertropical regions, which last from nine to ten weeks. To remain at Tent Home, where all the stores from the *Landlord* would be kept, would mean risking the precious cargo saved from the wreck. The encampment could not promise absolute safety. The rains must swell the river into a torrent, and if it overflowed its banks all the arrangements and fittings of Tent Home might be swept away.

Thus M. Zermatt was justifiably anxious about

finding a safe shelter, when chance came to his rescue in the following circumstances.

On the right bank of Jackal River, a little to the rear of Tent Home, there arose a wall of thick rock, in which with pick and hammer, and perhaps with mine, a grotto could be excavated. Fritz, Ernest, and Jack set about the task, but the work was making poor progress when, one morning, the tool that Jack was wielding went right through the rock.

"I have gone through the mountain!" the lad cried out.

The fact was there was a vast hollow inside the solid mass. Before entering it, in order to purify the air, bunches of burning grass were thrown inside, followed by rockets found in the *Landlord's* powder chest. Then by the light of torches, father, mother, and sons gazed with wonder and admiration at the stalactites which hung from its vault, the crystals of rock salt which jewelled it, and the carpet of fine sand with which its floor was covered.

A dwelling place was speedily fitted up within it. It was furnished with windows taken from the ship's stern gallery and escape pipes to carry off the smoke from the stoves. On the left hand were the work-shop, the stables and the cattle-sheds; to the rear, the store-rooms, separated by partitions of planking.

On the right hand there were three rooms: the first allotted to the father and mother; the second intended to serve as a dining room; the third occupied by the four boys, whose hammocks were hung from the roof.

A few weeks more, and this new installation left nothing to be desired.

Later on, other establishments were founded in the midst of the grass lands and the woods to the west of the coast line, which ran seven miles between Falconhurst and False Hope Point. The farmstead of Wood Grange was created, near Swan Lake; then, a little further inland, the farmstead of Sugar-cane Grove; then, on a little hill near the cape, the villa of Prospect Hill; and finally, the hermitage of Eberfurt, at the entrance to the defile of Cluse, which bounded the Promised Land on the west.

The Promised Land was the name given to the fertile country protected on the south and west by a lofty barrier of rock which ran from Jackal River to the shore of Nautilus Bay. On the east extended the coast between Rock Castle and False Hope Point. On the north lay the open sea. This territory, seven and a half miles wide by ten miles long, would have been adequate to the needs of quite a little colony. It was there that the family kept the domestic animals and the wild animals which they had tamed—an onager, two buffaloes, an ostrich, a jackal, a monkey, and an eagle. There the plantations of native growths flourished, with all the fruit trees of which the *Landlord* had carried a complete assortment, oranges, peaches, apples, apricots, chestnuts, cherries, plums, and even vines, which, under the warm sun of this land, were destined to produce a wine far superior to the palm wine of intertropical regions.

Beyond doubt nature had befriended the shipwrecked family; but their contribution in hard work, energy, and intelligence, was considerable. From these sprang the prosperity of this land, to which, in memory of their own fatherland, they gave the name of New Switzerland.

Within a year nothing remained of the wrecked vessel. An explosion carefully prepared by Fritz scattered its last fragments, which were picked up at various points along the coast. Before this was done everything of value which it contained had been removed: the articles which had been intended for trade with the planters of Port Jackson and the savages of Oceania, the property of the passengers—jewels, watches, snuff-boxes, rings, necklaces, and money amounting to a large sum, which was, however, valueless on this isolated land in the Indian Ocean. But other articles taken from the *Landlord* were of incalculable benefit, iron bars, pig lead, cart wheels ready to be fitted, whetstones, pickaxes, saws, mattocks, spades, ploughshares, iron wire, benches, vices, carpenter's, locksmith's, and blacksmith's tools, a hand mill, a saw mill, an entire assortment of cereals, maize, oats, and the like, and quantities of vegetable seeds.

The family spent the first rainy season under favourable conditions. They lived in the grotto, and busied themselves in arranging it to the best advantage. The furniture from the ship—seats, presses, pier tables, sofas, and beds—were distributed among the rooms of this dwelling place, and now that it no longer consisted of tents the name of Rock Castle was substituted for the former one of Tent Home.

Several years passed. No ship was seen in these remote waters. Yet nothing had been omitted to draw attention to the situation of the survivors of the *Landlord*. A battery was installed on Shark's Island, containing two small four-pounder cannon. Fritz and Jack fired these guns from time to time, but never obtained any reply from the open sea.

There was no indication that New Switzerland was inhabited anywhere in the neighbourhood of this district. The country was almost certainly a rather large one, and one day while making a journey of exploration southwards as far as the barrier of rock which was pierced by the defile of Cluse, M. Zermatt and his sons reached the far end of a verdant valley, the "Green Valley." Thence a wide horizon spread before their eyes, bounded by a range of mountains at a distance estimated at five and twenty miles.

The possibility that this unknown land was roamed by savage tribes caused them grave anxiety. But none had been seen in the neighbourhood of the Promised Land. The only danger there was from the attacks of a few wild animals, outside the actual district— bears, tigers, lions, and serpents—amongst others one enormous boa-constrictor, which had penetrated as far as the outer premises of Rock Castle, and to which the ass fell a prey.

The following are some of the native products from which M. Zermatt derived much advantage, for he had a very full knowledge of natural history, botany, and geology. A tree resembling the wild fig-tree, from whose cracked bark a gum was distilled, yielded india-rubber, which rendered possible the manufacture of several articles, among them waterproof boots. From certain other trees, they gathered a kind of wax which was used in making candles. The cocoanuts, besides supply food, were converted into almost unbreakable bowls and cups. The cabbage palm yielded a refreshing drink, known as palm wine; the beans of a cacao furnished a rather bitter chocolate, and the sago-tree a pith which, when soaked and kneaded, yielded a most nutritious flour constantly used in cooking. There was never any lack of sweetening, thanks to the swarms of bees, which produced honey in abundance. There was flax from the lanceolate leaves of the *phormium tenax,* though the carding and spinning of this was not effected without some trouble. Plaster was obtained by making red hot and then reducing to powder fragments of the actual rock wall of Rock Castle. Cotton was found in seed pods full to bursting. From the fine dust of another grotto fuller's earth was taken and used to make soap. There were clove-apples of extraordinary succulence. From the bark of the *ravensara* an aromatic flavouring was obtained in which the savours of nutmeg and cinnamon were mingled. From a mica shot with long asbestos threads, discov-covered in an adjacent cave, a kind of glass was manufactured. Beavers and rabbits supplied fur for clothing. There were euphorbium gum, useful for various medicinal purposes, china-clay, mead for a refreshing beverage, and delicious jellies made from seaweed collected on Whale Island in accordance with a method which Mme. Zermatt had learned at Cape Town.

To all this wealth must be added the resources rendered available to bold hunters by the fauna of New Switzerland. Among the wild animals from which they had, though very occasionally, to defend themselves were the tapir, lion, bear, jackal, tiger-cat, tiger, crocodile, panther, and elephant; while the depredations of the apes were so serious as to necessitate a general massacre. Among the quadrupeds, some of which were capable of domestication, were the onager and the buffalo, and among the winged tribe were an eagle, which became Fritz's hunting bird, and an ostrich which Jack trained to be his favourite mount.

As for game, both furred and feathered, there was abundance in the woods round about Wood Grange and the hermitage at Eberfurt. Jackal River supplied excellent crayfish. Among the rocks on the shore molluscs and crustaceans swarmed. And finally, the sea teemed with herrings, sturgeon, salmon, and other fish.

During this long period no journeys of exploration were carried out beyond the country between Nautilus Bay and Deliverance Bay. The coast beyond False Hope Point was explored later, to a distance of about twenty-five miles. Besides the pinnace M. Zermatt now possessed a long-boat, built under his direction. And further, at Fritz's request, they made a light canoe of the Greenlander pattern known as a kayak, using the whalebone taken from a whale which had been stranded at the entrance to Flamingo Bay for the ribs of the craft and the skins of dog-fish for her hull. This portable canoe, which careful caulking and tarring rendered quite water-tight, was provided with openings in which two paddlers could sit; the second could be hermetically closed when only the first was occupied.

Ten years passed without any incidents of serious importance. M. Zermatt, now forty-five years of age, enjoyed invariable good health and possessed a moral and physical endurance which had been developed to a higher degree by the uncertainties of an existence so far removed from the ordinary. Betsy, the energetic mother of four sons, was entering upon her forty-third year. Neither her physical strength nor her courage was abated, nor yet her love for her husband and children.

Fritz, now twenty-five, and the possessor of astonishing strength, suppleness, and skill, with a frank countenance, open face and amazingly keen eyes, had improved enormously in character.

Ernest, of graver bent than his twenty-two years warranted, and more skilled in mental than in physical exercises, was a great contrast to Fritz, and had educated himself highly by drawing upon the library taken from the *Landlord*.

Jack at twenty bubbled over with the joy of life. He was vivacity and perpetual motion incarnate, as adventurous as Fritz and as passionately fond of sport.

Although little Frank had now become a big boy of sixteen, his mother still petted and made much of him as if he were only ten.

Thus the existence of this family was as happy as could be, and many a time Mme. Zermatt used to say to her husband:

"Ah, my dear, would it not be real happiness if we could always live with our children, and if, in this solitude, we were not obliged to pass away one after another, leaving the survivors to sorrow and forlornness! Yes, I would bless the God who has given us this paradise on earth! But, alas, a day will come when we must close our eyes."

That was, and had ever been, the gravest preoccupation of Betsy's mind. Often did she and M. Zermatt confide to one another their only too well-founded apprehensions on this score. But this year, an unexpected event happened which was destined to modify their present and perhaps their future situation.

On the 9th of April, about seven o'clock in the morning, when M. Zermatt came out of the house with Ernest, Jack and Frank, he looked in vain for his eldest son, whom he supposed to be engaged in some work outside.

Fritz was often absent, and there was nothing in his being away now to make his father or his mother uneasy, although Mme. Zermatt was always rather nervous when her son ventured out on the open sea beyond Deliverance Bay.

It was practically certain that the intrepid young fellow was at sea, since the canoe was not in its shelter.

As the afternoon was wearing on M. Zermatt, with Ernest and Jack, took the boat to Shark's Island, there to watch for Fritz's return. It was arranged that M. Zermatt should fire a cannon if he were delayed in getting home, in order that his wife might not be left in a state of uncertainty.

There was, however, no occasion for this. Father and sons had barely set foot on the island when Fritz came round False Hope Point. Directly they saw him, M. Zermatt, Ernest, and Jack took to their boat again. They landed in the bay at Rock Castle at the same moment that Fritz jumped out onto the beach.

Fritz was then obliged to narrate the events of his voyage, which had lasted for nearly twenty-four hours. For some time past he had been contemplating an exploration of the northern coast. So that morning he had taken his eagle, Blitz, and put his canoe in the water. He took some provisions, an axe, a harpoon, a boat-hook, fishing lines, a gun, a pair of pistols, a game-bag, and a flask of mead. The wind blowing off shore, the ebb tide carried him rapidly beyond the cape, and he followed the line of shore, sloping somewhat towards the south-west.

Behind the point, and behind a succeeding mass of enormous rocks piled up by nature in awful disorder as the result of some violent volcanic convulsion, a spacious bay was hollowed out in the coast, bounded on the far side by a perpendicular promontory. This bay furnished an asylum for all kinds of sea-birds, which made the welkin ring with their cries. On the shore huge amphibians snored in the sun, seabears, seals, walruses and others, while countless myriads of graceful nautiluses rode on the surface of the water.

Fritz was not anxious to have any dealings with these formidable sea-monsters in his frail boat. So, pushing out towards the mouth of the bay, he continued his voyage westward.

After rounding a point of singular shape, to which he gave the name of Cape Snub-nose, he entered a natural archway, the foot of whose pillars was washed by the surf. Here there were thousands of swallows, whose nests were plastered to the crannies of the walls and roof. Fritz detached several of these nests, which were of strange construction, and put them in a bag.

"These swallows' nests," said M. Zermatt, interrupting his son's story, "are a very valuable article of commerce in China."

Outside the archway Fritz found another bay, contained between two capes situated about four miles apart. These were linked together, so to speak, by a sprinkling of reefs with an opening only wide enough to permit the passage of a ship of three or four hundred tons at most.

Behind the bay, as far as eye could see, rolled broad savannahs watered by clear streams, woods, marshes, and landscapes of every variety. The bay itself held treasure of inexhaustible value in the shape of pearl oysters, some magnificent samples of which Fritz brought back with him.

After partly rounding the inside of the bay, and

crossing the mouth of a river teeming with aquatic plants of every kind, the canoe reached the promontory opposite the archway.

Fritz then decided that he must not carry his expedition any further. The hour was getting late, so he resumed his course to the coast, making for False Hope Point, which he rounded before the gun on Shark's Island had been fired.

This was the story the young man told of the voyage which resulted in the discovery of Pearl Bay. But when he was alone with M. Zermatt, he amazed his father by telling him more in confidence.

Among the countless birds which wheeled and wound above the promontory—sea-swallows, sea-gulls and frigate-birds—there were also several pairs of albatrosses, one of which Fritz knocked down with a blow from his boat-hook.

While he was holding the bird on his knees, Fritz saw a scrap of coarse linen tied round one of its feet, and on this was legibly written in English:

"Whoever you may be to whom God may send this message from an unhappy woman, look for a volcanic island which you will know by the flames escaping from one of its craters. Save the unfortunate woman who is alone on the Burning Rock!"

Somewhere in the waters of New Switzerland, a hapless girl or woman was living, had perhaps been living for several years, upon an island, with none of the resources which the *Landlord* had provided for the shipwrecked family!

"What did you do?" M. Zermatt asked.

"The only thing that could be done," Fritz replied. "I tried to restore the albatross, which was only stunned by the blow from the boat-hook, and I succeeded in doing so by pouring a little mead down its beak. On a piece of my handkerchief I wrote with the blood of a sea otter these words in English: 'Put your trust in God. Perhaps His help is near.' Then I tied the piece of handkerchief to the albatross's foot, feeling sure that the bird was a tame one, and would go back to Burning Rock with my message. The minute I set it free the albatross flew off towards the west, so fast that I soon lost sight of it, and it was quite impossible for me to go after it."

M. Zermatt was deeply concerned. What could he do to rescue this unfortunate woman? Where was the Burning Rock? In the near neighbourhood of New Switzerland or hundreds of miles to the west? The albatross is powerful and tireless in flight, and can travel vast distances. Had this one come from some far distant sea which the pinnace could not reach?

Fritz was warmly commended by his father for having confided the secret to him only, since its disclosure might only have upset the other boys and Mme. Zermatt to no good purpose. The shipwrecked girl on Burning Rock might now be dead. The note had no date on it. Several years might have passed since the message was tied to the foot of the albatross.

So the secret was kept. Unhappily it was only too plain that no attempt could be made to discover the English girl on her island.

However, M. Zermatt resolved to explore Pearl Bay

and ascertain the value of the oyster beds it contained. Betsy agreed, though rather reluctantly, to remain at Rock Castle with Frank. Ernest and Jack were to accompany their father.

The next day but one, the 11th of April, the long-boat left the little cove by Jackal River and was rapidly borne by the current towards the north. Several of the pet animals joined the ship's company: the monkey, Nip the Second, Jack's jackal, the old dog Floss, and lastly Brownie and Fawn, two dogs in the prime of life.

Fritz, in his canoe, went in front of the boat, and having rounded False Hope Point he took the westerly course through the midst of the rocks where the walruses and other amphibian creatures of this shore abounded.

But it was not these creatures that attracted M. Zermatt's attention so much as the countless nautiluses already observed by Fritz. The whole bay was covered with these graceful creatures, their little sails spread out to catch the breeze, like a fleet of moving flowers.

After covering some seven miles from False Hope Point, Fritz pointed out at the far end of Nautilus Bay Cape Snub-nose, a cape which really was exactly like a nose of that shape. Four miles further on the archway curved up, and beyond that was Pearl Bay.

As they went through this archway Ernest and Jack collected a quantity of nests of the esculent swallow, though the birds defended them with fury.

When the boat had passed through the narrow strait

between the archway and the ridge of reefs, the spacious bay was revealed in its full extent, twenty to twenty-five miles in circumference.

It was a pure delight to sail over the surface of this splendid sheet of water, from the midst of which three or four wooded islands emerged. The bay was enclosed by verdant pasture lands, dense groves, and picturesque hills. On the west, there ran into it a pretty river, whose bed was hidden among the trees.

The boat touched shore in a little creek, close to the pearl oyster bed. As evening was closing in, M. Zermatt pitched camp by the edge of a stream. A fire was lighted, and some eggs were roasted in its ashes; these, with pemmican, potatoes, and maize biscuits, furnished the repast. Then, as a matter of precaution, all found quarters in the boat, leaving to Brownie and Fawn the duty of defending the camp against the jackals which could be heard howling all along the stream.

Three days, from the 12th to the 14th, were spent in fishing for oysters, all of which held pearls. In the evening Fritz and Jack went out after duck and partridge in a little wood on the right bank of the watercourse. They were obliged to be on their guard. Boars were plentiful in this wood, and there were other more formidable animals.

Indeed, in the evening of the 14th, a huge lion and lioness appeared, roaring and waving their tails in fury. After the lion had fallen, shot through the heart by Fritz, the lioness fell too, but not before, with a blow of her paw, she had broken the skull of poor old Floss, to her master's keen regret.

Thus it was established that some wild beasts inhabited this portion of New Switzerland, to the south and west of Pearl Bay, and outside the Promised Land. It was a happy chance that hitherto none of these creatures had forced their way into that district through the defile of Cluse; but M. Zermatt determined to block up this defile, which cut through the rampart of rock, as effectually as he could.

In the meanwhile a general instruction was issued, especially to Fritz and Jack, whose passion for hunting sometimes led them into imprudent excursions, that care should be taken to avoid such encounters as this.

The whole of this day was devoted to emptying the oysters piled up on the shore, and as this mass of molluscs was beginning to throw off exhalations that were anything but healthy, M. Zermatt and his sons determined to leave next morning at daybreak. It was necessary to return to Rock Castle, for Mme. Zermatt would be anxious. So the boat set out, preceded by the canoe. But when they reached the archway, Fritz passed a note to his father, and then sped away in the direction of the west. M. Zermatt could not fail to understand that he was going off to find the Burning Rock.

CHAPTER V

M. ZERMATT felt very anxious when he thought of the risks his son was about to run. But as he could neither stop him nor go with him the boat was obliged to continue its course towards False Hope Point.

When he got back to Rock Castle M. Zermatt decided still to say nothing to his children, or even to his wife. It would only have meant exciting useless fears, and possibly raising idle hopes. He only talked about an exploration to be conducted towards the west side of the shore. But when the absent one had not come back, at the end of three days, M. Zermatt was so uneasy that he resolved to go to look for him.

At daybreak on the 20th of April the *Elizabeth* got under way. She had been properly provisioned for this voyage, and had on board father, mother, and the three sons.

A better wind could not have been wished for. A good breeze blew from the south-west, allowing the pinnace to sail along the coast. In the afternoon she rounded the rocks of the archway and entered Pearl Bay.

M. Zermatt dropped anchor near the oyster bed, at the mouth of the river, where traces of the last camp were still to be seen. They were all preparing to go ashore when Ernest exclaimed:

"A savage!   A savage!"

And there indeed, towards the west of the bay, between the wooded islets, was a canoe moving about, seemingly mistrustful of the pinnace.

Never as yet had there been any ground for believing that New Switzerland was inhabited. Now, in view of a possible attack, the *Elizabeth* put herself on the defensive, with cannon loaded and guns ready to fire. But as soon as the savage had approached within a few cables' length, Jack cried out:

"It is Fritz!"

Fritz it was, alone in his canoe. Not having recognised from a distance the pinnace, which he had not expected to see in these waters, he was advancing cautiously, having even taken the precaution to blacken his face and hands.

When he had joined his family and embraced his mother and brothers, not without leaving a few smuts upon their cheeks, he led his father to one side.

"I have succeeded," he said.

"What?   The English girl on Burning Rock?"

"Yes, she is there, quite close, on an island in Pearl Bay," Fritz replied.

Without a word to his wife or children, M. Zermatt turned the pinnace towards the island pointed out by Fritz near the western shore of the bay. As they approached they could see a little wood of palms close to the beach, and in the wood a hut built in the Hottentot fashion.

They all landed, and Fritz fired a pistol in the air. Then they saw what looked like a young man come down from a tree in whose branches he was hiding.

But it was not a young man. It was a girl of about twenty, dressed like a midshipman. She was Jenny Montrose, the young English girl of the Burning Rock.

Mme. Zermatt, Ernest, Jack, and Frank now learnt the circumstances in which Fritz had discovered the situation of the deserted creature on a volcanic island in the open sea outside Pearl Bay, and how he had replied in a note which the young girl had never received, for the albatross did not return to Burning Rock.

How can one hope to describe the reception Jenny Montrose had, or the tenderness with which Mme. Zermatt folded her in her arms? While they had to wait for her to tell her story, Jenny had already heard from Fritz the story of New Switzerland and of the shipwrecked passengers on the *Landlord*.

The pinnace immediately left Pearl Bay, with all the family, now augmented by the young English girl. On both sides English and German were spoken sufficiently well for mutual understanding, and it was as though Jenny had at once become a member of the Robinson family.

Of course the *Elizabeth* carried home the few useful articles which Jenny had made with her own hands during her stay on Burning Rock. It was only natural that she should cling to these things, which had so many memories for her.

Also there were two living creatures, two faithful

companions from which the young girl could never have parted—a cormorant that she had trained to fish, and a tame jackal.

The *Elizabeth* was favoured with a fresh breeze which enabled her to carry every stitch of her canvas. The weather was so settled that M. Zermatt could not resist the desire to put in at the various establishments in the Promised Land as each came into view, when the pinnace had rounded False Hope Point.

The villa on Prospect Hill was the first, situated on that green hill, whence a view extended right to Falconhurst. The night was spent there, and it was a long time since Jenny had enjoyed so quiet a sleep.

Fritz and Frank, however, started at earliest dawn in the canoe in order to get everything ready at Rock Castle for the proper reception of the young English girl. Some time afterwards the pinnace put to sea again, and put in first at Whale Island, where a colony of rabbits was swarming. M. Zermatt insisted on Jenny accepting this island for her own—a present which she gratefully accepted.

From this point the passengers on the *Elizabeth* might have taken the land route and visited the farmstead at Wood Grange and the aerial dwelling, Falconhurst. But M. Zermatt and his wife wanted to leave Fritz the pleasure of taking their new companion to these.

Accordingly the pinnace continued to follow the windings of the shore as far as the mouth of Jackal River. When she reached the opening into Deliverance Bay she was received with a salute of three guns from the battery on Shark's Island. At the same moment Fritz and Frank hoisted the red and white flag in honour of the young girl.

When the salute had been returned by the two small guns aboard the pinnace M. Zermatt came alongside just as Fritz and Frank landed from the canoe. Then the entire family went up the beach to gain Rock Castle.

Jenny was overcome with wonder and admiration as she entered the fresh and verdant verandah and saw the arrangement and the furniture of the various rooms; when, too, she saw the dining table carefully laid by Fritz and his brother, with bamboo cups, cocoanut plates, and ostrich egg vessels side by side with utensils of European manufacture taken from the *Landlord*.

The dinner consisted of fresh fish, roast fowl, peccary ham, and fruit, with mead and canary wine as drinks.

Jenny Montrose was given the place of honour, between M. Zermatt and his wife. Tears of joy sprang to her eyes when, on a banner garlanded with flowers hung above the table, she read these words:

"Welcome to Jenny Montrose! God bless her entrance into the home of the Swiss Family Robinson!"

Then she told her story.

Jenny was the only child of Major William Montrose, an officer in the Indian army. While she was still quite young, a child indeed, she had followed her father from garrison to garrison. Deprived of her mother at the age of seven, she was brought up under her father's watchful care, and equipped to meet all the struggles of life unaided, if her last support should ever fail her. She was thoroughly instructed in everything right for a girl to know, and physical exercises had been an important part of her education—riding and hunting in particular.

In the middle of the year 1812 Major Montrose, now promoted Colonel, was ordered to return to Europe on board a man-of-war bringing home time-expired men from the Anglo-Indian army. He had been appointed to the command of a regiment in a distant expedition, and there was every probability that he would not return until he retired. This made it necessary for his daughter, now seventeen, to journey to her native country and make her home with an aunt in London. There she was to await the return of her father when at last he should rest from the fatigues of a life devoted to the service of arms.

As Jenny could not travel on a troopship, Colonel Montrose put her, with a maid to attend her, in the charge of a friend of his, Captain Greenfield, commander of the *Dorcas*. This ship sailed a few days before the one which was to take the colonel.

The voyage was ill-starred from the very first. On leaving the Bay of Bengal the *Dorcas* encountered storms of fearful violence; later she was chased by a French frigate, and compelled to seek refuge in the harbour of Batavia.

When the enemy had left these waters, the *Dorcas* set sail once more, and steered her course for the Cape of Good Hope. Her passage was a most difficult

one at this stormy season. Contrary winds continued
to blow with astonishing persistence. The *Dorcas* was
put out of her course by a storm which swept up from
the south-west. For an entire week Captain Greenfield
was unable to take his bearings. In fact he could not
have told whereabouts in the Indian Ocean he had
been carried by the storm, when during the night his
ship struck a reef.

An unknown coast rose some little distance off and
the crew, jumping into the first boat, made an attempt
to reach it. Jenny Montrose, with her maid and a few
passengers, got into the second boat. The ship was
breaking up already, and had to be abandoned as
speedily as possible.

Half an hour later the second boat was capsized
by a huge wave just as the first boat was disappearing
in the darkness.

When Jenny recovered consciousness she found herself upon a beach where the surf had laid her, probably the sole survivor of the wreck of the *Dorcas*.

The girl did not know what length of time had
elapsed since the boat was swamped. It was almost
a miracle that she had strength enough left to drag
herself into a cave, where, after she had eaten a few
eggs, she found a little rest in sleep.

When she awoke she dried in the sun the man's
clothes which she had put on at the time the ship
struck, in order to be less hampered in her movements,
and in one of the pockets of which there was a tinder-
box which would enable her to make a fire.

Jenny walked all along the shore of the island but

could not see any of her shipmates. There was nothing but fragments of the ship, a few pieces of wood from which she used to keep up her fire.

But, so great was the physical and moral strength of this young girl, so potent was the influence of her almost masculine education, that despair never took hold of her. She set her home within the cave in order. A few nails taken from the wreckage of the *Dorcas* were her only tools. Clever with her fingers, and of an inventive mind, she contrived the few things that were absolutely necessary. She succeeded in making a bow and fastening a few arrows, with which to hunt the furred and feathered game, and so provide for her daily food. There were a few animals which she was able to tame, a jackal and a cormorant, for instance, and these never left her side.

In the centre of the little island upon which she had been cast by the sea there rose a volcanic mountain from whose crater smoke and flames constantly belched. Jenny climbed to the top of this, a hundred fathoms or so above the level of the sea, but could see no glimpse of land on the horizon.

Burning Rock, which was about five miles in circumference, had on its eastern side only a narrow valley through which a little stream ran. Trees of various kinds sheltered here from too keen winds, covered it with their thick boughs and foliage; and on one of these mangroves Jenny established her dwelling place, just as the Zermatt family had done at Falconhurst.

Hunting in the valley and neighbourhood, fishing

in the stream and among the rocks with hooks fashioned out of nails, edible pods, and berries from different trees—these, supplemented by a few cases of preserved food and casks of wine, cast up on the shore during the three or four days following the wreck, enabled the young English girl to make an addition to the roots and shellfish which were her only food at first.

How many months had Jenny Montrose lived in this fashion on Burning Rock until the hour of her deliverance came?

At the beginning she had not thought of keeping count of time. But she was able to calculate roughly that two years and a half had passed since the wreck of the *Dorcas*.

Throughout all those months, rainy season and hot weather alike, not a day passed when she did not search the horizon. But never once did a sail appear on the background of the sky. From the highest point of the island, however, when the atmosphere was clear, she fancied two or three times that she could detect land to the eastward. But how was she to cover the intervening distance? And what was this land?

Although in this intertropical region the cold was not severe, Jenny's sufferings were great during the rainy season. Ensconced within her cave, which she was unable to leave either to hunt or to fish, she was still obliged to find food for herself. Happily the eggs, of which there were numbers among the rocks, the shellfish densely packed at the mouth of the cave, and the fruit stored in readiness for this season, made her food supply secure.

More than two years had passed when the idea occurred to her, like an inspiration from on high, to fasten to the foot of an albatross which she had caught a note telling of her deserted state upon the Burning Rock. She was quite unable to indicate its position. As soon as she set the bird free it took flight towards the north-east. What likelihood was there of its ever coming back to Burning Rock?

Several days went by without its reappearing. The faint hope the girl had had from this venture gradually faded away. But she would not lose all hope. If the help that she waited for did not come from this source, it would from some other.

Such was the story which Jenny told to the Zermatts.

They still had to learn the circumstances in which Fritz had discovered the Burning Rock.

When the boat left Pearl Bay, Fritz, who was in front of it in his canoe, passed a note to his father acquainting him with his intention to go to find the young English girl. So after passing the archway, instead of following the coast to the east, he went off in the opposite direction.

The shore was sown with reefs and fringed by enormous rocks. Beyond were masses of trees as fine as those at Wood Grange and Eberfurt. Numerous watercourses found their outlet in little bays. This north-west coast was unlike that between Deliverance Bay and Nautilus Bay.

Fritz was compelled by the heat, which was very

great the first day, to go ashore in order to find a little shade. He had to be rather cautious, for the hippopotami which lived at the mouth of the streams could easily have reduced the canoe to fragments.

Arriving at the outskirts of a dense wood, Fritz drew his light boat to the foot of a tree. Then, tired out he sank to sleep.

Next morning the voyage was continued until midday. When he put in to shore on this occasion Fritz was obliged to repulse the attack of a tiger which he wounded in the flank while his eagle tried to tear out the eyes of the brute. Two pistol shots stretched it dead at his feet.

But, to Fritz's bitter regret, the eagle, disembowelled by a blow from the tiger's claw, had ceased to breathe. Poor Blitz was buried in the sand, and his master resumed his voyage, grieved by the loss of his faithful hunting companion.

The second day had been spent following the winding coastline. No smoke out at sea indicated the presence of the Burning Rock. Now, as the sea was calm, Fritz determined to go farther out, in order to see if any smoke was visible above the southwestern horizon. Accordingly he drove his canoe in that direction. His sail bellied out in the brisk breeze off the land. After sailing for a couple of hours he was preparing to put about when he thought he could perceive a faint smoke.

At once Fritz forgot everything, the uneasiness his prolonged absence would cause at Rock Castle, his own fatigue, and the risks he would run in venturing out so far to sea. Driven by paddle as well as the wind, the canoe flew over the sea.

An hour later Fritz found himself within half-a-dozen cable-lengths of an island topped by a volcano, from which smoke and flame were escaping.

The eastern coast of the island seemed to be quite barren. But as he wound round it Fritz saw that it was intersected by the mouth of a stream at the extremity of a green valley.

The canoe was driven into a narrow creek and pulled up on the strand.

On the right hand was a cave, at the entrance to which a human being was lying, sunk in a deep sleep.

Fritz gazed at her with profound emotion. She was a girl of seventeen or eighteen, dressed in coarse sailcloth, which yet was clean and decently arranged. Her features were charming, and her face was very gentle. Fritz did not dare to waken her, and yet it was salvation which would greet her when she woke.

At last the girl opened her eyes. At the sight of a stranger she uttered a cry of alarm.

Fritz reassured her with a gesture, and then said in English:

"Do not be frightened, miss. I intend you no harm. I have come to save you."

And before she had time to reply he told her how an albatross had fallen into his hands, bearing a note begging help for the Englishwoman on the Burning Rock. He told her that a few miles to the east there was a land where a whole shipwrecked family was living.

Then, after throwing herself on her knees to thank God, the girl stretched out her hands to him in gratitude. She told her story briefly and invited Fritz to visit her wretched abode.

Fritz accepted the invitation, but stipulated that the visit must be a short one. Time pressed, and he was longing to take the young English girl to Rock Castle.

"To-morrow," she said, "we will start to-morrow, Mr. Fritz. Let me pass this one night more upon Burning Rock, since I shall never see it again."

"Very well, to-morrow," the young man answered.

And together they shared a meal provided from Jenny's stores, and the food carried in the canoe.

At length Jenny said her evening prayers and withdrew inside the cave, while Fritz lay down at the entrance to it, like a faithful watchdog.

Next day at earliest dawn they put into the canoe the little articles which Jenny did not want to leave behind, not forgetting her cormorant and her jackal. The young girl, in her man's dress, took the stern seat in the light vessel. The sail was hoisted, the paddles were wielded, and an hour later the last trails of smoke from the Burning Rock were lost on the far horizon.

Fritz had intended to make direct for False Hope Point. But the canoe, being heavily loaded, struck a snag of rock, and it was necessary to repair it. So Fritz was obliged to put into Pearl Bay, and he took his companion to the island, where the pinnace picked them up.

That was the narrative which Fritz related.

The addition of Jenny Montrose to the family circle increased its happiness. The weeks went by, busy with the up-keep of the farmsteads and the care of the animals. A beautiful avenue of fruit trees now connected Jackal River with Falconhurst. Improvements had been carried out at Wood Grange, at Sugar-cane Grove, at the hermitage at Eberfurt, and at Prospect Hill. Many delightful hours were spent in this last-named villa, built of bamboo on the plan of the Swiss chalet. From the top of the hill the eye could range on one side over a large part of the Promised Land, and on the other over a vista of twenty-five miles, bounded by the line where sea and sky met.

June brought again the heavy rains. It was necessary to leave Falconhurst and return to Rock Castle. These two or three months were always rather trying, made depressing, as they were, by the constant bad weather. A few trips to the farms to attend to the animals, and a few hours hunting which took Fritz and Jack out into the immediate neighbourhood of Rock Castle, represented the whole of the outdoor business of each day.

But they were not idle. Work went on under the direction of Mme. Zermatt. Jenny helped her, bringing to bear all her ingenious Anglo-Saxon energy, which was different from the rather more methodical Swiss system. And while the young girl studied German with M. Zermatt, the family studied English with her, Fritz speaking that language fluently at the end of a few weeks. How could they have made any but rapid progress with such a teacher?

So there was no complaint of dull days during the rainy season. Jenny's presence lent the evenings a new charm. No one was in a hurry for bed now. Mme. Zermatt and Jenny busied themselves with needlework. Sometimes the young girl was asked to sing, for she possesesd a charming voice. She learned the songs of Switzerland, those mountain melodies which will never grow old, and it was enchanting to hear them from her lips. Music was varied by reading aloud, when Ernest drew upon the best works in the library, and it seemed that time for bed always came too soon.

In this domestic atmosphere M. Zermatt, his wife, and his children, were as happy as mortal man can be. Yet they could not entirely forget their fears for the future, the improbability of rescue coming from outside, or their old homeland. Jenny, too—must not her heart have been rent sometimes when her thoughts turned to her father? Nothing had ever been heard of the ship that was taking her home, the *Dorcas*, and was it not the obvious conclusion that she had foundered with all hands?

The unlooked-for event which altered their situation so profoundly has already been described.

CHAPTER VI

PLANNING AND WORKING

DURING the first few days following the departure of the *Unicorn* deep depression reigned at Rock Castle. M. and Mme. Zermatt were inconsolable at having let two of their children go, although they realised the necessity of doing so.

But it is vain to ask of a parent's heart more than it is able to give. Fritz, that gallant young fellow, was gone, Fritz, the stout right arm of his family, in whose eyes he represented the future. Gone, too, was Frank, following in the footsteps of his eldest brother.

Ernest and Jack were left, it is true. Ernest had never lost his taste for study and, thanks to his reading, his education was as solid as it was practical. Jack shared Fritz's love of hunting and fishing and riding and sailing, and, keenly eager to wrest her last secrets from New Switzerland, he would take his brother's place in daring explorations.

And lastly, she, too, was gone, the charming and beloved Jenny, whose absence Betsy regretted as much as that of a dear daughter. It was heart-breaking to see their places in the rooms of Rock Castle, their seats at table and in the hall where all assembled in the evenings, empty.

They would all come back, no doubt, and then the grief of the parting and the sadness of their absence would be forgotten. They would all come back, and new friends with them—Colonel Montrose, who would be unwilling to be separated from his daughter after he had given her as wife to her rescuer, and Dolly Wolston, and her brother James with his wife and child. They would all be glad to settle in this land. And other emigrants would soon be coming to populate this remote colony of Great Britain.

Yes: in a year at latest, one fine day a ship would appear out beyond False Hope Point, sailing from the west, not to disappear in the north or east! She would shape her course into Deliverance Bay. Most likely she would be the *Unicorn*. But whatever ship she was, she would bring Colonel Montrose and his daughter, Fritz and Frank, Mr. and Mrs. Wolston's children!

The situation was entirely altered. The inhabitants of this New Switzerland were no longer merely the shipwrecked survivors of the *Landlord*, who had found refuge on an unknown land. The position of this land was definitely established now in latitude and longitude. Lieutenant Littlestone had its exact bearings. He would report them to the Admiralty, and the Admiralty would give the necessary orders for taking possession. When she left New Switzerland the corvette uncoiled behind her, as it were, a cable thousands of miles in length, a cable which bound New Switzerland to the old world, and which nothing could break thereafter.

As yet, indeed, only a portion of its northern coast was known, the thirty or forty miles, at most, between Unicorn Bay and the seas to the east of Burning Rock. Even the three deep bays, Deliverance, Nautilus and Pearl, had not been completely explored. In the whole course of these eleven years M. Zermatt and his sons had scarcely set foot beyond the great rampart of mountain outside the defile of Cluse. They had confined their excursions to the middle line of the Green Valley, and had never ascended the opposite heights.

Owing to the presence of the Wolstons the number of inhabitants of Rock Castle had not been diminished by the departure of the *Unicorn.*

Mr. Wolston, at this time forty-five years of age, was a man of sound constitution. He had been weakened by fever contracted in New South Wales, but the healthy climate of New Switzerland and the care which would be lavished on him there would soon restore him to health and strength. His engineering knowledge and experience could not fail to be of the greatest service, and M. Zermatt fully intended to use them in effecting improvements which he had not been able to carry out hitherto. But first of all Mr. Wolston, to whom Ernest felt himself drawn by a certain resemblance of tastes and character, must regain his health.

Mrs. Wolston, Merry, was a few years younger than Mme. Zermatt. The two women could not fail to like each other, and their friendship would grow as they knew each other. Household duties engaged them together at Rock Castle, and they would share the work when visiting the farmsteads at Wood Grange, the hermitage at Eberfurt, and Sugar-cane Grove.

Hannah Wolston was only seventeen. Her health, like her father's, had been impaired, and it was certain that her stay in the Promised Land would strengthen her constitution and bring back the colour to her pale cheeks. She gave promise of developing into a very attractive woman, being fair, with pretty features, a complexion which would soon recover its bloom, a pleasant look in her blue eyes and a graceful carriage. She presented a great contrast to her sister, the sparkling Dolly, with her fourteen years, and her fresh and ringing laugh, which would have filled the rooms of Rock Castle, a brunette who was always singing, always chattering, and full of merry repartee. But she, too, would come back soon, the bird that had flown away, and her warbling would again delight all this little world.

Meantime the enlargement of Rock Castle was a matter of pressing necessity. When the *Unicorn* returned this dwelling would be too small. If only Colonel Montrose and Jenny, Fritz and Frank, James Wolston and his sister, wife, and child, were reckoned, they could not live there together unless some parts of the great cave were specially adapted to their use. If any fresh colonists came with them new houses would have to be built. There would be plenty of room for these along the right bank of Jackal River, the shore towards Flamingo Bay, or the shady road between Rock Castle and Falconhurst.

M. Zermatt had many long talks with Mr. Wolston on this subject, talks in which Ernest eagerly took part, making sound suggestions.

During this time Jack, who now undertook alone the duties he had formerly shared with his eldest brother, made it his constant business to supply the needs of the larder. Followed by his dogs, Brownie and Fawn, he went hunting every day in the woods and plains, where game, furred and feathered, abounded. He ransacked the marshes, where wild duck and snipe furnished a change for the daily bill of fare. Coco, Jack's jackal, was an ardent rival of the dogs, whose constant companion he was on these hunting expeditions. Sometimes the young hunter bestrode his onager, Lightfoot, who abundantly justified his name; sometimes the buffalo, Storm, who swept like a storm across the forest land. Strict injunctions had been laid upon the daring young fellow never to venture outside the confines of the Promised Land, and never to go through the defile of Cluse, opening into the Green Valley, where he would run the risk of encountering fierce animals. Yielding to his mother's urgent entreaty, he had promised not to be away longer than a day at a time, and always to come home for the evening meal. But in spite of his promises Betsy could not hide her fears when she saw him vanish like an arrow from a bow beyond the trees near Rock Castle.

For his part, Ernest preferred the peaceful occupation of fishing to hunting. He would settle himself by the side of Jackal River or at the foot of the rocks in Flamingo Bay. There were quantities of crustaceans, molluscs, and fish there—salmon, herrings, mackerel, lobster, crayfish, oysters, and mussels. Sometimes Hannah Wolston would join him, not a little to his satisfaction.

The young girl was unsparing of her attentions to the cormorant and the jackal brought from Burning Rock. It was to her that Jenny had committed them before she went away, and they were in good hands. When she came back Jenny would find her two faithful companions in the pink of health, and at liberty to come and go as they pleased in the paddocks of Rock Castle.

While the cormorant agreed very well with the other inhabitants of the poultry yard, the jackal was on bad terms with Jack's jackal, which had tried in vain to make friends. The two creatures were jealous of each other, and were forever scratching and quarrelling.

"I give up trying to make them agree," Jack said one day to Hannah, "and I hand them over to you."

"Trust me, Jack," Hannah replied. "With a little patience I hope to bring them together."

"Try, my dear girl, for jackals should always be friends."

"It seems to me, Jack, that your monkey, too——"

"Nip the Second? Oh, all he wants is to bite Jenny's pet!"

And really, Nip the Second did appear to be very ill-disposed towards the newcomer. Tame as these

creatures were with human beings, it would be difficult
to establish harmony between them.

The days slipped by. Betsy and Merry never had
an idle hour. While Mme. Zermatt was mending
clothes, Mrs. Wolston, who was a very clever needle-
woman, was making dresses and petticoats out of the
materials that had been treasured from the wreck of
the *Landlord*.

The weather was superb, the heat still not excessive.
In the forenoon the breeze blew off the land, in the
afternoon off the sea. The nights remained fresh and
restful. The last week of October, the April of the
southern latitudes, was about to retire before November, the month of renewal, the month of spring in
that hemisphere.

The two families paid frequent visits to the farms,
sometimes on foot, sometimes in the cart drawn by
its team of buffaloes. More often than not Ernest
rode the young ass, Rash, and Jack bestrode the ostrich.
Mr. Wolston got much benefit from these walks. He
had fewer and lighter attacks of fever.

They used to go from Rock Castle to Falconhurst
by the fine road planted ten years before, which was
now completely shaded by chestnut, walnut, and
cherry trees. Sometimes the stay at the aerial country-
seat was prolonged for four and twenty hours; and
it was delightful, when they had climbed the winding
staircase inside, to step out onto the platform sheltered
beneath the foliage of the magnificent mangrove. The
dwelling-place seemed rather small now; but in Mr.
Wolston's opinion there was no need to consider its

enlargement. And one day M. Zermatt answered his argument thus:

"You are quite right, my dear Wolston. To live among the branches of a tree was all very well for the Robinsons, whose first care was to find a refuge from wild beasts, and that was our case at the beginning of our life on this island. But now we are colonists, real colonists."

"And besides," Mr. Wolston pointed out, "we have to get ready for the return of our children, and we have none too much time to put Rock Castle into a condition to receive them all."

"Yes," said Ernest, "if there are any enlargements to be made it is at Rock Castle. Where could we find a more secure home during the rainy season? I agree with Mr. Wolston; Falconhurst has become insufficient, and during the summer I think it would be better to move into Wood Grange or Sugar-cane Grove."

"I should prefer Prospect Hill," Mme. Zermatt remarked. "It would be quite easy with supplementary arrangements."

"An excellent idea, mamma!" Jack exclaimed. "The view from Prospect Hill is delightful, right over the sea to Deliverance Bay. That hill is simply marked out as the site for a villa."

"Or a fort," M. Zermatt replied; "a fort to command that point of the island."

"A fort?" Jack repeated enquiringly.

"Well, my boy," M. Zermatt answered, "we must not forget that New Switzerland is going to become an English possession, and that it will be to the interest of the English to fortify it. The battery on Shark's Island would not be strong enough to defend the future town which will probably be built between Flamingo Bay and Rock Castle. So it seems to me indispensable that Prospect Hill should be used in the near future for a fort."

"Prospect Hill, or a little farther forward, on False Hope Point," Mr. Wolston suggested. "In that case the villa might be preserved."

"I should like that much better," Jack declared.

"And so should I," Mme. Zermatt added. "Let us try to keep all these memorials of our early days, Prospect Hill as well as Falconhurst. I should be very sorry to see them disappear."

Of course, Betsy's feeling was a very natural one. But the situation had changed. While New Switzerland belonged to the shipwrecked survivors of the *Landlord* only, there had never been any question of putting it in a state of defence. When it became a dependency of England, it must have coast defences.

And all things considered, could its first occupants really regret the consequences involved by the arrival of the *Unicorn* in these waters of New Switzerland?

"No," was M. Zermatt's conclusion, "so let us leave the future to bring about gradually all the various changes it requires."

Moreover, there were other things to be done that were much more urgent than the repairs at Falconhurst and Prospect Hill. It was nearly time to get in all the crops, to say nothing of the attention that

had to be given to the animals at Wood Grange, the
hermitage at Eberfurt, and Sugar-cane Grove.

When they paid their first visit to Whale Island
M. Zermatt and Mr. Wolston had been amazed at the
number of rabbits it contained.   There were hundreds
of these most prolific rodents.   Fortunately the island
produced quite enough herbaceous plants and roots
to guarantee their food supply.   So Jenny, to whom
M. Zermatt had made a present of this island, would
find it in a highly prosperous condition when she
returned.

"You were very wise to enclose your rabbits there,"
Mr. Wolston remarked.   "There will be thousands of
them some day, and they would have eaten up every
field in the Promised Land!   In Australia, where I
come from, these creatures threaten to become a
worse plague than the locusts in Africa, and if the
most stringent measures are not taken against the depredations of the breed, the entire surface of Australia
will be consumed." [1]

During these latter months of the year 1816 it was
obvious more than once that Fritz and Frank were
badly missed, although the Wolstons did not spare
their efforts.   The harvest season was always a very
busy one.   An immense amount of work was involved
in the proper farming of the fields of maize and tapioca
and of the rice plantation beyond the marsh near
Flamingo Bay, in the cropping of the fruit trees, both

[1] Mr. Wolston was not deceived in speaking like this; seventy
years later the extraordinary increase of the rabbits had become
such a menace to Australia that the most active steps had to be
taken for their destruction.

the European species and the indigenous species, such as bananas, guavas, cacaos, cinnamons, and others, in the extraction and preparation of sago, and finally in the harvesting of the grain, wheat, rice, buckwheat and barley, and the cutting of the sugar-canes, which grew in such abundance on the farm fields of Sugarcane Grove. All this made heavy work for four men, although the three women helped them bravely. And it would all have to be begun over again in a few months, for the soil was so prolific that there was no danger of its being exhausted by two crops every year.

On the other hand, it was important that Mme. Zermatt, Mrs. Wolston, and Hannah should not give up entirely their domestic work. And for this reason, while Mr. Wolston and M. Zermatt and his two sons went off to work out of doors, they most commonly remained at Rock Castle.

Fertile as the soil of the Promised Land was, however, there was yet the possibility that its yield might be prejudicially affected by an excessive drought during the summer. What was lacking was a system of irrigation suitably carried all over the surface of this area of several hundred acres. The only watercourses were the Jackal and Falconhurst Rivers to the east, and to the west the Eastern River, which ran into the south end of Nautilus Bay. This defect had struck Mr. Wolston, and one day, the 9th of November, after the midday meal, he brought the conversation round to this subject.

"Nothing would be easier," he said, "than to fix

up a water wheel, using the Jackal River fall a mile
and a half above Rock Castle. There are two ship's
pumps among the material you took out of the *Landlord,* my dear Zermatt. Well, the wheel, once it is
fixed, could work them with quite sufficient force,
could pump the water up into a reservoir and carry
it through pipes as far as the fields at Wood Grange
and Sugar-cane Grove."

"But the pipes," said Ernest; "how can we make
them?"

"We would do on a big scale what you have already
done on a small scale to bring water from Jackal
River to the kitchen garden at Rock Castle," Mr.
Wolston replied. "Instead of using bamboos, we
would use trunks of the sago tree, cleared of their
pith. An installation like that would not be beyond
our powers."

"Splendid!" Jack declared. "When we have made
our land more fertile still it will produce more; it
will produce too much, and we shall not know what to
do with our crops, for after all, there is no market yet
at Rock Castle."

"There will be one, Jack," M. Zermatt replied,
"as there will be a town by and by, and then several
towns, not only in the Promised Land, but all
over New Switzerland. We must look ahead, my
son."

"And when there are towns," Ernest added, "there
will be inhabitants whose food supply must be secured.
So we must get out of the soil all that it is capable of
yielding."

"We shall get it all right," Mr. Wolston added reassuringly, "by means of this system of irrigation, which I will study if you like."

Jack held his tongue and did not give in. It was by no means an agreeable idea to him that the English colony would some day number a considerable population, and if Mme. Zermatt's inmost heart could have been read the same regret at the thought of the future might have been found there.

However this may be, in the few hours of leisure left to them occasionally by their work in the fields, Mr. Wolston, M. Zermatt and Ernest, who found this kind of task most interesting, studied the question of irrigation. They ascertained accurately the line and level of the country, and were convinced that its disposition was favourable to the construction of a canal.

Rather more than half-a-mile to the south of Wood Grange lay Swan Lake, filled by the rains during the rainy season, but attaining during the dry season a low water mark which rendered it useless. The trenches that might have been cut would not have enabled the water at summer level to drain away. But if they succeeded in keeping a constant surplusage in the lake, by drawing upon Jackal River, it would be easy to divert it over the surrounding land and bring fresh elements of fertility to it by a carefully considered system of irrigation.

The distance between the waterfall and the southern extremity of the lake was a good two and a half miles, it is true, and to build a conduit of that length could not fail to be a task of much magnitude. It would necessitate the felling of a great many sago trees.

Happily, another examination of the ground, carried out by Ernest and Mr. Wolston, demonstrated the fact that the length of the conduit could be materially reduced.

One evening, when the two families were sitting together in the common hall after a busy day both in and out of doors, Ernest said:

"Papa, Mr. Wolston and I have found out all about the levels. If we raise the water from Jackal River thirty feet, that will be enough to carry it four hundred yards to the place where the ground begins to slope again down to Swan Lake. A trench cut from that point will serve as a canal for the water and will take it direct into the lake."

"Good!" said M. Zermatt. "That will simplify the task enormously."

"And then Swan Lake will form the reservoir for irrigating the fields at Wood Grange, Sugar-cane Grove, and even the hermitage," Mr. Wolston added. "Besides, we will only supply it with enough water for the actual requirements of the irrigation system, and if a surplusage should accumulate we could easily drain it off towards the sea."

"Quite so," said M. Zermatt. "We shall deserve the thanks of all future colonists when once we have completed this canal."

"But not of the old ones, who were satisfied with what nature had given them!" Jack remarked. "Poor old Jackal River! They are going to tire it out turning a wheel; they are going to take a bit of it away; and all for the material advantage of people we do not even know!"

"It is plain that Jack is not an advocate of colonisation," said Mrs. Wolston.

"Our two families settled in this district, and their existence assured—what more could we wish for, Mrs. Wolston?"

"Good!" said Hannah Wolston. "But Jack will change his ideas with all the improvements you are going to introduce."

"Do you think so?" Jack answered with a laugh.

"When shall you begin this great undertaking?" Betsy enquired.

"In a few days, dear," M. Zermatt assured her. "After we have got in our first harvest we shall have three months' leisure before the second."

This being settled, a most laborious task ensued, lasting for five weeks from the 15th of November to the 20th of December.

Expeditions had to be made to Prospect Hill for the purpose of felling several hundred sago trees in the adjacent woods. There was no difficulty in hollowing them out, and their pith was carefully collected in bamboo barrels. It was the hauling of the trees that constituted the really hardest part of the work. This devolved upon M. Zermatt and Jack, assisted by the two buffaloes, the onager, and the young ass, which drew a kind of trolley or truck, like those used later in Europe. It was Ernest who hit upon the idea of suspending these heavy lengths of timber to the axle-tree of the two wheels of the waggon, previously detached from the body for that purpose. If the tree-trunks did scrape along the ground, they only did so at one end, and their hauling was effected under much easier conditions.

All the same, buffaloes, onager and ass had plenty to do, so much, indeed, that one day Jack said:

"It is a pity, papa, that we have not got a pair of elephants in our service! What a lot of fatigue our poor beasts would be saved!"

"But not the worthy pachyderms themselves," M. Zermatt replied—"converted into our poor beasts in their turn."

"Oh, elephants have plenty of strength," Jack retorted; "they would drag these sago-tree trunks along like so many matches! There are some in New Switzerland, and if we could only——"

"I am not very keen on these creatures getting into the Promised Land, Jack. They would soon get our fields into a pretty mess!"

"No doubt, papa. But if we should have an opportunity of meeting them in the savannahs of Pearl Bay, or in those plains where the Green Valley opens out——"

"We would take advantage of it," M. Zermatt answered. "But don't let us create the opportunity. It is better not to."

While M. Zermatt and his son were proceeding with these many hauling journeys, Mr. Wolston and Ernest were busy making and fixing the pumping machine. In the construction of the water-wheel the engineer displayed great skill, and particularly interested Ernest, who had a great bent for everything connected with mechanics.

This wheel was set up at the foot of the waterfall in Jackal River, in such a way as to work the *Landlord's* pumps. The water, brought up to a height of thirty feet, would be stored in a reservoir hollowed out between the rocks on the right bank, and this would be fitted with the water-pipes made from the sago-tree trunks, the first of which were soon laid along the river bank.

The work was carried on so steadily and methodically that about the 20th of December it was finished, including the trench or drain cut through the surface, of the ground to the southern end of Swan Lake.

"Shall we have an opening ceremony?" Hannah Wolston asked that evening.

"I rather think so!" Jack replied. "Just as if it were a matter of opening a canal in our own old Switzerland! What do you say, Mamma?"

"Just as you like, dears," Betsy answered.

"Then that is settled," said M. Zermatt. "The ceremony shall begin to-morrow with the starting of our machinery."

"How shall it end?" Ernest asked.

"With an excellent dinner in honour of Mr. Wolston."

"And of your son Ernest," said Mr. Wolston, "for he deserves great praise for his keenness and intelligence."

"I am delighted with your praise, sir," the young fellow replied, "but I had a good teacher."

The next day, about ten o'clock, the canal was formally opened in the presence of the two families who had assembled near the waterfall. The wheel, set in motion by the fall, revolved regularly, the two pumps worked and the water was let into the reservoir, which was filled in an hour and a half. Then the sluices were opened and the water travelled through the conduit, a distance of four hundred yards.

Everybody hastened to this spot, and there was much clapping of hands when the first trickles of water entered the portion of the canal which was open to the sky. After Ernest had thrown in a little buoy, the members of both families got into the waggon, which was waiting, and drove off towards Swan Lake, Jack speeding in front mounted on his ostrich.

The waggon made such good speed that, although it had a détour to make, it reached the far end of the canal at the same moment that the buoy floated out onto the surface of the lake.

Loud cheers greeted it; the work had been brought to a satisfactory conclusion. It would only be necessary to make a few breaches in the banks for the water, even in the height of the drought, to irrigate generously all the surrounding country during the hot weather.

Three months had now passed since the *Unicorn* had sailed. If nothing occurred to delay her she ought to be seen again off Deliverance Bay in three times that time.

Not a day passed without some talk about the absent ones. They were followed at every stage of their voyage. Now they had reached the Cape of Good Hope, where James Wolston was waiting for his sister Dolly. Now the corvette was working up the Atlantic, along the African coast. Now she was arriving at Portsmouth; Jenny and Fritz and Frank were landing and reaching London. There Colonel Montrose was clasping in his arms the daughter whom he had never thought to see again, and, with her, him who had rescued her from the Burning Rock, whose union with her he would sanction with his blessing.

Thus ended the year 1816, which had been marked by events whose consequences must profoundly alter the situation of New Switzerland.

CHAPTER VII

THE START OF AN EXPEDITION

ON the 1st of January good wishes were exchanged between the Zermatts and the Wolstons. They also gave one another presents, valuable chiefly for the goodwill of the givers—such trifles as time transforms into souvenirs. There were mutual congratulations, too, and much handshaking when the day dawned, a day observed as a holiday all over the world, when the new year

> Makes its bow upon the stage
> Of the unknown future age,

as a French poet has said. This New Year's day was very different from the twelve that had preceded it since the survivors of the wreck of the *Landlord* had first set foot on the beach at Tent Home. Heartfelt joy now entered into their emotions. It was a chorus of pure happiness and merriment they raised, and Jack took part in it with the lively enthusiasm which he put into everything.

M. Zermatt and Mr. Wolston embraced each other. They were old friends now, and had had time to learn to appreciate and esteem one another in the common life they led together. M. Zermatt treated

Hannah as if he were her father, and Mr. Wolston, Ernest and Jack as if they were his sons. It was the same with the two mothers who made no difference between their respective children.

Hannah Wolston must have been particularly touched by the congratulations which Ernest offered to her. It will be remembered that this young man was somewhat addicted to poetry. Once before, when the worthy donkey had had its fatal encounter with the enormous boa-constrictor, he had adorned its tomb with a few quite respectable lines. On the present occasion, in honour of this maiden, his inspiration stood him in good stead, and Hannah's cheeks flushed warmly when the young poet congratulated her on having recovered her health in the good air of the Promised Land.

"Health—and happiness, too," she answered, kissing Mme. Zermatt.

The day, which was Friday, was observed like a Sunday in that thanks were offered to the Most High, whose protection of the absent ones was invoked, while heartfelt gratitude was expressed for all His blessings.

Then Jack exclaimed:

"And what about our animals?"

"Well; what about our animals?" M. Zermatt enquired.

"Turk, and Brownie and Fawn; our buffaloes, Storm and Grumbler; our bull, Roarer; our cow, Paleface; our onager, Lightfoot; our asses, Arrow and Fleet and Swift; our jackal, Coco; our ostrich, Whirlwind; our monkey, Nip the Second; and indeed all our friends two and four footed."

"Come, come, Jack," said Mme. Zermatt, "you are not suggesting that your brother should write poetry for the whole farm and poultry yard, are you?"

"Of course not, Mamma, and I don't suppose the excellent creatures would appreciate the most beautiful verses in the world. But they do deserve that we should wish them a happy new year and give them double rations and fresh litter."

"Jack is quite right," said Mr. Wolston; "to-day all our beasts——"

"Including Jenny's jackal and cormorant," said Hannah Wolston.

"Well said, my dear," said Mrs. Wolston. "Jenny's pets shall have their share."

"And since to-day is the first day of the year the whole world over," said Mme. Zermatt, "let us think of those who have left us, who are certainly thinking of us."

And affectionate thoughts were wafted by both families to the beloved passengers on the *Unicorn*.

All the animals were treated according to their high deserts, and sugar was lavished upon them as well as caresses.

Then the whole party sat down in the dining-room at Rock Castle to an appetising luncheon, the gaiety of which was increased by a few glasses of old wine presented by the commander of the corvette.

There was no question of doing any of the usual daily work on a holiday like this, so M. Zermatt proposed a walk to Falconhurst, a short two and a half miles that could be travelled without much fatigue beneath the shade of the fair avenue which connected the summer and winter residences.

The weather was splendid, although the heat was great. But the double row of trees along the avenue barred the sun's rays with their dense foliage. It was just a pleasant trip along the shore, with the sea upon the right hand and the country on the left.

A start was made about eleven o'clock so as to allow of a whole afternoon's rest at Falconhurst and a return in time for dinner. The two families had not stayed at Wood Grange this year, nor yet at Prospect Hill or the hermitage at Eberfurt, because these farmsteads required enlargements which would not be undertaken until the *Unicorn* came back. The arrival of new colonists would probably necessitate other changes in the Promised Land.

After leaving the kitchen garden and crossing Jackal River by Family Bridge, the party went along the avenue of fruit trees, which had grown with tropical luxuriance.

There was no need to hurry, as an hour would take them to Falconhurst. The dogs, Brownie and Fawn, gambolled in front. On either hand fields of maize, millet, oats, wheat, barley, cassava, and sweet potatoes displayed their rich stores. The second harvest promised to be a good one, without taking into account that which would be reaped on the land farther to the north, irrigated from Swan Lake.

"It was a fine idea to utilise that water from Jackal

River, which until then was wasted, since the sea had no need of it!" Jack remarked thoughtfully to Mr. Wolston.

Every few hundred yards a halt was made, and the talk was resumed with new enjoyment. Hannah gathered some of the pretty flowers whose perfume scented the whole avenue. Hundreds of birds fluttered among the branches laden with fruit and leaves. Game of all kinds sped across the meadow lands, hares, rabbits, grouse, hazel hens, snipe. Neither Ernest nor Jack had been allowed to bring a gun, and it seemed as if the winged tribe knew this.

Before they had started Mme. Zermatt, seconded by Hannah, had urged the point.

"I beg," she said, "I beg that to-day all these unoffending creatures may be spared."

Ernest had agreed with good grace. He had no burning desire to shine as a hunter. But Jack had protested. To go out without his gun, if he were to be believed, was like being deprived of an arm or a leg.

"I can take it, even if I don't use it," he said. "I promise not to fire, not even if a covey of partridges gets up within half a dozen yards."

"You would not be able to keep your promise, Jack," Hannah replied. "With Ernest there would be no need for anxiety, but you——"

"And suppose some wild beast appeared, a panther, a bear, a tiger, a lion? There are some on our island."

"Not in the Promised Land," Mme. Zermatt answered. "Come, Jack, give in to us this time.

You will still have three hundred and sixty-four days in the year."

"Isn't it Leap Year by any chance?"

"No," Ernest replied.

"No luck!" the young sportsman exclaimed.

It was about an hour later when the two families stopped at the foot of Falconhurst, after crossing the mangrove wood.

M. Zermatt's first care was to ascertain that the fence which enclosed the poultry yard was in sound condition. Neither the monkeys nor the wild boars had indulged their instinct to destroy. There really would have been no need for Jack to make reprisals on these marauders on this occasion.

The party began by taking a rest on the semi-circular terrace of clay made above the roots of the huge mangrove and rendered waterproof by a mixture of resin and tar. They all took a little refreshment there from the barrels of mead which were stored under the terrace. Then they went up the winding staircase, built inside the tree, to the platform forty feet above the ground.

It was an unfailing pleasure to the Zermatts to be among the broad leaves of the tree. Was not this their first nest, the one which held so many memories for them? The nest had become a fresh and delightful habitation, with its two trellised balconies, its double floor, its rooms roofed in with nicely fitted bark, and its light furniture. Henceforward it would be no more than a mere resting place. More spacious buildings were to be erected at Prospect Hill. But M.

Zermatt meant to preserve the old "falcon's nest" as long as the gigantic tree would hold it in its arms, until, worn out by years, it fell to pieces from old age.

That afternoon, while they chatted on the balcony Mrs. Wolston made a remark which called for consideration. She was a woman of such enlightened piety, and so steeped in religious feeling, that no one was surprised when she spoke in this way.

"I have often marvelled, my dear friends, and I marvel still at all you have done in this corner of your island. Rock Castle, Falconhurst, Prospect Hill, your farms, your plantations, your fields, all prove your intelligence to be as great as your courage in hard work. But I have already asked Mme. Zermatt how it is that you have not got——"

"A chapel," Betsy answered quickly. "You are right, Merry dear, and we do undoubtedly owe it to God to build to His glory——"

"Something better than a chapel—a temple," exclaimed Jack, whom nothing ever dismayed; "a monument with a splendid steeple! When shall we begin, Papa? There is material enough and to spare. Mr. Wolston will draw the plans and we will carry them out."

"Excellent!" replied M. Zermatt with a smile; "but if I can see the temple with my mind's eye, I cannot see the pastor, the preacher."

"Frank will be that when he comes back," said Ernest.

"Meantime do not let that worry you, M. Zermatt,"

Mrs. Wolston put in. "We will content ourselves with saying our prayers in our chapel."

"It is an excellent idea of yours, Mrs. Wolston, and we must not forget that new colonists will be coming very soon. So we will look carefully into the matter in our spare time during the rainy season. We will look for a suitable site."

"It seems to me, dear," said Mme. Zermatt, "that if we cannot use Falconhurst as a dwelling place any longer, it would be quite easy to alter it into an aerial chapel."

"And then our prayers would be half way to heaven already, as Frank would remark," Jack added.

"It would be a little too far from Rock Castle," M. Zermatt replied. "I think it would be better to build this chapel near our principal residence, round which new houses will gradually gather. But, as I said before, we will look carefully into the idea."

During the three or four months which remained of the fine weather all hands were employed in the most pressing work, and from the 15th of March until the end of April there was not a single holiday. Mr. Wolston did not spare himself; but he could not take the place of Fritz and Frank in providing the farmsteads with fodder for the winter keep. There were now a hundred sheep, goats and pigs at Wood Grange; the hermitage at Eberfurt and Prospect Hill, and the cattlesheds at Rock Castle would not have been large enough to accommodate all this stock. The poultry was all brought into the poultry yard before the rainy season, and the fowls, bustards, and pigeons were attended to there every day. The geese and ducks could amuse themselves on the pond, a couple of gunshots away. It was only the draught cattle, the asses and buffaloes, and the cows and their calves that never left Rock Castle. Thus, irrespective of hunting and fishing, which were still very profitable from April to September, supplies were guaranteed merely from the produce of the yards.

On the 15th of March, however, there was still a good week before the field work would require the service of all hands. So, during that week, there would be no harm done by devoting the whole time to some trip outside the confines of the Promised Land. And this was the topic of conversation between the two families in the evening.

Mr. Wolston's knowledge was limited to the district between Jackal River and False Hope Point, including the farms at Wood Grange, the hermitage at Eberfurt, Sugar-cane Grove and Prospect Hill.

"I am surprised, Zermatt," he said one day, "that in all these twelve years neither you nor your children have attempted to reach the interior of New Switzerland."

"Why should we have tried, Wolston?" M. Zermatt replied. "Think! When the wreck of the *Landlord* cast us on this shore, my boys were only children, incapable of accompanying me on a journey of exploration. My wife could not have gone with me, and it would have been most imprudent to leave her alone."

"Alone with Frank, who was only five years old,"

Mme. Zermatt put in. "And besides, we had not abandoned hope of being picked up by some ship."

"Before all else," M. Zermatt went on, "it was a matter of providing for our immediate needs and of staying in the neighbourhood of the ship until we had taken out of her every single thing that might be useful to us. At the mouth of Jackal River we had fresh water, fields that could be cultivated easily on its right bank, and plantations all ready grown not far away. Soon afterwards, quite by chance, we discovered this healthy and safe dwelling place at Rock Castle. Ought we to have wasted time merely satisfying our curiosity?"

"And besides," Ernest remarked, "might not leaving Deliverance Bay have meant exposing ourselves to the chance of meeting natives, like those of the Nicobars and Andamans perhaps who are such fierce savages?"

"At all events," M. Zermatt went on, "each day brought some task that sheer necessity forbade us to postpone. Each new year imposed upon us the work of the year before. And gradually, with habits formed and an accustomed sense of well-being, we struck down roots in this spot, if I may use the phrase; that is why we have never left it. So the years have gone by, and it seems only yesterday that we first came here. What would you have had us do, Wolston? We were very well off here, in this district, and it did not occur to us that it would be wise to go out of it to look for anything better."

"That is all perfectly reasonable," Mr. Wolston answered, "but for my part, I could not have resisted for so many years my desire to explore the country towards the south, east and west."

"Because you are an Englishman," M. Zermatt replied, "and your native instinct urges you to travel. But we are Swiss, and the Swiss are a peaceful, stay-at-home people who never leave their mountains without regret; and if circumstances had not compelled us to leave Europe——"

"I protest, Papa!" Jack answered. "I protest, so far as I am concerned. Thorough Swiss as I am, I should have loved to travel all over the world!"

"You ought to be an Englishman, Jack," Ernest declared, "and please understand that I do not blame you a bit for having this inborn desire to move about. Besides, I think that Mr. Wolston is right. It really is necessary that we should make a complete survey of this New Switzerland of ours."

"Which is an island in the Indian Ocean, as we know now," Mr. Wolston added; "and it would be well to do it before the *Unicorn* comes back."

"Whenever Papa likes," exclaimed Jack, who was always ready to take a hand in any new discovery.

"We will talk about that again after the rainy season," M. Zermatt said. "I have not the least objection to a journey into the interior. But let us acknowledge that we were highly favoured in being permitted to land upon this coast which is both healthy and fertile. Is there another equal to it?"

"How do we know?" Ernest answered. "It is true, the coast we passed in the pinnace, when we doubled Cape East on our way to Unicorn Bay, was nothing but naked rocks and dangerous reefs, and even where the corvette was moored there was nothing but sandy shore. But beyond that, to the southward, it is quite likely that New Switzerland presents a less desolate appearance."

"The way to make sure of that," said Jack, "is to sail all round it in the pinnace. We shall know then what its configuration is."

"But if you have never been beyond Unicorn Bay to the eastward," Mr. Wolston insisted, "you have been much further along the northern coast."

"Yes, for something like forty miles," Ernest answered; "from False Hope Point to Pearl Bay."

"And we had not even the curiosity to go to see Burning Rock," Jack exclaimed.

"A desert island, which Jenny never wanted to see again," Hannah remarked.

"The best thing to do," M. Zermatt decided, "will be to explore the territory near the shore of Pearl Bay, for beyond that there are green prairies, broken hills, fields of cotton trees, with leafy woods."

"Where are the truffles!" Ernest put in.

"You glutton!" Jack exclaimed.

"Yes, truffles," M. Zermatt replied, laughing, "and where there are creatures too that dig the truffles up."

"Not forgetting panthers and lions!" Betsy added.

"Well," said Mr. Wolston, "the net result of all that is that we must not venture that way or any other without taking precautions. But since our future colony will be obliged to spread beyond the Promised Land, it seems to me that it would be better to explore the interior than to sail round the island."

"And to do so before the corvette comes back," Ernest added. "My view, indeed, is that it would be best to cross the defile of Cluse and go through the Green Valley so as to get right up to the mountains that one can see from the rising ground at Eberfurt."

"Did they not seem a very long way off from you?" Mr. Wolston asked.

"Yes; about twenty-five miles," Ernest replied.

"I am sure Ernest has mapped out a journey already," said Hannah with a smile.

"I confess I have, Hannah," the young man answered, "and I am longing to be able to draw an accurate map of the whole of our New Switzerland."

"My good people," said M. Zermatt, "this is what I suggest to begin to satisfy Mr. Wolston."

"Agreed to in advance!" replied Jack.

"Wait, you impatient fellow! It will be ten or twelve days before we are required for the second harvest, and if you like we will spend half that time in visiting the portion of the island which skirts the eastern shore."

"And while M. Zermatt with his two sons and Mr. Wolston are on this trip," Mrs. Wolston objected disapprovingly, "Mme. Zermatt, Hannah and I are to remain alone at Rock Castle; is that it?"

"No, Mrs. Wolston," M. Zermatt answered; "the pinnace will hold us all."

"When do we start?" cried Jack. "To-day?"

"Why not yesterday?" M. Zermatt answered, with a laugh.

"Since we have surveyed the inside of Pearl Bay already," said Ernest, "it really is better to follow up the eastern coast. The pinnace would go straight to Unicorn Bay and then southwards. We might perhaps discover the mouth of some river which we might ascend."

"That is an excellent idea," M. Zermatt declared.

"Unless perhaps it were better to make a circuit of the island," Mr. Wolston remarked.

"The circuit of it?" Ernest replied. "Oh, that would take more time than we have to give, for when we made our first trip to the Green Valley we could only make out the faint blue outline of the mountains on the horizon."

"That is precisely what it is important to have accurate information about," Mr. Wolston urged.

"And what we ought to have known all about long ago," Jack declared.

"Then that is settled," said M. Zermatt in conclusion; "perhaps we shall find on this east coast the mouth of a river which it will be possible to ascend, if not in the pinnace at any rate in the canoe."

And the plan having been agreed upon, it was decided to make a start on the next day but one.

As a matter of fact, thirty-six hours was none too long a time to ask for preparation. To begin with, the *Elizabeth* had to be got ready for the voyage, and at the same time provision had to be made for the feeding of the domestic animals during an absence which might perhaps be protracted by unforeseen circumstances.

So one and all had quite enough to get through.

Mr. Wolston and Jack made it their business to inspect the pinnace which was moored in the creek. She had not been to sea since her trip to Unicorn Bay. Some repairs had to be done, and Mr. Wolston was clever at this. Navigation would be no new thing to him, and Jack, too, could be relied upon, as the fearless successor to Fritz, to handle the *Elizabeth* as he handled the canoe.

M. Zermatt and Ernest, Mme. Zermatt, Mrs. Wolston and Hannah, were entrusted with the duty of providing the cattlesheds and the poultry yard with food, and they did it conscientiously. There was a large quantity left of the last harvest. Being graminivorous, the buffaloes, onager, asses, cows and the ostrich would lack nothing. The fowls, geese, ducks, Jenny's cormorant, the two jackals, the monkey, were made as sure of their food supply. Brownie and Fawn were to be taken, for there might be need to hunt on this trip, if the pinnace put in at any point on the coast.

All these arrangements of course made visits necessary to the farmsteads at Wood Grange, the hermitage at Eberfurt, Sugar-cane Grove, and Prospect Hill, among which the various animals were distributed. All these places were carefully kept in a state to receive visitors for a few days. But with the help of the waggon, the delay of thirty-six hours, stipulated for by M. Zermatt, was not exceeded.

There really was no time to be lost. The yellowing crops were on the point of ripening. The harvest could not be delayed beyond a fortnight, and the pinnace must be back by that time.

At last, in the evening of the 14th of March, a case of preserved meat, a bag of cassava flour, a cask of mead, a keg of palm wine, four guns, four pistols, powder, lead, enough shot for the *Elizabeth's* two small cannon, bedding, linen, spare clothes, oilskins, and cooking utensils were put on board.

Everything being ready for the start, all that had to be done was to take advantage, at the very first break of day, of the breeze which would blow off the land in order to reach Cape East.

After a peaceful night the two families went on board, at five o'clock in the morning, accompanied by the two dogs which gambolled and frolicked to their hearts' content.

As soon as the party had all taken their place on deck, the canoe was triced up aft. Then, with mainsail, foresail, and jib set, with M. Zermatt at the helm and Mr. Wolston and Jack on the look-out, the pinnace picked up the wind, and after passing Shark's Island speedily lost sight of the heights of Rock Castle.

CHAPTER VIII

EXPLORERS OF UNKNOWN COASTS

AS soon as she had cleared the entrance to the bay the pinnace glided over the surface of the broad expanse of sea between False Hope Point and Cape East. The weather was fine. The grey-blue sky was tapestried with a few clouds through which the sun's rays filtered.

At this early morning hour the breeze blew off the land and was favourable to the progress of the *Elizabeth*. It would not be until she had rounded Cape East that she would feel the wind from the sea.

The light vessel was carrying all her brig sails, even a flying jib and the pole sails of her two masts. To the swing of the open sea, with full sails, and a list to her starboard quarter, she clove the water, as still as that of a lake, and sped along at eight knots, leaving a long track of rippling foam in her wake.

What thoughts thronged Mme. Zermatt's mind, what memories of these twelve years that had passed! She saw again in fancy the tub boat roughly improvised for their rescue, which the least false stroke might have capsized; that frail contrivance making for an unknown shore with all that she loved within it, her husband, and her four sons, of whom the youngest was barely five years old; then she was landing

121

at the mouth of Jackal River, and the first tent was set up at the spot which was Tent Home before it became Rock Castle.

And what fears were hers whenever M. Zermatt and Fritz went back to the wreck! And now here she was, upon this well-rigged, well-handled pinnace, a good sea-boat, sharing without a tremor of fear in this voyage of discovery round the eastern coast of the island.

What changes, too, there had been in the last five months, and what changes, more important still, perhaps, could be anticipated within the very near future!

M. Zermatt was manœuvring so as to make the best use of the wind which tended to die away as the *Elizabeth* drew farther away from the land. Mr. Wolston, Ernest, and Jack stood by the sheets ready to haul them taut or ease them as need might be. It would have been a pity to become becalmed before coming off Cape East, where the pinnace would catch the breeze from the open sea.

Mr. Wolston said:

"I am afraid the wind is scanting; see how our sails are sagging!"

"The wind certainly is dropping," M. Zermatt answered, "but since it is blowing from aft let us put the foresail one side and the mainsail the other. We are sure to gather some pace that way."

"It should not take us more than half an hour to round the point," Ernest remarked.

"If the breeze drops altogether," Jack suggested,

"we have only to put out the oars and paddle as far as the cape. With four of us at it the pinnace won't stay still, I should imagine."

"And who will take the tiller while you are all at the oars?" Mme. Zermatt enquired.

"You will, mamma, or Mrs. Wolston, or even Hannah," Jack replied. "Why not Hannah? I am sure she would shove the tiller to port or starboard as well as any old salt?"

"Why not?" answered the girl, laughing. "Especially if I have only to do what you tell me, Jack."

"Good! It is as easy to manage a boat as it is to manage a house, and, of course, all women are adepts at that from the start," Jack answered.

There was no need to resort to the oars, or to what would have been much simpler—towing by the canoe. As soon as the two sails had been set crosswise the pinnace obeyed the breeze more readily and made appreciable progress towards Cape East.

Various signs went to show that beyond the cape the wind from the west would make itself felt. The sea on this side was vivid green a couple of miles from the shore. Sometimes little waves, deploying in white lines, gleamed with bright reflections. The voyage proceeded gaily, and it was scarcely half past eight when the *Elizabeth* was athwart the cape.

The sails were trimmed again and the little vessel put on a faster pace, lightly rocked by a sea that distressed no one on board.

As the breeze was plainly settled, M. Zermatt suggested that they should go up again towards the north-east, so as to go round the mass of rocks on which the *Landlord* had been broken.

"We can do it easily," said Mr. Wolston, "and for my own part I should very much like to see the reef onto which the storm threw you, so far off the course from the Cape of Good Hope to Batavia."

"A wreck that cost many lives," said Mme. Zermatt, whose face clouded at the memory. "My husband, my children, and myself were all who escaped death."

"So it has never been known whether any of the crew was picked up at sea or found refuge on any neighbouring land?" Mr. Wolston enquired.

"Never," M. Zermatt answered, "according to what Lieutenant Littlestone declared; and for a long time the *Landlord* was supposed to have been lost with all hands."

"As for that," Ernest observed, "it must be pointed out that the crew of the *Dorcas*, on which Jenny took her passage, had better luck than ours had, since the boatswain and two sailors were taken to Sydney."

"That is true," M. Zermatt replied. "But can we be positive that no survivors from the *Landlord* succeeded in finding a refuge on some one of these shores in the Indian Ocean, and even that after all these years they are not there still, as we are in New Switzerland?"

"There is nothing impossible in that," Ernest declared, "for our island is only seven or eight hundred miles from Australia. As the west coast of Australia is seldom visited by European ships the shipwrecked people might have had no opportunity of being rescued from the natives."

"The conclusion to be drawn from it all," said Mr. Wolston, "is that these seas are dangerous and that storms are frequent here. In only a few years there have been the loss of the *Landlord* and the loss of the *Dorcas*."

"Quite so," replied Ernest. "But let us remember that at the time those wrecks occurred, the position of our island was not marked on the charts, and it is not surprising that several ships were lost upon the reefs by which it is surrounded. But very soon now its bearings will be on record as exactly as those of the other islands of the Indian Ocean."

"The more's the pity!" cried Jack. "Yes: the more's the pity, since New Switzerland will now become known."

The *Elizabeth* was manœuvring by this time off the west side of the reef, and as she had been obliged to beat up against the wind in order to round the farthest rocks she now had only to sail before the wind in this direction.

M. Zermatt pointed out to Mr. Wolston on the opposite side of the reef the narrow gap into which an enormous wave had thrust the *Landlord*. The breach made in the timbers of the ship, first with the axe and then by an explosion, had permitted the removal of the things that she contained, prior to the time when a final explosion by gunpowder had accomplished her total destruction.

Of the ruined fragments of the ship, nothing remained upon the reef, the tide having washed everything to the shore, things which could float of themselves and also those which had previously been made floatable by means of empty casks, such as boilers, pieces of iron, copper and lead, and the four-pounder cannon, two of which were now on Shark's Island, and the rest in the battery at Rock Castle.

As they skirted the edge of the rocks, the party on the pinnace tried to see if there were any pieces of wreckage visible beneath the clear and calm water. Two and a half years previously Fritz, when he had gone in his canoe on a trip to Pearl Bay, had been able to discern at the bottom of the sea a number of large cannon, gun-carriages, cannon balls, pieces of iron, and fragments of the keel and capstan, which it would have required a diving-bell to raise. Even if he had had the opportunity of employing such a contrivance, however, M. Zermatt would not have been much better off. Now, none of these things was visible on the bottom. A thick carpet of sand mixed with long sea-weeds covered the last remnants of the *Landlord*.

After making the round of the reef, the *Elizabeth* bore away obliquely towards the south, in such a way as to draw close to Cape East. M. Zermatt steered a careful course, for one point ran out to sea surrounded by reefs.

Three-quarters of an hour later, after passing this point, which in all probability marked the eastern extremity of New Switzerland, the pinnace was able to follow the line of the coast for a mile and more, getting the wind from the north-west over land.

While sailing thus, M. Zermatt could not fail to observe once more how deserted an appearance the eastern coast of the island presented. There was not a tree upon the cliffs, not a trace of vegetation at their foot, not a stream trickling among the naked and deserted beaches. Nothing but rocks calcined by the sun. What a contrast to the verdant shores of Deliverance Bay and their extension onwards as far as False Hope Point!

M. Zermatt spoke:

"If after the wreck of the *Landlord* we had fallen upon this eastern coast, what would have become of us, and how should we have found anything to live upon?"

"Necessity would have compelled you to go into the interior," Mr. Wolston answered. "And in making your way round Deliverance Bay you would certainly have come to the spot where the tents of Tent Home were pitched."

"That is so, Wolston," M. Zermatt replied, "but think of the effort involved, and think of the despair we should have been a prey to during those first days."

"Who can tell, too," Ernest put in, "if our tub boat would not have been smashed on these rocks? How different from the mouth of Jackal River, where we were able to land without any risk or difficulty!"

About eleven o'clock the *Elizabeth* reached Unicorn Bay, and half an hour later dropped anchor at the foot of a rock near the spot where the English corvette had been moored.

M. Zermatt's plan, of which all approved, was to land in this corner of the bay and spend the rest of the day there, then to start again at daybreak next morning to continue the voyage along the coast line.

When the anchor was fast the stern of the pinnace was brought in by a hawser, and the landing was effected on fine, hard sand.

The bay was surrounded by a limestone cliff about a hundred feet in height from the foot to the top, which could only be gained by means of a narrow gap in the centre of it.

The party walked over the beach, which still bore traces of the last encampment. Here and there a few prints could still be seen in the sand above high water mark, with bits of wood left from the repairs to the corvette, holes made by the tent pegs, lumps of coal scattered among the shingle, and ashes from the fires.

All this prompted M. Zermatt to make the following remarks, fully justified by the circumstances:

"Just imagine if this were our first visit to the east coast of the island; with all these indisputable proofs before us of a landing, which the marks show to have been recent, think of the regrets and disappointment we should have felt! A ship had anchored here, her crew had camped within this bay, and we did not know anything about it! And after leaving this utterly deserted shore, could we have ventured to hope that she would ever come back?"

"That is very true," Betsy replied. "How was it that we learned of the arrival of the *Unicorn?*"

"By chance," said Jack; "pure chance!"

"No, my boy," M. Zermatt answered; "whatever Ernest may have said, it was due to our custom of firing our guns at Shark's Island every year at this season, to which the corvette replied with three guns."

"I must acknowledge that I was wrong," Ernest confessed.

"And think of our anxiety and our despair," M. Zermatt went on, "during the next three days, when the storm prevented us from going back to the island to repeat our signals, and think of our fear that the ship might have left again before we could reach her!"

"Yes, indeed," said Mr. Wolston, "that would have been a frightful disappointment! Fancy knowing that a ship had anchored in this bay and that you had not been able to communicate with her! And yet, in my opinion, your chances of being restored to your own home were still greatly increased."

"That is certain," Ernest said emphatically, "for our island was no longer unknown, seeing that the ship must have ascertained its position, which would have been entered in the charts. Some day or other a ship would have come to take possession of this land."

"Well, finally and in conclusion," said Jack, "the *Unicorn* did come, the *Unicorn* was observed, the *Unicorn* was visited, the *Unicorn* has gone, the *Unicorn*

will come back, and what we have to do now, I think,
is——"

"Have lunch?" Hannah Wolston put in, laughing.

"Exactly," Ernest answered.

"Let us sit down then," Jack claimed, "for I am
hungry enough to eat my plate—and I could digest it!"

They settled themselves at the top of the beach,
near the gap in the cliff, where there was shelter from
the rays of the sun. Provisions were fetched from the
pinnace, potted meat, smoked ham, cold chicken, cassava cakes, and bread baked the day before. To drink
they had mead, of which there were several casks in
the pinnace's store room, and a few bottles of Falconhurst wine to be uncorked later.

After the provisions and utensils had been brought
ashore, Mrs. Wolston with Mme. Zermatt and Hannah
laid the cloth on a smooth stretch of fine sand spread
over thick bunches of very dry seaweed. Then all
enjoyed a good luncheon, which would satisfy them
until the six o'clock dinner.

But it would not have been worth while to under-
take the toil of a voyage like this merely in order to
land on this beach, go aboard again, and anchor at
some other point along the shore only to leave it, too,
in the same conditions. The Promised Land could only
be a very small portion of New Switzerland.

So directly the meal was finished Mr. Wolston said:

"I suggest that we spend this afternoon pushing into
the interior of the island."

"And at once," exclaimed Jack. "We ought to be a good two miles away already."

"You would not have talked like that before lunch," Hannah remarked with a smile; "you ate enough for four people."

"And now I am ready to walk four times as far as anyone else," Jack answered; "ready to go to the end of the world—our small world, I mean."

"But if you go so far, so very far, my dear boy," said Mme. Zermatt, "we shall not be able to follow you."

"Upon my word," said M. Zermatt emphatically, slapping his son on the shoulder, "I am at my wits' end to know how to curb Jack's impatience! There is absolutely no way of holding him in. Why, I think even Fritz never showed such——"

"Fritz?" Jack retorted. "Well, isn't it my duty to try to take his place in everything? When he comes back he won't be what he was before he went away."

"Why not?" Hannah asked.

"Because he will be married, father of a family, papa and grand-papa, too, if he does not come back soon."

"Do you think so, Jack?" Mrs. Wolston laughed. "Fritz a grandfather after one year's absence?"

"Well, grandfather or not, he will be married."

"And why shouldn't he be what he was, even then?" Hannah insisted.

"Let Jack talk, Hannah," Ernest answered. "His turn will come to make an excellent husband just as Fritz's will."

"Just as yours will, my boy," Jack retorted, with a shrewd look at Ernest and the young girl. "For my own part I should be mightily surprised at such a thing; I think nature specially cut me out to be an uncle, the very best of uncles, an Uncle of New Switzerland! But there is no question to-day, so far as I am aware, of parading in bridal array before the Mayor of Rock Castle; the question is, are we to explore beyond this cliff?"

"I think," said Mrs. Wolston, "that Mme. Zermatt, Hannah, and I had better stay here while you make your trip, which is sure to be very tiring if it lasts until the evening. This beach is absolutely deserted, and we need not be afraid of any unpleasant visitors. Besides, it would be quite easy for us to return to the pinnace. If you leave us like this at the camp there will be no risk of your being delayed or stopped."

"I believe you would be perfectly safe here, my dear Merry," said M. Zermatt, "and yet I should not be easy at leaving you."

"Right!" Ernest exclaimed, "I ask nothing better than to stay too, while——"

"Ah!" cried Jack, "there's our student all over! To stay—no doubt to shove his nose into his musty books! I am sure he has stuffed one or two volumes into the bottom of the hold. Well, let him stay, but on condition that Hannah comes with us."

"And your mother and Mrs. Wolston too," M. Zermatt added. "Upon consideration that is much better. They will stop when they are tired."

"And then Ernest will be able to keep them company," said Jack, laughing again.

"Don't let us waste time," said Mr. Wolston. "The difficulty might have been to scale this cliff, which I should guess to be a hundred or a hundred and fifty feet high. But, fortunately, the pitch of this gap is not very steep, and that will take us onto the upper level. When once we are on the top we will decide what is best to be done."

"Let's go! Let's go!" Jack repeated.

Before starting M. Zermatt went to examine the *Elizabeth's* mooring. He satisfied himself that there would be no danger of her grounding at low tide or of striking against the rocks at high tide.

Then they all moved towards the gap. Each of the men carried a gun, a shot bag, a powder flask, and some ball cartridge prepared by Jack. The young sportsman quite expected indeed to bag some game, perhaps some wild animal of known or unknown species, in this part of New Switzerland.

Brownie and Fawn hunted in front. The party followed them up a slanting track, the steepness of which was lessened by its many windings. In the rainy season the gap doubtless served as a shoot for the water from the platform above, which then would form a torrent. But now, at the height of summer, its bed was dry. It was necessary to be careful in walking between these rocks, which might easily have fallen like an avalanche if the least shock had upset their equilibrium.

Quite half-an-hour was required to reach the top of the cliff.

The first to step out onto the top was the eager Jack.

Before him, towards the west, a vast plain extended as far as eye could see.

Jack stood wonderstricken. He turned about to gaze round. When Mr. Wolston joined him he exclaimed:

"What a country! What a surprise, and what a disappointment!"

The discomfiture was general when M. Zermatt and the others emerged upon the plateau.

Mrs. Wolston and Mme. Zermatt, with Hannah near them, sat down at the foot of a great block of rock. There was not a tree to give the least shelter from a raging sun, no grass on which to lie down. The stony ground, strewn haphazard with great rocks, unadapted to any vegetable growth, was carpeted in places with some of those wild mosses which do not require soil. As M. Zermatt declared, it was a desert of Arabia Petræa adjoining the fertile district of the Promised Land.

It was indeed an amazing contrast to the region lying between Jackal River and False Hope Point, and to the country beyond the defile of Cluse, the Green Valley, and the land abutting on Pearl Bay. And Mme. Zermatt's question may well be echoed, what would have been the plight of the shipwrecked family if the tub boat had deposited them on the eastern coast of the island?

From this cliff as far as Deliverance Bay, which

could be discerned five miles away to the west, the eye saw nothing but a desert country, without verdure, without a tree, without a single stream. Upon its surface no four-footed creature could be descried. It seemed to be forsaken even by the birds of land and sea.

"This is the end of our excursion," said M. Zermatt, "at any rate in this portion of our island."

"Beyond all question," Mr. Wolston replied; "I think it is quite useless to brave this tropic heat to reconnoitre a stony country with which nothing can be done."

"How capricious and fantastic nature is!" Ernest remarked. "She only proceeds by contrasts! Down there, all her productive energy in action: here, the most appalling sterility!"

"I think the best thing we can do," said Mme. Zermatt, "is to go down to the beach again and return to the ship."

"I also think so," said Mr. Wolston.

"Very well," said Jack, "but not until we have climbed to the top of the last rocks."

And he pointed to a heap of rocks which rose up on the left, sixty feet or so above the ground level. In less than five minutes he was at the top of it. Then after looking all round the horizon he called to Mr. Wolston and to his father and brother to come and join him.

Did it mean that he had made some discovery in the south-west, in which direction he was pointing?

Mr. Wolston and M. Zermatt were soon up beside him, though not without some trouble.

In this direction the littoral did really present an entirely different aspect.

About five miles from Unicorn Bay the cliff dropped abruptly and ended at a broad valley, probably watered by one of the main rivers of the island. On the further side of this depression were rolling, verdant masses of dense woods. In the breaks in these and beyond them the country displayed a most luxuriant vegetation to the extreme limits of the south and south-west.

The arid district seemed to be confined to the immediate area of some twelve to fifteen square miles contained between Cape East and Deliverance Bay.

If ever a country called for exploration, it was certainly that which now was seen for the first time. What surprises and what opportunities might it not have in store, although it could never surpass the Promised Land!

"Let us go," said Jack.

"Let us go," Mr. Wolston echoed, eager to hurry towards the new valley.

But five long miles over ground strewn with boulders, following a way among the rocks—think of the time needed to do them, and the fatigue, to say nothing of the danger of sunstroke on this shadeless tableland!

So M. Zermatt was obliged to restrain the impatience of Mr. Wolston and Jack.

"Not to-day," he said. "It is getting too late. Let us wait until to-morrow. Instead of crossing this district on foot, we will go by sea. The valley we can see almost certainly ends in some section of the sea-shore, in some creek where a river runs out. If the pinnace finds a good anchorage there we will devote one or two days to a really serious exploration of the interior."

It was the wisest course, and no one could raise an objection to it.

After a parting glance all round, M. Zermatt, with Mr. Wolston and Jack, went down and explained to the others what had been decided. The exploration, postponed until the morrow, would be carried out under conditions which would enable the whole party to take part in it without danger or fatigue.

It now only remained to descend the path through the gap in the cliff, and it took but a few minutes to reach the foot.

Though there was an entire absence of game on the shores of Unicorn Bay, as Jack complained, there were swarms of fish in its waters and of crustaceans among its rocks, with which Ernest expressed himself as being entirely satisfied. With the help of Hannah he set some nets and got some good fishing, with the result that for dinner there was a supplementary dish of large crabs with most excellent flesh and of small fried soles of good quality.

After dinner they took a final stroll as far as the end of the beach and about nine o'clock all the party went on board the *Elizabeth* again.

CHAPTER IX

NEXT morning M. Zermatt's first thought was to scan the eastern horizon. Behind a light veil of mist, soon to be dispersed, the solar disk was looming, enlarged by the refraction. A magnificent day was heralded. There was nothing to indicate any atmospheric disturbance. For three or four days the barometer had been set fair. The atmosphere was rendered a little opaque by the dust, unweighted by humidity, which it held in suspension. Further, the breeze, which was rather fresh, seemed to be settled in the north-west. The sea would be calm for quite a couple of miles out. So the pinnace would be able to continue her voyage along the line of coast in perfect safety.

At six o'clock everybody was on deck and the hawsers were cast off. With her foresail, mainsail, and jibs all hauled aboard and gathered, the little vessel cleared the point and took the open sea, where the wind was more appreciably felt. Half an hour later, with her course set southwards and Mr. Wolston at the helm, the *Elizabeth* was following the meanderings of the coast at a distance of ten cable-lengths, so that the eye could see its least details from the indentations of the beach to the top of the rocky cliffs.

As far as could be calculated, it must be from ten to twelve miles from Unicorn Bay to the valley which had been observed to the southward. Two or three hours would suffice to accomplish that distance. The tide, which had been on the flood since sunrise, was setting in that direction and would probably be slack by the time the *Elizabeth* reached her destination.

On both sides of the *Elizabeth* swift companies of magnificent sturgeons were darting and playing in the water, some of them measuring seven to eight feet in length. Jack and Ernest were wild to harpoon them, but M. Zermatt would not allow them to do so. No good purpose would have been served by delaying the voyage for this sport. Mackerel and weevers, which could be taken while sailing, were another matter. So some lines were trailed from the stern and brought up several dozen of those excellent fish, which, boiled in salt water, would make their appearance at luncheon at the first stop.

There was no change in the appearance of the coast. It still presented an unbroken front of limestone or granite, a lofty wall rising from the sand, pierced with caverns in which the roaring of the sea must have been appalling when the waves rushed into them, driven before the gales blowing from the open sea. The impression made upon the mind by this coast was one of profound gloom.

Yet, as the ship got further south a certain animation became noticeable, due to the incessant flight of frigate birds, booby birds, sea-gulls, and albatrosses, whose cries were deafening. Sometimes they came within gunshot. Jack was itching to shoot, and he might not have been able to resist his temptation if Hannah had not interceded for the inoffensive creatures.

"Perhaps Jenny's albatross is among all these others," she suggested. "What a pity it would be, Jack, if you were to kill that poor creature!"

"Hannah is right," said Ernest.

"As usual," Jack answered, "and I promise not to shoot another albatross until we have found the one that brought the message from Burning Rock."

"Would you like me to tell you what I think?" Hannah went on.

"Of course!" Jack replied.

"Well, that we shall see that albatross again some day."

"Naturally, since I shan't have killed it."

About nine o'clock the pinnace was almost abreast of the depression formed by an abrupt bend of the cliff towards the interior. The ridge of the coast was becoming lower. Broad mounds, less rugged of aspect, connected it now with the sandy beach, which was broken by large protuberances of a blackish hue. There were many reefs, covered at high tide, in some cases running out several cable-lengths from the shore. The *Elizabeth* approached them cautiously. Mr. Wolston leaned over the bow and observed the water attentively, noting every suspicious agitation and every change of colour which might indicate the proximity of a reef.

Suddenly Jack cried:

"Ah, at any rate no one can say that this coast is deserted! There are people over there, and fine people, too!"

All eyes turned towards the beach and the rocks where Jack's keen eyes detected numbers of living creatures.

"What do you mean, my boy?" his mother asked. "You see men there—savages perhaps?"

It was of savages, the fierce Indo-Malay savages, that Mme. Zermatt was always and quite reasonably, most afraid.

"Come, Jack, answer!" said his father.

"Don't be uneasy! Don't be uneasy!" Jack replied. "I did not say anything about human beings. These have got two legs, but they have feathers too."

"Then they are penguins?" Ernest enquired.

"Or auks."

"It is easy to confuse them, Jack," said Ernest, "for those birds are closely allied in the order of palmipedes."

"Let us say in the goose family, to save any dispute," M. Zermatt answered; "and goose is the best name for these stupid birds."

"Perhaps that is why they are sometimes mistaken for men," Jack suggested slyly.

"Wag!" Hannah exclaimed.

"Only from a distance," M. Zermatt added. "And really, just look at their necks with a ring of white feathers, their small wings hanging down like two little arms, their upright heads, their black feet, and the regular lines in which they are drawn up! They look like a regiment of soldiers in uniform. Do you remember, boys, what a number of penguins there used to be on the rocks at the mouth of Jackal River?"

"Rather!" said Ernest; "I can still see Jack rushing into the midst of the foe, with water up to his waist, and hitting out so stoutly that he knocked over half-a-dozen of the penguins with his stick!"

"Exactly," Jack acknowledged. "And as I was only ten years old at the time didn't I show promise?"

"You have fulfilled the promise, too," added M. Zermatt with a smile. "The poor creatures that we ill treated thus evidently made haste to abandon the beach at Deliverance Bay, and came to take refuge on this coast."

Whether this was so or not, it was the fact that the auks or penguins had absolutely deserted the shores of the bay within the first few months after the settlement at Rock Castle.

Continuing on her way along the line of coast, the *Elizabeth* passed by wide stretches where at low water vast sheets of salt deposit must be left high and dry. There must have been enough to employ a hundred hands salt-raking, and the future colony would be able to collect there all the salt it could possibly require.

From the foot of the cliff, which ended here in a sharp angle, a promontory ran out beneath the water. The pinnace was obliged to sheer off more than a mile to sea. When she again put in towards the coast, it was to make for the creek where the valley debouched which had been seen from the heights above Unicorn Bay.

"A river! There is a river!" cried Jack, perched at the top of the foremast.

M. Zermatt was examining the shore through a telescope, and this is what he saw:

On the right hand, the cliff bent sharply and went back along the slope of the interior. On the left hand, the coast line ended in a cape at least ten or fifteen miles away. The whole campaign was verdant with grass lands and woods, rising tier on tier to the limits of the horizon. Between these two points curved the creek, forming a natural harbour, screened by curtains of rock from the adverse easterly winds, and apparently having easily navigable passages.

Across this creek was a calm and limpid river shaded by fine trees. It appeared to be navigable, and as far as could be judged from this distance, its course bent towards the south-west.

This was manifestly the spot for the pinnace to put in at, as there was an excellent anchorage. So her head was turned towards the passage which gave entrance to it, and, with all sail taken in except the mainsail and jib, she beat up against the wind, on the starboard tack. The floodtide, which had still an hour to run, helped her. The sea was absolutely calm. At lowest ebb perhaps a reef might show here and there amid the splashing surf.

No precaution that prudence dictated was neglected. M. Zermatt at the tiller, Mr. Wolston and Ernest posted at the bow, and Jack astride the cross bars, all kept their eyes on the passage up the middle of which the *Elizabeth* was moving. Mme. Zermatt, with

Mrs. Wolston and her daughter, sat upon the poop. All maintained silence, under the two-fold influence of curiosity and of vague anxiety in approaching this new country in which human beings were about to set foot probably for the first time. The silence was only broken by the murmur of the water along the hull, mingled with the flapping of the sails which were spilling the wind, the directions called out by Jack and the cries of gulls and sea-mews flying wildly towards the rocks surrounding the creek.

It was eleven o'clock when the anchor was dropped beside a kind of natural quay on the left of the river mouth, where an easy landing was available. A little behind, some tall palm trees offered a sufficient protection from the rays of the sun which had now almost reached the meridian. After luncheon an organised exploration of the interior could be arranged.

The mouth of this river appeared to be as deserted as the mouth of Jackal River had been when the shipwrecked people first came ashore there. It did not look as if human foot had ever been set there before. The only difference was that instead of a narrow, winding, and unnavigable stream, a watercourse was here displayed which must certainly run far back into the middle portion of the island.

Jack jumped ashore the moment the *Elizabeth* had anchored, and, hauling on to a hawser made fast to her stern, drew her alongside of the rocks. This rendered it unnecessary to use the canoe to land by, and in a few minutes all were upon the beach. After carrying the provisions up to the shade of the clump of trees, the first business was the satisfaction of an alarming appetite, sharpened by a voyage of several hours in the keen air.

But eating did not wholly interfere with the interchange of question and answer.

"Is it perhaps not a pity that we did not rather anchor on the left bank of the river?" said Mr. Wolston. "The bank is low on this side, whereas on the other the buttress of the cliff towers a hundred feet above it."

"And I should not have had any difficulty in climbing to the top," Jack declared. "From there at least we should have been able to get a first view of the country."

"There is nothing easier than to cross the creek in the canoe," M. Zermatt answered. "But why should we be sorry? On the other bank I can only see stones and sand as far as the desert which reaches from Cape East to this bay. On this side, on the contrary, we have vegetation, trees and shade, and, beyond, opens out the country which we saw from the sea, and which it will be easy to explore. In my opinion we could not have chosen better."

"And we do approve of the choice, don't we, Mr. Wolston?" said Betsy.

"Quite, Mme. Zermatt; and we go over to the other bank whenever we like."

"I should like to add," said Mrs. Wolston, "that we are so very comfortable where we are——"

"That you would like to stay here!" Jack finished gaily. "Come, that's settled! Let us abandon Rock Castle, Falconhurst, the Promised Land, and let us come and found the ultimate capital of New Switzerland here at the mouth of this magnificent river."

"Jack is off again!" Ernest answered. "But in spite of his joking, it is clear that the size of this river and the depth of the creek into which it runs do offer greater advantages for the establishment of a colony than the mouth of Jackal River does. But we must explore this region thoroughly, study its resources, and ascertain whether or not it is frequented by any dangerous animals."

"That is talking like a wise man," said Hannah Wolston.

"As Ernest always talks," his brother retorted.

"In any case," M. Zermatt added, "splendid and rich as this country may be, we could not abandon the Promised Land."

"Certainly not," said Mme. Zermatt emphatically. "It would break my heart to leave it altogether."

"I quite understand you, Betsy dear," Mrs. Wolston replied, "and I would never consent to separate from you in order to live here."

"Well," said Mr. Wolston, "there is no question of doing that, but only of walking about the immediate neighbourhood after lunch."

The question being stated in terms like that, all were unanimous in hailing Mr. Wolston's proposal. Yet his wife and daughter and Mme. Zermatt would have excused themselves from taking part in an expedition which could not fail to be a tiring one, if after some reflection M. Zermatt had not said:

"I should not like to think of you alone in this

place, even for only a few hours, and you know, Betsy, that I have never left you at Rock Castle without putting you in charge of one of the boys. In the event of danger during our absence, what would become of you? I should not be easy for a minute. But we can arrange everything; since the river is navigable, why should we not all go up it together?"

"In the canoe?" Ernest asked.

"No; in the pinnace, which, moreover, I would prefer not to leave anchored here while we are away."

"Agreed," Betsy replied; "we are all three ready to go with you."

"Will the *Elizabeth* be able to make way against the stream?" Mr. Wolston enquired.

"We shall have the current with us," M. Zermatt answered, "if we wait for the flood tide. The tide will turn soon, and in six hours we shall be able to take advantage of it."

"Will it not be too late to make a start then?" Mrs. Wolston suggested.

"Well, yes, it would be too late," M. Zermatt replied. "So it seems to me it would be wiser to finish the day here, spend the night on board, and get under way with the flood tide at daybreak."

"And until then?" Jack enquired.

"Until then," M. Zermatt answered, "we shall have time to inspect the creek and the immediate neighbourhood. But, as the heat is very great, I advise the ladies to await our return at the camp."

"Willingly," said Mrs. Wolston, "provided you do not go very far away."

"It is merely a matter of a walk along the right bank of the river, from which we will not wander," M. Zermatt promised.

This plan permitted of an investigation of the lower valley being made before penetrating into the hinterland.

M. Zermatt and Mr. Wolston, with Ernest and Jack, climbed up onto the bank again, and reached some slightly swelling ground which connected the watercourse with the country on the western side.

This territory presented a very fertile appearance—woods, here and there, in dense masses; plains carpeted with thick grass, where thousands of ruminants might have found sustenance; a veritable network of little streams all running towards the main river; and lastly, like a barrier on the southwestern horizon, the mountain range which had already been remarked in that direction.

"Talking of that," said M. Zermatt, "I must admit that the range is not so far away as we supposed when we saw it for the first time from the heights above the Green Valley. Probably it was a haze that gave it its bluish tint, and I estimated the distance at more than thirty miles. It was an optical illusion. Ernest understands that, I expect."

"Quite, Papa; that day the distance looked twice what it really is. If we estimate the distance of that range from the Green Valley at eighteen or twenty miles we shall be pretty near the truth, I believe."

"I think so, too," said Mr. Wolston. "But is it actually the same range?"

"Oh, yes, it is the same," Ernest answered; "I do not think New Switzerland is large enough to contain another of that size."

"Why not?" Jack asked. "Why should not our island be as large as Sicily, or Madagascar, or New Zealand, or Australia?"

"And why should it not be a continent?" exclaimed Mr. Wolston, laughing.

"You seem to think that I always exaggerate everything," Jack retorted.

"You do, my boy," said M. Zermatt; "after all, that only means you are over-imaginative. But just think: if this island were as large as you suppose, and probably wish, it could hardly have escaped the observation of navigators."

"Of the old and the new world too," Ernest added. "Its position in this part of the Indian Ocean is much too valuable, and if it had been known, you may be quite sure that England, for example——"

"Don't stand upon ceremony, my dear Ernest," said Mr. Wolston good-humouredly. "We English are born colonisers, and claim a right to colonise everything we come across."

"And so, to make an end of it," M. Zermatt resumed, "from the day our island had been discovered it would have figured in the Admiralty charts and no doubt would have been called New England instead of New Switzerland."

"Anyhow," said Mr. Wolston, "it will not have lost anything by the waiting since you, its first occupant, have surrendered it to Great Britain."

"And since the *Unicorn* is going to bring it the official certificate of adoption," added Jack.

It had still to be ascertained whether the range rose in the centre of the island or at the extreme end of its southern coast.

When this point had been established Ernest would be in a position to complete his map of New Switzerland. And this natural desire was justification for Mr. Wolston's suggestion that they should explore the country as far as the foot of the mountains, and even make the ascent of these. But this plan could only be carried into effect at the beginning of the next dry season.

Ernest had taken and recorded with approximate accuracy the bearings of all the portions of the island that had been visited. The coast line on the north was about thirty miles in length; on the east it ran in an almost straight line from Cape East to the mouth of Deliverance Bay; next came that bay, hollowed out somewhat like a leather bottle, and joining the rocky coast between Falconhurst beach and the reefs of False Hope Point; beyond this, to the westward, Nautilus Bay was scooped out, terminated by Cape Snub-nose, and receiving the waters of the Eastern River; lastly, in broad, sweeping curves, the vast Pearl Bay was cut out of the littoral, between the archway and the opposite promontory, behind which, ten miles out at sea in the south-west, lay Burning Rock.

Thus the Promised Land, contained between the sea on one side and Nautilus Bay on the other, and en-

closed by a long wall of mountains extending from
the mouth of Deliverance Bay to the innermost point
of Nautilus Bay, was inaccessible except through the
defile of Cluse on its southern boundary. This district
of about ten square miles contained Jackal River, the
stream at Falconhurst, Swan Lake, the dwelling places
of Rock Castle and Falconhurst, and the farmsteads
at Wood Grange, Sugar-cane Grove, and the hermitage
at Eberfurt.

The exploration was now carried out along the banks
of the water-course, from which M. Zermatt did not
care to move away. This was quite to Ernest's mind,
and he said:

"When we get back from this trip I shall be able
to trace the course of part of this river and of the
valley it irrigates. In view of the fertility of this new
territory, it is unquestionable that our island could
support several thousand colonists."

"As many as that?" exclaimed Jack, not attempting
to conceal his vexation at the idea that his "second
fatherland" might be so densely populated some day.

"Further," Ernest went on, "since it is always well
for a town to be built near the mouth of a river, future
inhabitants will most likely decide to settle here beside
this creek."

"Well, we won't dispute it with them," M. Zermatt
remarked. "Not one of us could ever make up his
mind to leave the Promised Land."

"Especially as Mme. Zermatt would never consent
to do so," Mr. Wolston observed. "She has formally
proclaimed that."

"Mamma is right," Jack exclaimed. "And ask all our good servants, furred and feathered; ask Storm, and Grumbler, and Swift, and Paleface, and Bull and Arrow, and Nip the Second, the Lightfoot, and Whirlwind, and Turk, and then ask Brownie and Fawn, who are here present, if they would ever consent to move into a new house! Give them a vote, and have a scrutiny, and as they are the majority I know what the popular decision will be!"

"Be sensible, Jack," M. Zermatt answered. "There is no need for us to consult any of our dumb brutes."

"Not such brutes as the name might lead you to suppose!" Jack retorted, running and shouting to excite the two young dogs to wilder frolic.

About six o'clock M. Zermatt and his companions returned to the encampment, by way of the coast, which was bordered by long beaches with a background of resinous trees. Dinner was taken on the grass, and the diners enjoyed a dish of fried gudgeon taken from the fresh water of the river with the lines which Ernest had got ready for Hannah. This river appeared to be full of fish, and in the streamlets which flowed into it higher up there were swarms of crayfish, some dozens of which they promised to catch before leaving.

After dinner no one evinced any desire to return on board the pinnace, and it was only the absence of a tent that rendered the wish to sleep on the shore impracticable. It was a magnificent evening. A light breeze laden with the fragrance of the country, sweet as the savour stealing from a bowl of rose-leaves, perfumed and refreshed the entire atmosphere. After a long day under a tropical sun it was pure joy to draw this life-giving, life-restoring air deep into the lungs.

There was every guarantee of fine weather. A light haze shaded the horizon out at sea. The atmospheric dust held in the higher regions of the air just dimmed the scintillation of the stars. Beneath those stars the party walked and talked over their plans for the morrow. Then, about ten o'clock, all went on board the *Elizabeth* and each and all made ready to regain their berths except Ernest who was to take the first watch.

Just as they were going below Mme. Zermatt made a remark:

"There is one thing you have forgotten," said she.

"Forgotten, Betsy?" said Mr. Zermatt enquiringly.

"Yes: to give a name to this river."

"Quite right," M. Zermatt admitted; "it is an oversight that would have vexed Ernest in his map-making."

"Well," said Ernest, "there is a name already indicated for it. Let us call the river Hannah."

"Excellent!" said Jack. "Would you like that, Hannah?"

"Of course I should," the young girl replied, "but I have another name to suggest, and it deserves the compliment."

"What is it?" Mme. Zermatt asked.

"Our dear Jenny's family name."

Every one agreed, and henceforward Montrose River figured on the map of New Switzerland.

CHAPTER X

THE next morning about six o'clock, at low tide, the points of a few rocks which had not been visible the day before were exposed round the edge of the creek. It was ascertained, however, that even at lowest ebb practicable passages remained forty to fifty fathoms in width. This meant that the Montrose river was navigable at all stages of the tide. The depth of water near the rocks where the *Elizabeth* was moored was so great that she was still floating five or six feet above the sandy bottom.

About seven o'clock ripples were breaking along the rocks, forerunners of the flood tide, and the pinnace would soon have swung round upon her anchor if she had not been held by the hawser aft.

Mr. Wolston and Ernest, who had been ashore since daybreak, came back at this moment, after inspecting the condition of the creek lower down. They merely had to jump on deck to rejoin M. and Mme. Zermatt and Mrs. Wolston and her daughter. Jack had gone out hunting with his two dogs, and was still absent. A few gunshots notified his presence in the neighbourhood and suggested his success in his sport. It was not long before he put in an appearance, with his game bag bulging with a brace of partridges and half a dozen quails.

"I have not wasted my time or my powder," he remarked as he flung the brilliant-plumaged game down in the bows.

"Our congratulations," his father replied; "and now do not let us waste any more of the flood tide. Cast off the hawser and jump aboard."

Jack obeyed, and leaped onto the deck with his dogs. The anchor being apeak already, it was only necessary to trice it up to the cathead. The pinnace was immediately caught by the tide, and, driven by a light breeze blowing in from the sea, she entered the mouth of the Montrose river. Then with the wind behind her she began to ascend it, keeping to the middle of the channel.

The breadth of the stream from one bank to the other was not less than two hundred and fifty or three hundred feet. There was no indication of its narrowing, as far as the eye could see the banks ahead. On the right hand still ran the escarpment of the cliff, gradually diminishing in height while the ground rose in a barely perceptible slope. On the left, over the rather low bank, the eye travelled over plains broken by woods and clumps of trees, the tops of which were turning yellow at this season of the year.

After half an hour's good travelling, the *Elizabeth* reached the first bend of the Montrose, which, making a loop of about thirty degrees, now wound towards the south-west.

Beyond this bend the banks were not more than ten or twelve feet high—the height of the highest tides. This was proved by the layers of grass deposited among the tangled reeds, sharp-edged like bayonets. Inasmuch as on this date, the 19th of March, the equinoctial tides attained their maximum height, the conclusion was that the bed of the river was deep enough to contain all the sum of its waters, and that it never overflowed the surrounding country.

The pinnace was moving at from eight to ten knots an hour, which meant that she might expect to cover somewhere near twenty miles during the time the flood tide lasted.

Ernest had taken note of her speed and remarked:

"That is more or less the distance at which we have calculated the mountains rise in the south."

"Quite so," Mr. Wolston replied; "and if the river washes the foot of the range we shall have no difficulty in reaching it. In that case we need not postpone our projected trip for three or four months."

"Still, it would take more time than we can spare now," M. Zermatt answered. "Even if the Montrose did take us to the foot of the range we should not have reached our goal. We should still have to ascend to the summit, and in all probability that would involve much time and trouble."

"Besides," Ernest added, "when we have ascertained whether the river continues its course towards the south-west, we have yet to learn whether the stream is broken by rapids or barred by any obstacles we cannot pass."

"We shall soon see," M. Zermatt replied. "Let us go on while the flood tide carries us, and we will make up our minds on the other point in a few hours' time."

Beyond the bend the two banks were much less

steep, and enabled a wide view to be obtained of the region traversed by the Montrose.

Game of every kind swarmed in the grass and among the reeds along the banks; bustards, grouse, partridges and quails. If Jack had sent his dogs foraging along the banks and in the adjacent country, they could not have gone fifty yards without putting up rabbits, hares, agoutis, peccaries, and water-cavies. In this respect this district equalled that round Falconhurst, and the farmsteads—even in regard to the monkey tribe, which capered from tree to tree. A little way off, herds of antelope raced by, of the same species as that which was penned on Shark's Island. Herds of buffalo, too, were seen in more than one spot in the direction of the range, and sometimes distant glimpses were caught of herds of ostriches, half running, half flying as they sped away. On this occasion, M. Zermatt and his two sons did not mistake them for Arabs, as they had mistaken the first ostriches they saw from the heights above the hermitage at Eberfurt.

Jack was impatient at being pinned to the *Elizabeth's* deck and unable to jump ashore, at having to watch all these birds and animals going by without being able to speed them with a shot. Yet there would have been no good in bringing down any of the game, since it was not required.

"We are not hunters to-day," his father reminded him; "we are explorers, and, more particularly, geographers on a mission in this part of New Switzerland."

The young Nimrod did not see the matter in that light, and made up his mind to beat the country with

his dogs as soon as the pinnace reached her first anchorage. He would further the cause of geography
in his own fashion; that is, he would survey partridges
and hares instead of the points of the compass. This
last was the job for the learned Ernest who was so
anxious to add to his map the new territory that lay
to the south of the Promised Land.

Of carnivorous animals and of those wild beasts
which, as has been said, were so numerous in the
woods and plains at the end of Pearl Bay and at the
entrance to the Green Valley, not a trace was seen
along the banks of the Montrose during the course of
this voyage. By great good fortune no lions or tigers,
panthers or leopards, showed themselves. Jackals could
be heard, indeed, howling in the outskirts of the
nearest woods. The conclusion was that these beasts,
which belong to a subgenus of the Canidæ family,
between the wolf and the fox, constituted the majority
of the fauna of the island.

It would be an oversight not to make mention of
the many waterfowl seen, duck, teal, and snipe, which
flew from one bank to another or took cover among the
reeds. Jack would never willingly have thrown away
such opportunities of exercising his skill. So he fired
a few successful shots, and no one found fault with
him for doing so, unless, perhaps, it was Hannah, who
always begged quarter for these inoffensive creatures.

"Inoffensive, perhaps, but excellent—when they are
cooked to a turn!" Jack retorted.

And it really was matter for congratulation that at
luncheon and dinner the bill of fare was supplemented

by the wild fowl which Fawn retrieved from the stream of the Montrose.

It was a little after eleven o'clock that the *Elizabeth* reached a second bend in the river which turned further to the west, according to Ernest's expectation. From its general direction it could be deduced with sufficient certainty that it came down from the range, still some fifteen miles or more away, from which it was manifestly fed largely.

"It is annoying that the tide has almost finished running," said Ernest, "and that we cannot go any farther."

"Really annoying," M. Zermatt replied, "but it is slack now, and the ebb will be perceptible quite soon. Well, as this is the season of the highest tides, it is clear that the flood tide never reaches much beyond this bend of the Montrose."

"Nothing could be clearer," Mr. Wolston agreed. "So now we must decide whether we shall moor here or whether we shall take advantage of the ebb to go back to the creek, which the pinnace could reach in less than two hours."

The spot was charming, and every one was much tempted to spend the day there. The left bank formed a tiny cove, into which a little tributary of fresh and running water fell. Above it bent some mighty trees, with dense foliage, in which myriad chirpings and rustlings of wings were heard. It was a clump of enormous Indian fig-trees, almost identical with the mangrove-trees at Falconhurst. Behind this were groups of evergreen oaks, through whose shade the

sun's rays could not pierce. Right at the back, under
the dome of guava trees and cinnamons, down the
whole length of the tributary stream, a fresh breeze
stole, swaying the lower branches like so many fans.

"What a perfectly delightful spot!" Mme. Zermatt
exclaimed. "Expressly designed to be the site of a
villa! A pity it is so far from Rock Castle!"

"Yes: much too far, my dear," M. Zermatt replied.
"But the site will not be wasted, you may be quite
sure, and we must not take everything for ourselves.
Would you leave nothing for our future fellow-
citizens?"

"You may be quite sure, Betsy," Mrs. Wolston said,
"that this part of the island, watered by the Montrose
river, will be much sought after by new colonists."

"Meanwhile," said Jack, "I vote we camp here until
evening, and even till to-morrow morning."

"That is what we have to decide," M. Zermatt
declared. "We must not forget that the ebb can take
us back to the creek in a couple of hours, and that
we should be back at Rock Castle by to-morrow
evening."

"What do you think about it, Hannah?" Ernest
asked.

"Let your father decide," the girl answered. "But
I quite agree that this spot is delightful, and it would
be pleasant to stay in it for one afternoon."

"Besides," Ernest continued, "I should like to take
a few more bearings."

"And we should like to take a little nourishment,"

Jack exclaimed. "Let us have lunch! Of your pity, let us have lunch!"

It was agreed that they should spend the afternoon and evening in this loop of the Montrose. Then, at the next ebb tide, about one o'clock in the morning, when the night was clear—there would be a full moon —the pinnace would go down the river without the least risk. After leaving the creek she would either go to Unicorn Bay and anchor there, or would round Cape East and make Rock Castle, as the state of the sea and the direction of the wind might dictate.

As soon as the pinnace was made fast by her bows to the foot of a tree, her stern immediately swung round down stream, clear proof that the ebb tide was beginning to run.

After luncheon Mme. Zermatt, Mrs. Wolston, and Hannah agreed to settle themselves down in the encampment while the exploration of the surrounding country was effected. It really was important to make a more complete survey of this region. So it was arranged that M. Zermatt and Jack should go and hunt along the little tributary, remaining comparatively close to its mouth, and that Mr. Wolston and Ernest should take the canoe and go as far up the river as they could, to return in time for dinner.

The canoe, paddled by Mr. Wolston and Ernest, set off up river, while M. Zermatt and Jack went along the bank of the winding streamlet which ran down from the north.

Beyond this loop the Montrose bent towards the south-west. The canoe kept on its way along banks bordered by leafy forest trees and rendered almost inaccessible by tangled grasses and interlaced reeds. It would have been impossible to effect a landing there, and it was not necessary. The important thing was to ascertain the general direction of the river by ascending it as far as possible. Moreover, the field of vision was soon enlarged. A mile or so further up, the forest mass grew less dense. Further on again, broad plains succeeded, deformed with rocky excrescences, which appeared to reach unbroken right to the foot of the mountains.

The surface of the Montrose river shone like a mirror. There was good reason to regret leaving the shadow of the trees which bordered it lower down. Moreover, in the midst of a broiling atmosphere, where there was now scarcely a breath of air, paddling was really hard work. Fortunately, the force of the stream was not increased by the tide running down, for the flood did not reach beyond the last loop or elbow. They only had to contend with the normal flow of the river. The waters were low now. Matters would be different in a few weeks' time, during the rainy season, when the mountain range would send down its contribution through the natural issue of the Montrose.

In spite of the heat, Mr. Wolston and Ernest paddled along energetically. Among the fantastic bluffs of the river, behind the points, there were occasional backwaters which they chose to take, so as to economise their labour.

"It is not impossible," said Mr. Wolston, "that we

might reach the foot of the range in which the Montrose must have its source."

"So you cling to your idea, sir?" Ernest replied, shaking his head.

"Yes, I do, and it is most devoutly to be wished it may be so, my dear boy. You will never know your island thoroughly until you have surveyed its entire extent from the top of those mountains, which, I may further remark, do not appear to be very lofty."

"I estimate their height at from twelve to fifteen hundred feet, Mr. Wolston, and I agree with you that from the top of them it will be possible to see all over New Switzerland, unless it is much larger than we suppose. What is there beyond that range? The only reason why we do not know already is that during these past twelve years we have never felt pinched for room in the Promised Land."

"Quite so, my dear boy," Mr. Wolston replied; "but it is a matter of real concern now to ascertain the actual size and importance of an island which is destined to be colonised."

"That will be done, sir, next dry season, and before the Unicorn comes back, you may be quite sure. To-day, however, I think it will be wisest to limit ourselves to just these few hours' exploring; that will be enough to enable us to ascertain the general course of the river."

"Yet with a little perseverance, Ernest, we might perhaps be able to reach the range, and climb its northern slope."

"Provided the climb is not too steep, sir."

"Oh, well, with a good pair of legs———"

"You ought to have brought Jack instead of me," said Ernest with a smile. "He would not have gainsaid you; he would have urged you to push on as far as the mountains, even if you could not have got back before to-morrow or the day after; and a nice state of anxiety we should all have been in, during your long delay!"

"Well, yes, you are quite right, my dear boy," Mr. Wolston admitted. "We must keep our promise since we have given it. One more hour's going, and then our canoe shall return with the stream. No matter! I shall not rest until we have planted the flag of old England on the highest peak of New Switzerland!"

Mr. Wolston's ambition, so warmly declared, was that of a good Englishman, at a time when Great Britain was sending her sailors over all the seas in the wide world to extend her colonial possessions. But he saw that it would be better to defer taking possession of the island until later, and he refrained from pressing the matter further now.

They went on their way in the canoe. The further they penetrated towards the south-west, the more open, treeless, and sterile the country became. The grass lands were succeeded by barren tracts strewn with stones. Hardly any birds flew over this naked area. There was no sign of animal life except the howling of packs of jackals, which kept out of sight.

"Jack was well advised not to come with us this time," Ernest remarked.

"Yes, indeed," Mr. Wolston answered; "he would

not have had the chance for a single shot. He will have much better luck in the forest land that is watered by the little tributary of the Montrose."

"Anyhow, what we bring back as the result of our trip is the information that this part of the island is like the part above Unicorn Bay," said Ernest. "Who can say whether it is not much the same on the other side of the range? Most likely the fertile part of the island is the north and the middle only, between Pearl Bay and the Green Valley."

"So when we set out on our big excursion," Mr. Wolston replied, "I think it will be best to march straight south instead of going all round the coast to the east or west."

"I think so, too, sir, and the best way to get into the country will be through the defile of Cluse."

It was now nearly four o'clock. The canoe was five or six miles above the encampment when a sound of roaring waters became audible from higher up the stream. Was it a mountain stream rushing into the bed of Montrose? Or was it the Montrose itself, forming rapids there? Did some dam of rocks render it unnavigable in the upper reaches?

Mr. Wolston and Ernest, stationary at the moment in a back water under the shelter of a bluff, were just preparing to turn back. As the bank was too steep for them to see above it Mr. Wolston said:

"Let us take a few strokes more and turn the point."

"Certainly," said Ernest; "it looks as if the Montrose will not help a boat to get up to the foot of the mountains."

Mr. Wolston and Ernest began to paddle again with what strength they had left after their four hours' toil under a burning sun.

The river here made a bend towards the south-west, which was manifestly its general direction. A few moments later, some hundrd yards further up, a much longer reach came into view. It was dammed by a heap of rocks scattered from one bank to the other, with only narrow breaks between, through which the water poured in noisy falls that spread commotion fifty yards below.

"That would have stopped us if we had meant to go on," Ernest remarked.

"It might have been possible to carry the canoe beyond the dam," Mr. Wolston answered.

"If it is nothing more than a dam, sir."

"We will find out, my dear boy, for it is really important to know. Let us get ashore."

On the left hand there was a narrow gorge, quite dry at this season, which wound away across the upland. In a few weeks' time, no doubt, when the rainy season began, it would serve as the bed of a torrent whose roaring waters would join those of the Montrose.

Mr. Wolston drove the boat-hook into the ground; and he and Ernest stepped onto the bank, up which they went so as to approach the dam from the side.

It took them about a quarter of an hour to cover the intervening distance, the path being strewn with stones loosely held in the sand by coarse clumps of grass.

Scattered here and there, too, were pebbles of a

brownish tint, with rounded corners, very like shingle, and about the size of nuts.

When Mr. Wolston and Ernest reached the dam they discovered that the Montrose was unnavigable for a good mile and a half. Its bed was obstructed with rocks among which the water boiled, and the portage of a canoe up stream would be a very laborious business.

The country appeared to be absolutely barren right up to the foot of the range. For any trace of verdure it was necessary to look towards the northwest and north, in the direction of the Green Valley, the distant forests of which could just be seen on the boundary of the Promised Land.

So there was nothing for it but to retrace their steps, and this Mr. Wolston and Ernest did, greatly regretting that the Montrose was blocked in this portion of its course.

As they went along the winding gorge Ernest picked up a few of the brownish pebbles, which were heavier than their size seemed to warrant. He put a couple of the little stones in his pocket with the intention of examining them when he got back to Rock Castle.

It was with a good deal of vexation that Mr. Wolston turned his back on the south-western horizon. But the sun was getting low, and it would not have done to be belated so far from the encampment. So the canoe took to the stream once more, and, driven along by the paddles, made good speed down the river.

At six o'clock the whole party was gathered together again at the foot of the clump of evergreen oaks. M.

Zermatt and Jack were well satisfied with their sport, and had brought back an antelope, a brace of rabbits, an agouti, and several birds of various kinds.

The little tributary of the Montrose watered a very fertile tract of country, sometimes crossing plains which were admirably suitable for raising grain, sometimes running through dense woods. There were also game districts where the sound of the sportsman's gun had almost certainly just been heard for the first time.

A good dinner was waiting for the men after their excursion. It was served under the shadow of the trees, on the bank of the stream, whose running waters murmured over their sandy bed, sprinkled with aquatic plants.

At nine o'clock all went to their berths aboard the *Elizabeth* to sleep well and soundly.

It had been settled that the pinnace should make a start at the beginning of the ebb, that is to say about one o'clock in the morning, so as to get the full advantage of the tide running out. Thus the time for sleep was limited. But this could be made up for the following night, either at Unicorn Bay, if they were in there, or at Rock Castle if the *Elizabeth* arrived there within the twenty-four hours.

In spite of the remonstrances of his sons and of Mr. Wolston, M. Zermatt had decided to remain on deck, undertaking to awaken them at the time arranged. It was necessary never wholly to relax caution. At night wild beasts, unseen by day, leave their lairs, drawn to the water-courses by thirst.

At one o'clock M Zermatt called Mr. Wolston,

Ernest, and Jack. The first rippling of the ebb was just becoming audible. A light breeze blew off the land. The sails were hoisted, hauled aboard, and gathered, and the pinnace yielded to the two-fold action of the stream and wind.

The night was very clear, the sky strewn with stars like snowflakes hung in space. The moon, almost full, was sinking slowly down towards the northern horizon.

Nothing occurred to disturb this night voyage, although some hippopotami were heard grunting, when half the journey was done. It will be remembered from Fritz's narrative of his trip on the Eastern River, that these amphibian monsters were already known to be in occupation of the water-courses of the island.

As the weather was splendid and the sea calm, it was agreed that the pinnace should make use at once of the morning breeze which was just rising out at sea. M. Zermatt was glad to think that they might get back to Rock Castle in about fifteen hours, that is to say before nightfall.

In order to take the shortest route and make Cape East in a straight line, the *Elizabeth* was sailed a mile or more away out to sea. Her passengers were then able to get a more complete view of the coast for fully fifteen miles in a southerly direction.

M. Zermatt ordered the sheets to be hauled in, so as to work to windward, and the pinnace shaped her course for Cape East on the starboard tack.

Just at this moment Mr. Wolston, who was standing in the bows, raised his spyglass to his eyes. He wiped its glass and scrutinised one of the points of the coast with extreme attention.

Several times in succession he raised and then lowered the instrument, and everyone was struck by the interest with which he scanned the horizon to the south-east.

M. Zermatt handed over the tiller to Jack, and came forward with the intention of questioning Mr. Wolston, who removed the telescope from his eye and said:

"No; I am mistaken."

"What are you mistaken about, Wolston?" M. Zermatt enquired. "What did you think you saw over there?"

"Smoke."

"Smoke?" echoed Ernest, who had come up, disturbed by the reply.

For the smoke could only come from some camp pitched on that part of the shore. And that theory involved some disturbing questions. Was the island inhabited by savages? Had they come from the Australian shore in their canoes and landed, and would they attempt to penetrate into the interior? The inhabitants of Rock Castle would be in considerable danger if such people ever set foot within the Promised Land.

"Where did you see the smoke?" M. Zermatt asked sharply.

"There—above the last point that projects from the shore on this side."

And Mr. Wolston pointed to the extreme end of the

land, twelve miles or so away, which beyond that point turned off to the south-west and was lost to sight.

M. Zermatt and Ernest, one after the other, examined the indicated spot with the utmost care.

"Nothing at all," Ernest added.

Mr. Wolston watched for a few minutes more with the closest attention.

"No; I cannot distinguish the smoke now," he said. "It must have been some light greyish vapour—a little cloud lying very low, perhaps, which has just melted away."

The answer was reassuring. Yet as long as the point was within sight M. Zermatt and his companions never took their eyes off it. But they saw nothing which could cause them any uneasiness.

The *Elizabeth*, under full sail, was moving rapidly over a rather choppy sea, which did not check her way. At one o'clock in the afternoon she was off Unicorn Bay, which was left a couple of miles to larboard; then, approaching nearer to the coast, she made in a straight line towards Cape East.

The cape was rounded at four o'clock and as the flood tide was setting to the west of Deliverance Bay, an hour would suffice to cover that distance. Rounding Shark's Island, the *Elizabeth* made at full speed towards Jackal River, and thirty-five minutes later her passengers set foot on the beach at Rock Castle.

CHAPTER XI

IN THE SEASON OF RAINS

FOUR days and a half had been the length of its inhabitants' absence from Rock Castle. It might have been as long again without the domestic animals suffering thereby, as their sheds had been provisioned for a long period. Mr. Wolston would then have had time to carry his exploration to the foot of the range, to which he was comparatively close when at the dam across the river. Very probably too, he would have suggested to M. Zermatt that they should stay three or four days longer at the anchorage up the Montrose, if there had been no obstacle in the way of the canoe going up the course of the river.

But the voyage of exploration had not been without results. The pinnace had been able to reconnoitre the eastern coast for a distance of some twenty-five miles from Cape East. This, with the addition of an equal extent of littoral visited in the north as far as Pearl Bay, was the sum of what was known of the contour of the island. With respect to its perimeter on the west and south, the aspect it presented and the districts it bounded, whether barren or fertile, the two families could have no certain knowledge without making a voyage all round the island, unless indeed the ascent of the mountains should enable a view to be obtained of the whole of New Switzerland.

There was, of course, the probability that the *Unicorn* had made a survey of its dimensions and its shape when she resumed her voyage. And so, in the event of the expedition planned by Mr. Wolston not resulting in a complete discovery of the island, they would only have to wait for the return of the English corvette to know all about it.

Meantime, and for the next seven or eight weeks, every hour would be fully occupied with the work of haymaking and harvesting, threshing, grapegathering, and getting in the crops. No one would be able to take a single day off if they were to get all the farms in order before the broken weather, which constituted the winter in this latitude of the southern hemisphere.

So every one set to work, and, as a beginning, the two families moved to Falconhurst. By this removal they put themselves within easy reach of Wood Grange, Sugar-cane Grove, and Prospect Hill. The summer dwelling was lacking in neither space nor comfort, for new rooms had been built among the gigantic roots of the mangrove, and there was also, of course, the upper storey in the air which the surrounding foliage rendered so delightful. At the foot of the tree a large yard was provided for the animals, with sheds and out-houses, surrounded by an impenetrable hedge of bamboo and thorny shrubs.

It is unnecessary to describe in detail all the work which was undertaken and successfully accomplished during these two months. They had to go from one farm to another, store all the grain and fodder in the barns, gather all the ripe fruit and make all arrangements to protect the birds in the poultry-yards from the inclemency of the rainy season.

Thanks to the irrigation from Swan Lake, which was abundantly supplied by the canal, the yield of the farms had increased appreciably. This district of the Promised Land could have provided a hundred colonists with a safe living, and its present inhabitants had plenty of work to get in all the harvest.

In anticipation of the stormy weather, which would last for eight or nine weeks, they also had to safeguard the farmsteads, against damage by wind or rain. The gates and fences of the yards and fields, and the doors and windows of the buildings were tightly closed, caulked, and shored up. The roofs were weighted with heavy logs, to resist the fierce easterly squalls. Like precautions were taken in the case of the outhouses, barns, sheds, and fowl-houses, whose occupants, two-legged and four-legged, were too numerous to be brought into the outbuildings at Rock Castle. Moreover, the various buildings on Whale Island and Shark's Island were put into condition to withstand the tremendous gales to which they were directly exposed by their situation near the shore.

On Whale Island the resinous trees, the evergreen sea-pines, now formed thick woods. The nursery plantations of cocoa-trees and other species had thrived, since they had been protected by thorn hedges. There had been no risk of damage since then from the hundreds of rabbits which in the early days used to devour all the shoots. These voracious rodents found plenty of food among the seawrack. Jenny would certainly find the island, of which M. Zermatt had given her the sole possession, in perfect condition.

In the case of Shark's Island again, the plantations of cocoa-trees, mangroves, and pines had prospered greatly. The enclosures for the antelopes that were being tamed had to be strengthened. Of grass and leaves, which form the food of these ruminants, there would be no lack during the winter. Fresh water, thanks to the inexhaustible spring discovered at the far end of the island, would not run short. M. Zermatt had built a central shed of stout planks in which provisions of every kind were stored. Finally, the battery erected on the flat top of the little hill was covered in with a solid roof and protected by the trees over which the flagstaff rose.

On the occasion of this visit, in accordance with the custom at the beginning as at the end of the rainy season, Ernest and Jack fired the regulation two guns. This time no answering report was heard from the open sea, such as had happened six months before after the arrival of the English corvette.

When the two guns had been reloaded and primed, Jack exclaimed:

"Now it will be our turn to answer the *Unicorn*, when she salutes New Switzerland, and think of the delight with which we shall send her our answer!"

It was not long before the last crops were got into the barns and storerooms of Rock Castle; wheat, barley, rye, rice, maize, oats, millet, tapioca, sago, and sweet potatoes. Peas, kidney beans, broad beans, carrots, turnips, leeks, lettuce, and endive would be supplied in abundance from the kitchen garden, which had been rendered extraordinarily productive by proper attention to the rotation of the crops. Fields of sugar-cane and orchards of fruit trees were within a stone's throw of the dwelling place, on both banks of the stream. The gathering of the grapes in the vineyard at Falconhurst was finished in due time, and for the making of mead there was no lack of honey, or of the spices and rye-cakes required to assist its process of fermentation. There was also plenty of palm wine, not to mention the reserve store of Canary. Of the brandy left by Lieutenant Littlestone there were several kegs in the cool basement of the rocky cave. Fuel for the kitchen stove was provided by dry wood piled in the wood-sheds, and further, the gales might be relied upon to strew the beaches outside Rock Castle with branches, while the flood tides drove more onto the shore of Deliverance Bay. Moreover, there was no need to use this fuel to warm the hall and rooms. In the tropics, below the nineteenth parallel, the cold is never distressing. Fires were only needed for cooking, washing, and other housework.

The second fortnight of May arrived, and it was time for all this work to be finished. There was no mistaking the signs that heralded the approach of the bad weather. Each sunset the sky was covered with mists, which grew denser day by day. The wind gradually settled in the east, and when it blew from that quarter all the storms at sea swept madly upon the island.

Before withdrawing into Rock Castle M. Zermatt determined to spend the whole day of the 24th on a trip to the hermitage at Eberfurt, and Mr. Wolston and Jack were to go with him.

It was desirable to make sure that the defile of Cluse was effectively closed against the invasion of wild beasts. It was of the utmost importance to prevent their breaking through and causing wholesale destruction of the plantations.

This farmstead, the most remote one, was seven or eight miles from Rock Castle.

The party, mounted on the buffalo, the onager, and the ostrich, arrived at the hermitage in less than two hours. The enclosures were found to be in a good state of repair, but it was deemed prudent to strengthen the entrance with a few stout cross-bars. An invasion of carnivorous animals or pachyderms was not to be feared so long as they could not make their way through the defile.

No suspicious marks or tracks were detected, much to Jack's disappointment. That keen sportsman was always promising himself that he would capture at least a young elephant. After he had tamed and domesticated it he would certainly break it in for his own riding.

At last, on the 25th, when the first rains began to fall upon the island, the two families finally left Falconhurst and settled down in Rock Castle.

No country could have offered a more secluded abode,

sheltered from all inclemency of weather, or one more delightfully arranged. Endless had been the improvements since the day when Jack's pickaxe had "gone through the mountain"! The salt cavern had become a comfortable dwelling place. In the forefront of the rocky mass there was still the same arrangement of rooms *en suite*, with doors and windows cut through. The library, so dear to Ernest's heart, with two bays open to the east on the Jackal River side, was surmounted by a graceful pigeon-house. The vast saloon, with windows draped with green material lightly coated with india-rubber, and furnished with the principal articles, taken from the *Landlord*, still continued to serve as an oratory, pending the time when Mr. Wolston should have built his chapel.

Above the rooms was a terrace, to which two pathways gave access, and in front a verandah, with a sloping roof supported by fourteen bamboo pillars. Along these pillars pepper plants twined their shoots, with other shrubs which exhaled a pleasant scent of vanilla, mingled with bindweeds and climbing plants now in their full verdure.

On the other side of the cave, following up the course of the river, the private gardens of Rock Castle spread. They were surrounded by thorn hedges, and were divided into square beds of vegetables, fancy beds of flowers, and plantations of pistachios, almonds, walnuts, oranges, lemons, bananas, guavas, and every other species of fruit found in hot countries. The trees proper to the temperate climes of Europe, such as cherries, pears, wild cherries and figs, were to be found in the grand alley, which they lined the whole way to Falconhurst.

From the 25th onwards the rains never ceased. And with them burst the lashing, hissing squalls which drove from the sea over the table-lands of Cape East. All excursions out of doors were impossible thenceforward, and only the various occupations of the household could be carried on. But it was important work, the care and attention that had to be given to the animals, to the buffaloes, onager, cows, calves, and asses, and to the pets, like the monkey, Nip the Second; Jack's jackal, and Jenny's jackal, and cormorant, these last being especially pampered for her sake. Lastly, there was all the housework and preserve-making to attend to, and sometimes, when, very occasionally, the weather cleared for a short time, a little fishing could be got at the mouth of Jackal River and at the foot of the rocks below Rock Castle.

In the first week of June there was a vast increase in the gales and rains. It was imprudent to go out, except in water-proof oil-skins.

The entire neighbourhood, kitchen garden, plantations, and fields, was swamped under these torrential downpours, and from the top of the cliff above Rock Castle a thousand tiny streams broke away, making a noise like so many cascades.

Although no one set foot outside the house unless it was absolutely necessary, there was no dullness.

One evening M. Zermatt made the following calculation:

"Here we are at the 15th of June. The *Unicorn* left us on the 20th of October last year, so that is eight full months. Therefore she ought to be on the point of leaving European waters for the Indian Ocean."

"What do you think, Ernest?" Mme. Zermatt asked.

"If you take her stay at the Cape into account," Ernest answered, "I think the corvette might have reached an English port in three months. It will take her the same time to come back, and as it was understood that she was to be back in a year, that means that she will have had to remain half a year in Europe. So my conclusion is that she is still there."

"But probably on the eve of sailing," Hannah remarked.

"Most likely, Hannah dear," Ernest replied.

"After all," said Mrs. Wolston, "she might have cut her stay in England short."

"She might have done so, certainly," Mr. Wolston answered, "although six months would not be too long for all that she had to do. Our Lords of the Admiralty are not remarkably expeditious."

"Oh, but when it is a question of taking possession!" M. Zermatt exclaimed.

"That gets done!" Jack laughed. "Are you aware that it is a very handsome present we are making to your country, Mr. Wolston?"

"I quite agree, my dear boy."

"And yet," the young man went on, "what a chance it would have been for our dear old Switzerland to embark upon a career of colonial expansion! An island which possesses all the animal and vegetable wealth of the torrid zone—an island so admirably situated in the very middle of the Indian Ocean for trade with the Far East and the Pacific!"

"There goes Jack, off again, as if he were careering on Grumbler or Lightfoot!" Mr. Wolston said.

"But, Ernest," Hannah interposed, "what are we to conclude from your calculations about the *Unicorn?*"

"Why, that it will be in the first few days of July at latest that she will set sail on her voyage here with our dear ones and the colonists who may have decided to come with them. She will put in at the Cape, Hannah, and that will probably delay her until about the middle of August. So I do not expect to see her off False Hope Point before the middle of October."

"Four more long months!" Mme. Zermatt sighed. "We need patience when we think of all those whom we love upon the sea! May God guard them!"

The women, busy with their household work, never wasted a minute, but it must not be supposed that the men were idle. The rumbling of the forge and the purring of the lathe were constantly to be heard. Mr. Wolston was a very clever engineer, and, assisted M. Zermatt, sometimes by Ernest, and on rarer occasions by Jack, who was always out of doors if there was the least sign of the weather clearing up, he made a number of useful articles to complete the fittings of Rock Castle.

One scheme which was exhaustively discussed and finally agreed upon was the building of a chapel.

The question of the site furnished the subject for several debates. Some thought that the selected site ought to front the sea and be on one of the cliffs halfway between Rock Castle and Falconhurst, so that it could be reached from both houses without too long a walk. Others thought that on such a site the chapel would be too much exposed to the gales blowing in from the sea, and that it would be better to build it near Jackal River, below the fall. Mme. Zermatt, however, and Mrs. Wolston thought that that would be too far away. So it was decided to build the chapel at the far end of the kitchen garden, on a spot that was well sheltered by lofty rocks.

Mr. Wolston then suggested that more solid and durable material than wood and bamboo should be employed. Why not use blocks of limestone, or even pebbles from the beach, in the fashion often seen in sea-side villages? Lime could be produced from the shells and reef-coral which existed in such quantity on the shore, by raising them to a red heat to extract the carbonic acid. The work would be begun when weather permitted, and two or three months would be ample to bring it to a satisfactory conclusion.

In July, which was the heart of the rainy season in this latitude, the violence of the storms was intensified. It was seldom possible to venture out of doors. Squalls and gales lashed the coast with tremendous fury. One might fancy oneself bombarded with grape-shot when the hail fell. The sea towered in enormous rolling waves, roaring as they broke in the chasms of the coast. Often the spray swept right over the cliff and fell in thick sheets at the foot of the trees. There were occasions when the wind and the tide combined to produce a kind of tidal wave which drove the water of Jackal River right back to the foot of the fall.

M. Zermatt was in a continual state of anxiety about the adjacent fields. They even had to cut the pipes which connected the river with Swan Lake, to prevent the overplus of water from swamping the land round Wood Grange. The position of the pinnace and the longboat in the creek also gave rise to some apprehension. On many occasions they had to make sure that the anchors were holding, and to double the hawsers to prevent collision with the rocks. As a matter of fact, no damage was done in this particular. But what kind of state must the farms be in, especially Wood Grange and Prospect Hill, which were more exposed than the others owing to their proximity to the shore, which the hurricanes lashed with positively terrifying fury?

So M. Zermatt, Ernest, Jack and Mr. Wolston determined to take advantage of a day which gave a brief respite from the storm, to go as far as False Hope Point.

Their fears were only too well founded. The two farms had suffered much, and required a great deal of strengthening and repair which could not be undertaken at this season and was therefore postponed until the end of the rains.

It was in the library that the two families usually

spent their evenings. As has been said, there were plenty of books there, some brought from the *Land-lord;* others, more modern works, given by Lieutenant Littlestone, including books of travel and works on natural history, zoology and botany, which were read over and over again by Ernest; others, again, which belonged to Mr. Wolston, manuals of mechanics, meteorology, physics and chemistry. There were also books about hunting and sport in India and Africa which filled Jack with longing to go out to those countries.

While the storm moaned and roared outside, in-doors they read aloud. They conversed, sometimes in English, sometimes in German—two languages which both families now spoke fluently, although they some-times had to use their dictionaries. There were eve-nings when only one language was employed, English, Swiss, or German, or, though in this they had less facility, Swiss French. Ernest and Hannah were the only two who had made much progress in this beau-tiful language, which is so pure, so precise, so flexible, so happily fitted to express the inspiration of poetry, and so accurately adapted to everything relating to science and art. It was quite a pleasure to hear the young man and the girl conversing in French, although all that they said was not always understood by the others.

As had been said, July is the worst month in this portion of the Indian Ocean. When the storms abated, there supervened thick fogs, which enveloped the entire island. If a ship had passed within only a few cables' lengths, she could not have seen either the inland heights or the capes along the coast. It was not without reason that they feared lest some other ship might perish in these seas as the *Landlord* and the *Dorcas* had perished. The future would certainly make it incumbent upon the new colonists to light the coasts of New Switzerland and so make it easier to effect a landing there, at any rate in the north.

"Why should we not build a lighthouse?" Jack enquired. "Let us see: a lighthouse on False Hope Point, perhaps, and another on Cape East! Then, with signal guns from Shark's Island, ships would have no difficulty in getting into Deliverance Bay."

"It will be done, my dear boy," M. Zermatt answered, "for everything gets done in time. Fortunately, Lieutenant Littlestone did not need any lighthouses to see our island, nor any guns to help him to anchor opposite Rock Castle."

"Anyhow," Jack went on, "we should be quite equal, I imagine, to lighting the coast."

"Jack is certainly not afraid of attempting big things," Mr. Wolston said.

"Why should I be, Mr. Wolston, after all we have done as yet, and all we shall do under your instructions?"

"You know how to pay compliments, my boy," M. Zermatt remarked.

"And I am not forgetting Mrs. Wolston, or Hannah," Jack added.

"In any case," Hannah replied, "if I had not the

knowledge I would not fail through any lack of good will."

"And with good will——" Ernest went on.

"One can build lighthouses two hundred feet above the level of the Indian Ocean," Jack answered lightly. "So I rely upon Hannah to lay the first stone."

"Whenever you like, my dear Jack," she answered, laughing.

On the morning of the 25th of July, M. and Mme. Zermatt were in their room when Ernest came to them, looking even more serious than usual, his eyes shining brightly.

He wanted to acquaint his father with a discovery, which, if properly worked, might, he thought, have results of the very highest importance in the future.

In his hand he held something which he handed to M. Zermatt after a final look at it.

It was one of the pebbles he had picked up in the gorge on the occasion of his trip in the canoe, with Mr. Wolston, on the upper reaches of the Montrose River.

M. Zermatt took the pebble, the weight of which surprised him to begin with. Then he asked his son why he brought it to him with such an air of mystery.

"Because it is worth while to give it a little careful attention," Ernest replied.

"Why?"

"Because that pebble is a nugget."

"A nugget?" M. Zermatt said questioningly.

And going to the window he began to look at it in the better light.

"I am certain of what I allege," Ernest declared. "I have examined that pebble, have analysed some portions of it, and I can guarantee that it is largely composed of gold in a native state."

"Are you sure you are not mistaken, my boy?" M. Zermatt asked.

"Quite, Papa, quite!"

Mme. Zermatt had listened to this conversation without speaking a word, without even putting out her hand to take the precious object, the finding of which seemed to leave her quite indifferent.

Ernest continued:

"Now, as we were coming back down the Montrose gorge I noticed a number of pebbles like that. So it is certain that there are quantities of nuggets in that corner of the island."

"And what does that matter to us?" Mme. Zermatt demanded.

M. Zermatt looked at his wife, recognising all the scorn in her remark.

Then he said:

"My dear Ernest, you have not mentioned your discovery to any one?"

"To no one."

"I am glad: not because I have no confidence in your brother or in Mr. Wolston. But this is a secret that ought to be carefully considered before it is divulged."

"What is there to be afraid of, Papa?" Ernest asked.

"Nothing at present, but much for the future of the colony! Let the existence of these gold-bearing districts once be heard of, let it once be known that New Switzerland is rich in nuggets, and gold-miners will come in crowds, and in their train will come all the evils, all the disorder, all the crimes that gold-hunting involves! You may be quite sure that what did not escape you, Ernest, will not escape others, and that all the mineral treasures of the Montrose will be known some day. Well, let that be as far in the future as possible! You were right to keep this secret, my boy, and we will keep it too."

"That is wisely spoken, dear," Mme. Zermatt added, "and I quite approve of all you have said. No! Let us say nothing, and do not let us go back to that gorge up the Montrose. Let us leave it to chance, or rather to God, who orders all the treasures of this world and distributes them as He thinks fit!"

Father, mother, and son agreed. The desert region between the upper reaches of the river and the foot of the mountain range would not attract the new inhabitants of the island for a long time to come, and beyond question many evils would thus be avoided.

The rainy season was now at its height. For at least another three weeks they must exercise patience. After twenty-four hours' respite the gales burst out again with greater violence, under the influence of the atmospheric disturbances which convulsed the whole of the north of the Indian Ocean. It was now

August. Although this month only represents our February in the Southern hemisphere, it is then, between the Tropics and the Equator, that the rains and winds usually begin to abate and the sky to be cleared from the heavy vapours.

"For twelve years we have never experienced such a long series of gales," M. Zermatt remarked one day. "Even in May and July there were some weeks of lull. And the west wind always sets in again at the beginning of August."

"You will get a very sorry idea of our island, Merry dear," Mme. Zermatt added.

"Make yourself easy, Betsy," Mrs. Wolston replied. "Are we not accustomed in my country, England, to bad weather for six months in the year?"

"It is abominable!" said Jack emphatically. "An August like this in New Switzerland! I ought to have been out hunting three weeks ago, and every morning my dogs ask me what is the matter!"

"This spell will soon end now," Ernest declared. "If I may believe the barometer and the thermometer, it will not be long before we get into the period of thunderstorms, which generally is the end of the rainy season."

"Anyhow," said Jack, "this abominable weather is lasting too long. It is not what we promised Mr. and Mrs. Wolston, and I am sure Hannah is cross with us for having deceived her."

"No, I am not, Jack—really."

"And that she would be glad to go away!"

The young girl's eyes answered for her. They told

how happy she was in the cordial hospitality of the
Zermatts.   Her real hope was that nothing would
ever part her parents and herself from them!

As Ernest had remarked, the rainy season generally
ended in violent thunderstorms, which lasted for five
or six days.   The whole heavens were then illumined
by lightning, followed by peals of thunder as though
the starry vault were crashing in, peals which re-echoed
from a thousand points along the shore.

It was on the 17th of August that these storms
were announced by a rising of the temperature, an
increasing heaviness of the atmosphere, and a drifting
up in the north-west of livid clouds, denoting high
electric tension.

Rock Castle, from the shelter of its dome of rock,
set wind and rain at defiance.   There was nothing
to be feared there from the lightning, which is so
dangerous in open country or among trees, to which
the electric fluid is easily attracted.

The next day but one, in the evening, the skies were
rent by the most terrible ball of fire that had fallen
yet.   All gathered in the library sprang to their feet at
the noise of the dry and rending peal of thunder,
which went rolling on and on through the upper zones
of the air.

Then, after a minute's interval, dead silence reigned
outside.

The bolt had unquestionably fallen not far from
Rock Castle.

At this moment the report of an explosion was heard.

"What is that?" cried Jack.

"It is not thunder," said M. Zermatt.

"Certainly not," said Mr. Wolston, who had come to the window.

"Was it a gun fired outside the bay?" Ernest asked.

All listened with panting hearts.

Were they mistaken—was it an acoustic illusion, a final thunderclap?

If it was really the discharge of a piece of ordnance, it meant that a ship was off the island, driven there by the storm, and perhaps in distress.

A second report resounded. It was the same sound, and therefore came from the same distance, and this time no lightning had preceded it.

"Another," said Jack, "and there can be no doubt——"

"Yes," Mr. Wolston declared, "it was a gun we just heard!"

Hannah ran towards the door crying out as if involuntarily:

"The *Unicorn!* It can only be the *Unicorn!*"

For a few moments a stupefied silence reigned. The *Unicorn* off the island, and calling for help? No, no! That some ship might have been driven to the northeast, and be disabled and drifting among the reefs of False Hope Point or Cape East, was conceivable. But that it was the English corvette was not admissible. That would have necessitated her having left Europe three months earlier than they had expected. No, no! And M. Zermatt was so emphatic in his assertion of the contrary that all came round to his opinion: this could not be the *Unicorn*.

But it was none the less appalling to think that a ship was in distress near the island, that the gale was driving her onto the reef where the *Landlord* had been dashed to pieces, and that she was appealing for help in vain.

M. Zermatt, Mr. Wolston, Ernest, and Jack went out into the rain and climbed up the shoulder of cliff behind Rock Castle.

The darkness was so intense that they could not see farther than a very few yards in the direction of the sea. All four were obliged to return almost at once, without having seen anything on the surface of Deliverance Bay.

"And if we had seen, what could we do to help the ship?" Jack asked.

"Nothing," M. Zermatt answered.

"Let us pray for those in peril," said Mrs. Wolston; "may the Almighty protect them!"

The three women fell on their knees beside the window, and the men stood by them with bent heads.

As no other report of guns was heard, they were obliged to conclude that the vessel was either lost with all hands or had passed by the island out to sea.

No one left the great hall that night, and directly day appeared, the storm having ceased, all hurried out of the grounds of Rock Castle.

There was no sail in sight, either in Deliverance Bay or in the arm of the sea between False Hope Point and Cape East.

Nor was anything to be seen of any ship which

might have been dashed upon the *Landlord's* reef six or seven miles beyond.

"Let us go to Shark's Island," Jack suggested.

"You are right," M. Zermatt replied. "We shall see farther from the top of the battery."

"Besides," Jack added, "now or never is the time to fire a few guns. Who knows if they won't be heard at sea, and answered?"

The difficulty evidently would be to get to Shark's Island, for the bay must still be very rough indeed. But the distance was not much more than a couple of miles, and the longboat could risk it.

Mme. Zermatt and Mrs. Wolston, conquering their anxiety, did not oppose the idea. It might be a question of saving the lives of fellow-men.

At seven o'clock the boat left the little creek. M. Zermatt and Mr. Wolston, Ernest, and Jack all rowed energetically, helped forward by the ebb tide. A few bucketfuls shipped over the bows did not frighten them into turning back.

Directly they reached the island all four jumped out onto the low rocks.

What havoc they found! Trees lying uprooted by the wind, the antelopes' paddocks were destroyed, and the terrified animals rushing about all over the place!

M. Zermatt and the rest reached the foot of the little hill on which the battery stood, and Jack was naturally the first to appear at the top.

"Come along, come along!" he shouted impatiently.

M. Zermatt, Mr. Wolston and Ernest hurried up to him.

The shed under which the two guns were placed side by side had been burnt down during the night, and all that was left of it was a few ruins, which were still smoking. The flag-staff was split right down, and lay in the midst of a heap of half-burnt grass and brushwood. The trees, whose branches had been interlaced above the battery, were shivered right down to their roots, and the marks could be seen of flames that had consumed their upper branches.

The two guns were still upon their gun-carriages, which were too heavy for the gale to overturn them.

Ernest and Jack had brought quick-matches, and were also provided with several cannon-cartridges in order that they might be able to continue firing if they heard any reports from out at sea.

Jack, posted by the first gun, applied the light.

The match burnt right down to the touch-hole, but the charge did not go off.

"The charge has got damp," Mr. Wolston remarked, "and could not catch light."

"Let us change it," M. Zermatt replied. "Jack, take the sponge and try to clean out the gun. Then you can put a new cartridge in."

But when the sponge had been thrust into the gun, it went right down to the end of it, much to Jack's surprise. The old cartridge, which had been put in it at the end of the summer, was not there. It was the same with the second gun."

"So they have been fired!" Mr. Wolston exclaimed.

"Fired?" M. Zermatt repeated.

"Yes—both of them," Jack replied.

"But by whom?"

"By whom?" Ernest answered. "Why, by the thunder itself."

"The thunder?" M. Zermatt repeated.

"Not a doubt of it, papa. That last thunderbolt which we heard yesterday fell upon the hill. The hangar caught fire, and when the flames reached the two guns, the two charges exploded, one after the other."

This was the obvious explanation, in view of the burnt ruins which strewed the ground. But what anxious hours the good people at Rock Castle had spent during that interminable night of storm!

"Nice sort of thunder, turning gunner!" Jack exclaimed. "*Jupiter Tonans* is meddling with what is no concern of his!"

The cannon were reloaded, and the longboat left Shark's Island, where the hangar must be rebuilt as soon as the weather permitted.

But as no vessel had arrived in the waters of the island in the course of the previous night, so no vessel had been lost upon the reefs of New Switzerland.

CHAPTER XII

THE rainy season, which was very long drawn out that year, came to an end about the last week in August. The work of ploughing and sowing was immediately begun. As M. Zermatt did not propose to start upon the expedition to the interior before the third week in September, there would be ample time for this labour.

On this occasion the two families decided not to settle in at Falconhurst. The dwelling-place in the air had suffered damage during the recent storms, and some repairs were necessary. They would merely pass a few days there to attend to the sowing, the pruning of the vineyard, and what had to be done for the animals; and they would not make any longer stay at Wood Grange or Sugar-cane Grove or Prospect Hill.

"We must remember," said M. Zermatt, "that when our absent ones come back, with all the new friends that they will bring, Colonel Montrose, your son James and his wife, my dear Wolston, and perhaps some new colonists, additions will be absolutely necessary at Falconhurst and the other farms. Some additional pairs of hands will be uncommonly useful for all that work, which is bound to be heavy. Let us confine our attention now to our fields and stables and poultry-yards. We shall have quite enough to do in the next two months, while waiting for the *Unicorn*."

As Mme. Zermatt and Mrs. Wolston must stay at Rock Castle, they agreed to be responsible for everything both in and out of doors, the cattle, the birds on Goose Pond, and the vegetable garden. They gave Hannah permission to go with her father to the farms, and the girl and Ernest were equally pleased.

The waggon, drawn by the two buffaloes, and the three asses, was to be used in the transport across the Promised Land. M. Zermatt, Ernest, Mr. Wolston and Hannah were to drive in the waggon, while Jack, who always enjoyed acting as scout, was to ride before them on the onager, Lightfoot.

On the 25th of August, the first halt was made at Falconhurst. The weather was fine, with a light breeze blowing from Deliverance Bay. The heat, as yet, was not excessive. The journey along the shady avenue of trees which lined the river bank resembled a pleasant stroll.

There was no agricultural labour to be done at Falconhurst. The fields which had to be sown were at the other, more remote, farms. The whole time was devoted to the animals, to supplying them with fresh food, executing some necessary repairs to the sheds, and cleaning and dredging the little stream which watered this property.

The magnificent trees in the adjoining wood had withstood the fierce assaults of the storms, though not without the loss of a few branches. All this dead wood had to be collected and piled in the woodsheds in the yard.

It was discovered that one of the largest mangrove trees had been struck by lightning. Although the same fate had not befallen the tree which supported the aerial dwelling-place, Ernest thought it would be prudent to protect it by means of a lightning conductor reaching above the top of its highest branches and connected with the ground by a metal rod. He determined to look into the matter of this device, for the summer season was broken by many thunderstorms, and the electricity might have caused serious damage at Falconhurst.

All this work took three full days, and it was not until the fourth that M. Zermatt returned to Rock Castle. He left it again forty-eight hours later with his companions, and, riding and driving as before, they took the road to Wood Grange.

The distance between Rock Castle and that farm was covered in the morning. Directly they arrived, everybody set to work. It was here that the sheepfold was, with an annually increasing number of sheep and goats; and here, too, was a poultry-run with several hundreds of birds. There was damage to be repaired in the hayloft, where the feed from the last harvest had been stored.

The dwelling-house did not appear to have suffered at all from the bad weather. This, however, was not the mere shanty of the early days, made of flexible reeds and slender, pliable poles. It was a brick cottage now, coated outside with sand and clay, and inside with plaster, so that it was impervious to damp. The cotton plantations contiguous to Wood Grange appeared to be in excellent condition. So, too, did the marsh, now a regular rice-field, the soil of which had not been undermined by the rains. On the other side, Swan Lake was full almost to the top of its banks, even at its lowest, but there was nothing about it to suggest an inundation of the adjacent fields. The little lake was alive with countless flocks of aquatic birds, herons, pelicans, snipe, moorhens, and, most graceful of all, coal-black swans sailing in pairs upon its surface.

Jack brought down several dozen ducks, and a magnificent water-cavy, which he got in the underwood, and which the waggon would take back to Rock Castle.

The monkeys had ceased to trouble. Not a single one was to be seen. Since the massacre of so many of them they had wisely decided to decamp.

Having attended to the animals, they applied themselves to sowing the Wood Grange fields. The soil was so fertile that it required no ploughing or manuring. All that was necessary to freshen it in preparation for another crop was to harrow it with the harrow which the asses drew. But the sowing required a good deal of time and the co-operation of all hands, even Hannah's, and it was not possible to return to Rock Castle before the 6th of September.

Those who thus came back could not but compliment Mrs. Wolston and Mme. Zermatt on the zeal and energy they had displayed during their absence. The poultry-yard and the cattle-sheds were in perfect condition; the kitchen garden had been cleaned and weeded, and the vegetable plants pricked out in masterly style. The two good housewives had also gone in for a complete spring cleaning.

It was then decided that a final excursion should be made in the next few days to the other settlements in the district. The farms at Sugar-cane Grove and at Prospect Hill could be visited in the one trip. But to reach False Hope Point would certainly take a week, and they could not count upon being back before the middle of September.

"As for the hermitage at Eberfurt," M. Zermatt remarked, "we shall have an opportunity to visit that when we make our expedition into the interior of the island, for there is no other way out of the Promised Land except the defile of Cluse, and that is near our farm."

"Quite so," Mr. Wolston replied; "but isn't there any work to be done on the land over there which would suffer by the delay?"

"My dear Wolston," M. Zermatt answered, "all we have to do is wait until we are wanted for the haymaking and the harvesting, and that will not be for several weeks. So let us finish up with Sugar-cane Grove and Prospect Hill."

This agreed to, it was decided that Hannah should not go with her father this time, since the journey might take longer than a week, and Mrs. Wolston might miss her.

Ernest was disappointed, and asked whether his presence, too, at Rock Island was not also indispensable.

It was Jack who came to his aid. The day before the start, when everybody was assembled in the general hall, he made the following bold suggestion:

"Papa, I know quite well that Mrs. Wolston and Hannah and Mamma do not really run any risk by being left alone at Rock Castle—but when it is a question of leaving them for a whole week—who can say—well, perhaps——"

"Very true, Jack," M. Zermatt replied; "I shall not have an easy minute the whole time we are away, although there is no reason to anticipate any danger. Up to now we have never been separated for more than two or three days, and this time it will be for a whole week. It is a long time. Yet, it would be very inconvenient for us all to go together."

"If you like," said Mr. Wolston, "I will stay at Rock Castle."

"No, my dear Wolston, anyone rather than you," M. Zermatt replied. "You must go with us to Sugarcane Grove and Prospect Hill, because of all that is to be done there in the future. But if one of the boys is willing to stay with his mother I shall have no more anxiety. That has been done several times before. Now Jack——"

Jack, who could hardly keep back a smile, looked slyly at Ernest.

"What!" he exclaimed. "Is it me you ask to stay at home? Would you deprive a hunter of such an

opportunity of hunting big game?   If anyone has to
stay at Rock Castle, why should it be I rather than
Ernest?"

"Ernest or Jack, it is all the same," M. Zermatt
answered. "Is it not so, Mrs. Wolston?"

"Certainly, M. Zermatt."

"And with Ernest to keep you company, you would
not be afraid, nor you, Betsy, nor you, Hannah,
dear?"

"Not a bit afraid," replied the girl, blushing a little.

"Speak up then, Ernest," Jack said. "You don't
say if that plan suits you?"

The plan did suit Ernest, and M. Zermatt could
feel every confidence in that serious young man, who
was as careful as he was brave.

The start had been arranged for the following day.
At dawn, M. Zermatt, Mr. Wolston, and Jack said
good-bye, promising to make their absence as brief
as possible.

The shortest road between Rock Castle and Sugar-
cane Grove bore away on the left to the Wood Grange
Road, which ran along the coast.

The waggon, in which M. Zermatt and Mr. Wolston
drove, was loaded with bags of seed, utensils and
tools, and an adequate supply of provisions and
ammunition.

Jack, who had declined to be parted from Lightfoot, rode near the waggon, followed by his two dogs,
Brownie and Fawn.

They started in a north-westerly direction, leaving
Swan Lake upon the right. Wide prairies, natural

pasture grounds, extended as far as the canal cut from Jackal River, which was crossed, about two and a half miles from Falconhurst, by the original culvert.

There was no cart track in this direction like that which led to the Wood Grange farm; but frequent hauling of heavy timber had levelled the ground and destroyed the grass. So the waggon, drawn by the two sturdy buffaloes, made good speed without any very great trouble.

The seven or eight miles to Sugar-cane Grove were covered in four hours.

M. Zermatt, Mr. Wolston, and Jack reached the house in time for luncheon. Having eaten with excellent appetites, they set to work at once.

They had first to repair the fences that formed the enclosure in which the pigs had spent the rainy season. This had been invaded by some other members of the pig family, the tajacus, or musky peccaries, which had previously been seen at Sugar-cane Grove, and which lived on perfectly friendly terms with the domestic pigs. The tajacus were never driven away, for M. Zermatt knew that the flesh of these creatures could be turned to good account, provided the musky gland in the middle of the back was first removed.

All the plantations on this estate were found to be in first-class order, thanks to its distance from the sea.

When M. Zermatt and his sons first visited this place it was nothing but a marsh, which they then called Sugar-cane Marsh. That was in the early days

after their landing on the island. Now vast fields
of arable land surrounded the Sugar-cane Grove, succeeded by pastures where cows grazed. Where the
simple hut made of branches once stood there was
now a house sheltered by trees. At a little distance
away there was a thick copse, composed entirely of
bamboos, whose strong thorns could be employed as
nails, and would have torn to shreds the clothes of
anyone who made his way through them.

The stay at Sugar-cane Grove lasted a week, which
was entirely occupied in sowing millet, wheat, oats
and maize. Cereals throve quickly in this soil, which
was irrigated from Swan Lake. Mr. Wolston had cut
a trench from the western bank of the lake to this
spot, and the water spread over the surface of this
district by the natural process of finding its own level.
As a result of this device, Sugar-cane Grove might
be regarded as the richest of the three farms established in the Promised Land.

During this week Jack had plenty of sport. The
moment he could be spared, he went off with his dogs.
The larder was plentifully stocked with quails, grouse,
partridges, and bustards, with peccaries and agoutis.
Hyenas had previously been observed in the neighbourhood, but Jack met none, nor yet any other carnivorous animal. It was clear that the wild animals fled
before man.

While walking by the side of the lake, Jack, more
fortunate than his brother Fritz had been a few years
before, got the chance to bowl over an animal the
size of a large donkey, with a dark brown coat, a kind

of hornless rhinoceros, of the tapir species. It was an anta, and it did not fall to the first shot which the young hunter fired at twenty paces; but just as it was charging at Jack, a second bullet pierced its heart.

At last, in the evening of the 15th of September, all this work was finished. The next day, after the house had been fast closed and the enclosure shut up with a solid railing, the waggon set off towards the north on its way to Prospect Hill, in the neighbourhood of False Hope Point.

The farm was about five miles from that point, which stretches out like a vulture's beak between Nautilus Bay and the open sea. The greater part of the journey lay on a flat plain, where the going was easy. But the plain sloped appreciably as it approached the cliff.

Two hours after the start, beyond a green and rich stretch of country wonderfully refreshed by the rainy season, M. Zermatt, Mr. Wolston, and Jack came to the Monkeys' Wood, which had ceased to deserve that name since those mischievous creatures had disappeared. At the foot of the hill they called a halt.

The sides of Prospect Hill were not really so steep that the buffaloes and the onager could not climb them, by following a zigzag path which wound round them. There was one really strenuous effort to be made, and the waggon was at the top.

The house, being greatly exposed to the easterly and northerly winds which beat full upon the cape, had suffered a good deal from the recent storms. Its roof required some immediate repairs, for the gales had dismantled it in more than one place. But now, in good summer weather, it was quite habitable, and the party were able to instal themselves there for a few days.

In the poultry-yard, too, where the cocks and hens were clucking and running about, there was damage due to the bad weather to be attended to; and the mouth of the little stream of fresh water which rose near the top of the hill had to be cleared and opened.

In the plantations, and more especially the plantations of caper bushes and tea plants, the chief work was that of straightening the plants that had been beaten down by the force of the winds but were still rooted in the ground.

During their stay here the visitors took several walks to the end of False Hope Point. From this spot one could see over a vast extent of sea towards the east, and over part of Nautilus Bay to the west. How often in all these years had the shipwrecked people watched in vain for the sight of a ship beyond this cape!

When M. Zermatt and his two companions went there now, Jack was moved to say:

"It was twelve years ago, when we had given up all hope of ever finding any of our companions on the *Landlord*, that we gave this cape its fitting name of False Hope Point. If the *Unicorn* should come into sight over there to-day, would it not be fitting to change the name to Cape Welcome?"

"Very fitting, my dear boy," Mr. Wolston answered, "but it is not at all likely to happen. The *Unicorn* is still in mid-Atlantic, and it must be nearly two months before she can reach these waters of New Switzerland."

"One can never tell, Mr. Wolston," Jack replied. "But, failing the *Unicorn*, why should not some other ship come first to investigate, and then to take possession of the island? Of course, her captain would have good reason to call it False Hope Island, since it has been taken possession of already!"

But no ship did appear, and it was unnecessary to alter the name originally given to the cape.

On the 21st of September all the work at the villa at Prospect Hill was finished, and M. Zermatt decided to start for home next day at early dawn.

As they sat together that evening in the little balcony in front of the house, they witnessed a magnificent sunset below a clear horizon undimmed by the lightest haze. Ten miles away, Cape East rose from a foundation of shadow, broken sometimes by points of light as the surf broke against the rocks at its foot. The sea was absolutely calm, and spread in a curve as far as Deliverance Bay. Below the hill the grass lands, shaded by clumps of trees, blent their verdant carpet with the yellow tinted sands. Behind, twenty miles away to the south, the mountain range, to which Mr. Wolston's eyes often strayed, was shaded off, its edges scalloped with a line of gold by the last rays of the sun.

Next day the waggon went down the steep slopes of Prospect Hill and took the road once more, and in the afternoon it arrived at the gates of Rock Castle. The travellers were received with delight, although their expedition had not involved an absence of more than a couple of weeks.

That evening, when the two families were all together again in the large hall and M. Zermatt had finished his story of the expedition to the farms, Ernest laid upon the table a sheet of paper on which was a coloured drawing.

"Hullo, what is that?" Jack asked. "The plan of the future capital of New Switzreland?"

"Not yet," Ernest answered.

"Then I can't guess——"

"Why, it is the design for the inside decoration of our little chapel," said Hannah.

"That's it, Jack," said Ernest, "and I had to get on with it, for the walls are half built already."

The announcement caused great pleasure, and Ernest was warmly praised for his work, which was voted perfect both in its style and its arrangement.

"Will there be a steeple?" Jack demanded.

"Certainly," Hannah answered.

"And a bell?"

"Yes—the *Landlord's* bell."

"And Hannah is to have the honour of ringing it first," Ernest announced.

It was the 24th of September, the date when Mr. Wolston's plan was to be carried into effect.

What would be the results of this exploration of the interior of New Switzerland?

For twelve years the shipwrecked people had been satisfied with the district of the Promised Land. It had sufficed to assure them of a livelihood, and even of prosperity. So, quite apart from the anxiety she must naturally feel when any of her dear ones were absent, Mme. Zermatt, though she did not seek to explain it even to herself, had her doubts about this expedition.

That evening, when M. Zermatt joined her in their room, she opened her heart to her husband, who answered her thus:

"If we were still in the same condition that we have been since we came here I would grant you, my dear, that this journey of discovery was not necessary. Even if Mr. Wolston and his family had been cast by shipwreck on this island of ours, I should say to them: 'What has been enough for us ought to be enough for you, and there is no need to rush into adventure when the advantage is not certain, and when there may be dangers to be incurred'; but New Switzerland has now a place on the map, and in the interest of its future colonists it is important that its extent should be known, the formation of its coasts and its resources."

"Quite so, dear, quite so," Mme. Zermatt answered, "but could not all that exploration be done better by the new arrivals?"

"Well, there would be no real harm done by waiting," M. Zermatt admitted, "and the work might be undertaken under better conditions. But you know, Betsy, Mr. Wolston has this idea very much at heart, and Ernest is anxious to complete the map of New Switzerland. So I think it is right to satisfy them."

"I would not say no, dear, if it did not mean another separation," Mme. Zermatt replied.

"A separation for a fortnight at most!"

"Unless Mrs. Wolston and Hannah and I go too."

"That would not be wise, dear wife," M. Zermatt said firmly. "If not dangerous, the expedition may at least be arduous and fatiguing. It will mean walking across an arid desert under a broiling sun. The ascent of the range is sure to be difficult."

"And so we are all to stay at Rock Castle?"

"Yes, Betsy, but I do not propose that you shall be left there alone. I have thought a great deal about it, and this is what I have decided, and what will meet with general approval, I think. Mr. Wolston shall make the trip with our two boys, Ernest to take the observations, and Jack, because he would never consent to forego such an opportunity, to go exploring; and I will remain at Rock Castle. Will that suit you, Betsy?"

"What a question, dear!" Mme. Zermatt answered. "We can have every confidence in Mr. Wolston. He will not let himself be dragged into any indiscretion. Our two boys will run no risk with him."

"I think this plan will satisfy Mrs. Wolston and Hannah," M. Zermatt went on.

"Hannah will be rather sorry when our Ernest is away," said Mme. Zermatt.

"And Ernest will be sorry to go without her," M. Zermatt added. "Yes, those two young creatures are attracted towards each other, and some day Ernest will be united to the woman he loves in the chapel he has designed! But we will talk about that marriage again, at the proper time."

"It will please Mr. and Mrs. Wolston as much as it pleases us," Mme. Zermatt answered.

When M. Zermatt propounded his suggestion it was received with general approval. Ernest and Hannah were obliged to fall in with so reasonable a plan. The former acknowledged that ladies ought not to venture upon an expedition of this kind, and the latter recognised that Ernest's presence was indispensable.

The 25th of September was the date fixed for the start.

And now every one was busy getting ready for the journey. Mr. Wolston and the two young men had agreed to make the expedition on foot. It might well be that the country adjoining the base of the mountain range was as difficult as that through which the upper reaches of the Montrose River ran.

So they would go on foot, staff in hand, gun slung across back, with the two dogs in attendance. Jack was an excellent shot, and neither Mr. Wolston nor Ernest was to be despised, so the three hunters could rely upon being able to find plenty of food for themselves.

But the waggon and team of buffaloes had to be got ready to convey the two families to the hermitage at Eberfurt. M. Zermatt wished to take advantage of this opportunity to visit this farm, which lay at the far end of the Promised Land. The suggestion that the rest should accompany Mr. Wolston and Jack and Ernest as far as the end of the defile of Cluse was received with acclamation. It might, perhaps, be convenient to prolong the stay at Eberfurt if the

house should be found to require work at which everyone would be needed to lend a hand.

On the 25th, at a very early hour, the waggon left
Rock Castle, followed by the two dogs, Brownie and
Fawn. It was large enough to hold them all. The
stage was a good eight miles, but the buffaloes could
cover it before noon.

The weather was fine, the sky blue and dappled.
A few light fleecy clouds veiled the sun's rays and
tempered their heat.

About eleven o'clock, after travelling across a green
and fertile country, the waggon arrived at the hermitage of Eberfurt.

In the little wood which lay on the hither side of
it, a dozen or so monkeys were seen. It was imperative to drive them out of it, and they fled before a
few shots.

As soon as the waggon had come to a stop, the party
proceeded to instal themselves in the house. Being
well protected by the surrounding trees, it had suffered but slight damage from the bad weather. While
the three women set about preparing luncheon, the
men went off, about a gun-shot's range, to inspect
the defile of Cluse, which led into the hinterland of
the island.

Some important and arduous work had to be done
here, for powerful animals had attempted to break
through the barrier, and it was necessary to strengthen
it. It appeared that a herd of elephants had tried
to get through the defile, and if they had succeeded
they might have done great damage not only at Eber-

furt, but also to the farms at Sugar-cane Grove and Wood Grange. There might even have been occasion to defend Rock Castle from an attack by these formidable pachyderms.

It took the afternoon and the whole of the following day to fix the new beams and logs in place. All hands were needed to move these heavy weights and adjust them firmly. But when the job was done they had the satisfaction of knowing that the pass could not be forced.

The hermitage at Eberfurt was no longer the hut of Kamchatkan type, supported by four trees and raised twenty feet above the ground. There was now an enclosed and stockaded house, containing several rooms, sufficient to accommodate both families. On either hand were ample sheds built beneath the lower branches of the mangroves and evergreen oaks. It was there that the team of buffaloes was stabled, with plenty of fodder. There the well-trained, sturdy animals could chew the cud to their hearts' content.

Game swarmed in the neighbourhood—hares, rabbits, partridges, cavies, agoutis, bustards, grouse, and antelopes. Jack had a delightful time. Some of the game, after it had been roasted before the fire sparkling on the hearth, was reserved for the three men on their expedition. With their game-bags at their side, their knapsacks on their back, with tinder to light a fire, content with broiled meat and cassava cakes, with plenty of powder and shot, and with flasks full of brandy, they could not imagine any ground for anxiety on the score of their daily food. Besides, as they crossed the fertile plains, of which they had already caught glimpses over the Green Valley and to the south of Pearl Bay, they must surely find edible roots and fruits.

On the 27th of September, at a very early hour, the last good-byes were said in the defile of Cluse. For a whole fortnight there would be no news of the absent ones! How long the time would seem!

"No news?" said Ernest. "No, mamma; no, Hannah dear, you shall have news."

"By post?" Jack enquired.

"Yes, by aerial post," Ernest answered. "Don't you see this pigeon that I have brought in its little cage? Do you suppose I brought it only to leave it at Eberfurt? No, we will let it go from the top of the range, and it will bring you news of our expedition."

Everybody applauded this excellent idea, and Hannah vowed in her heart to watch every day for the coming of Ernest's messenger.

Mr. Wolston and the two brothers passed through a narrow outlet contrived between the posts in the defile of Cluse. It was carefully shut behind them, and in a few minutes they disappeared behind a bend in the barrier of rock.

CHAPTER XIII

THE MOUNTAIN RANGE

TO go afoot is ideal travelling. Going afoot allows a man to see all that there is to see, gives leave for dallying. Who goes afoot is satisfied with by-paths when the high road is no more. He may proceed as the humour takes him, pass where the lightest vehicle, the best trained steed, could find no way, ascend the shelving steeps, and scale the mountain tops.

Thus, though they might have to endure great fatigue, Mr. Wolston and the two young men had not hesitated to plunge on foot into the heart of the unknown districts of the hinterland, all the more willingly in anticipation of their projected climb to the summit of the range.

This plan only involved a tramp of eighteen or twenty miles, provided they were able to go in a bee line to the foot of the mountains. There was thus no question of any long journey. But it was all through entirely new country, which might hold surprises for the three explorers.

Jack was the most highly excited of the party. With his adventurous temper it was an enormous satisfaction to him to pass beyond the limits of the Promised Land and to travel over these wide plains, of which he as yet knew nothing. It was a fortunate thing that he was not mounted on onager, bull, or ostrich, and that he had brought only one dog, Fawn. Thus, Mr. Wolston would have some chance of restraining his impetuosity.

When they emerged from the defile the three turned first towards the little eminence which was called the Arabian Watch-tower, in memory of the troop of ostriches in which M. Zermatt and his boy had imagined they saw a troop of Bedouin Arabs on horseback, on the occasion of their first visit to the Green Valley. From this tower they turned off towards the Bears' Cave where, a few years before, Ernest had come so near being suffocated in the hug of one of these much too pressing creatures!

It was not their notion to follow up the course of the Eastern River, which ran from south to west.

That would have meant lengthening their route, since the slopes of the range rose towards the south.

This led Ernest to observe:

"What we can't do on the Eastern River might have been done on the Montrose. It would certainly have been much shorter for us if we could have gone up one of its banks."

"What I want to know," said Jack, "is why we could not have gone in the pinnace to the mouth of the Montrose? The canoe might have taken us from there as far as the barrage, which is twelve to fifteen miles at most from the range."

"Nothing would have been easier, my dear boy," Mr. Wolston replied. "But the desert country through which the Montrose runs has nothing of interest to show us. So it is ever so much better to go across the region which lies between Deliverance Bay and the mountains."

Their route continued down the Green Valley, which extended for about five miles parallel to the boundary wall of the Promised Land. This valley was about a couple of thousand yards in width, and contained dense woods, isolated clumps of trees, and grass lands rising in terraces up its sloping sides. In it was a stream which murmured as it ran among the reeds, and which flowed either into the Eastern River, or into Nautilus Bay.

Mr. Wolston and the two brothers were longing to get to the end of the Green Valley, so as to obtain their first glimpse of the country which opened up to the south. To the best of his skill and knowledge Ernest took their bearings as they went, by means of his pocket compass, and made notes of them, with the distances they covered.

About midday they halted in the shade of a clump of guava trees, not far from grass where euphorbia grew in abundance. A few partridges which Jack had shot as he went along, were plucked and cleaned and roasted over a fire, and, with some cassava cakes, formed the luncheon. The stream provided clear water, with which a dash of brandy from the flasks was mixed, and ripe guavas served admirably for dessert.

Invigorated and rested, the three men resumed their march. The far end of the valley was penned in between two lofty walls of rock. As it ran through this narrow gorge the stream was transformed into a torrent, and the outlet came into view.

An almost flat country, displaying all the luxuriant fertility of the tropics, spread as far as the first belts of the range. What a difference from the region watered by the upper reaches of the Montrose! A couple of miles away to the south-east, a liquid ribbon unrolled, gleaming in the sun, no doubt flowing to join the Montrose.

Southwards, as far as the foot of the mountains, for fifteen miles or more, plains and forests succeeded one another. The marching was often heavy. The ground was thickly covered with grass five and six feet high, with tall reeds studded with prickly plumes, and with sugar-canes waving in the breeze as far as eye could see. There was no doubt it would be possible to develop with vast profit all these natural products which, at this period, formed the principal wealth of over-sea dominions.

When Mr. Wolston and the two young men had walked for four solid hours, Ernest said:

"I vote we call a halt."

"What, already?" exclaimed Jack, who had as little desire to rest as his dog had.

"I agree with Ernest," said Mr. Wolston. "This seems a suitable spot, and we can spend the night at the edge of this copse of nettle-trees."

"Well, then, let us camp," said Jack, "and have dinner, too, for my stomach's empty."

"Must we light a fire and keep it up till daylight?"
Ernest asked.

"It would be wise," Jack declared; "that is the best
way to keep wild beasts off."

"No doubt," said Mr. Wolston, "but we should have
to keep watch in turns, and I think sleep is better.
I do not think there is anything for us to fear."

"No," said Ernest confidently; "I have not noticed
any suspicious tracks, and we have not heard a growl
since we left the Green Valley. We may as well spare
ourselves the weariness of keeping watch one after the
other."

Jack did not insist, and the travellers prepared to
appease their hunger.

The night gave promise of being one of those nights
when nature slumbers sweetly, and no breath disturbs
the peace. Not a leaf moved among the trees, not
the snapping of a twig broke the silence of the plain.

Fawn betrayed no symptoms of uneasiness. No
hoarse bark of jackals was heard from afar, although
those brutes were so numerous in the island. Upon
the whole, there did not seem to be the least imprudence in sleeping under the open sky.

Mr. Wolston and the two brothers dined off the
remains of their luncheon and a few turtle eggs, which
Ernest had found, roasted among the ashes, with the
addition of some of the fresh kernels of the fir-apples
which grew in quantities in the neighbourhood, and
which have the flavour of the hazel-nut.

The first to close his eyes was Jack, for he was the
most tired of the three. He had never stopped beat-

ing the thickets and the bushes, often at such a distance that Mr. Wolston had been obliged to call him back. But as he was the first to go to sleep, so, too, was he the first to wake at daybreak.

The three resumed their march at once. An hour later they had to ford a little stream which probably ran into the Montrose five or six miles further on. So at least Ernest believed, taking its south-westerly course into consideration.

There were still the same wide prairies, vast plantations of sugar-cane, and, in the damp places, many clumps of those wax-trees which bear the flower on one stalk and the fruit upon the other.

At last dense forests appeared instead of the trees that grew singly upon the flanks of the Green Valley, cinnamons, palms of various kinds, figs, mangroves, and many bearing no edible fruit, such as spruce and evergreen oak and maritime oak, all of magnificent growth. Except in the few spots where the wax-trees grew, there were no marshy places in this district. Moreover, the ground rose steadily—a fact which deprived Jack of his last hope of meeting any flocks of waterfowl. He would have to be satisfied with the game of plain and forest.

Mr. Wolston said:

"It is quite clear, my dear Jack, that we shall have nothing to complain of if we are reduced to sultana birds, partridges, quails, bustards and grouse, not to mention antelopes, cavies, and agoutis. But I think it would be wise only to lay in supplies just as we are going to make a halt, so as to not to overload our game-bags."

"You are quite right, Mr. Wolston," the ardent sportsman replied. "But when game comes within such easy range it is very difficult to resist."

But finally Jack fell in with Mr. Wolston's advice. It was as late as eleven o'clock when several gun-shots proclaimed the fact that the bill of fare for the first meal was just completed. People who like their game a little high would very likely have found fault with the brace of grouse and the three snipe that Fawn retrieved from the brushwood. But nothing was left of these birds, which were roasted before a fire of dry wood. As for the dog, he regaled himself upon the carcasses.

In the afternoon, however, a few more shots were necessary to drive away animals formidable if only because of their superior numbers. All three guns had to speak to put to flight a band of wild cats, of the kind that had been seen previously within the Promised Land, when the first visit was paid to the Green Valley. They made off with a heavy list of wounded, raising hideous cries which resembled mewing and howling mixed. It might be well to make careful provision against an attack by them during the next halt for the night.

This country was rich in birds, other than game— parrots, parrakeets, brilliant scarlet macaws, tiny toucans with green wings decked with gold, big Virginian blue-jays, and tall flamingoes. It was also thronged with antelopes, elands, quaggas, onagers, and buffaloes.

Directly they scented the presence of man from afar, these creatures galloped away at great speed.

The country, still rising steadily towards the range, had lost as yet none of its fertility, which was as great as that of the northern part of the island. Soon Mr. Wolston, Ernest, and Jack came to a wooded belt. As they drew near the foot of the mountains they saw a succession of lofty forests, seemingly of great density. Next morning they might expect a much more difficult and fatiguing march.

That evening the hungry men regaled themselves upon hazel-hens, of which all three had bagged a few from a covey which Fawn put up in the tall and tangled grass. Camp was pitched at the edge of a magnificent forest of sago-trees, watered by a tiny stream which the steep pitch of the ground converted into a torrent as it sped on its course towards the south-west.

On this occasion Mr. Wolston decided to organise a sharp watch on the outskirts of the camp. A fire was to be kept alive until dawn. This necessitated their taking it in turns to watch by it throughout the night, which was disturbed by the howling of animals within close distance.

The start next morning was made in the small hours. Another seven or eight miles, and the foot of the mountains would be reached—perhaps in the second stage that day, if no obstacle occurred to delay the march. And if the flanks of the range were practicable on their northern side, the ascent would only take the first few hours of the following morning.

The country now presented a very different appear-

ance from that seen on emerging from the Green Valley. To right and left, woods rose, tier on tier. They
consisted almost exclusively of resinous species, which
flourish in great altitudes, and were watered by brawl-
ing little streams which flowed towards the east. These
little streams, which contributed directly or indirectly
to the Montrose, would soon dry up under the heat of
summer, and already it was possible to cross them
ankle-deep.

The adventurers went on until eleven o'clock. A
halt was then called for rest and refreshment, after a
pretty tiring stage.

There had been no lack of game from the start.
Jack had even succeeded in bagging a young antelope,
the best portions of which he brought in, and the game-
bags were packed with what was left, to serve for the
evening dinner.

It was well that this precaution had been taken for
in the afternoon all game, both furred and feathered,
entirely disappeared.

The midday halt was passed at the foot of an enormous pine, near which Ernest lighted a fire of dead
branches. While one of the antelope's quarters was
roasting under Jack's vigilant eye, Mr. Wolston and
Ernest went off a few hundred yards to get a look at the
country.

"If this forest belt extends as far as the range,"
said Ernest, "it most likely covers the lower slopes.
At least, that is what I thought I could see this morning when we left our camp."

"In that case," Mr. Wolston replied, "we shall have

to make the best of it, and go through these forests. We could not get round them without greatly lengthening our route, and we might even have to go right to the east coast."

"Which must be something like twenty-five miles away," Ernest remarked, "if my estimate is right. I mean the part of the coast we went to in the pinnace, at the mouth of the Montrose."

"If that is so, my dear boy, we cannot think of reaching the range from the east. The west———"

"That is the unknown quantity, sir; besides, when the range is viewed from above the Green Valley, it seems to run out of sight to the westward."

"Well, then," said Mr. Wolston, "if we have no choice, let us risk it and break our way right through this forest to the other side. If we can't do it in one day, we will take two, or we will take three; but we will get to our goal."

The antelope's meat, done to a turn on the live embers, some cassava cakes, and a handful of fruit gathered close by, bananas, guavas, and cinnamon apples, formed the meal, for which an hour's halt sufficed. Then they picked up their arms and game-bags again, and all three plunged into the forest, guiding themselves by the pocket compass.

Marching was easy enough among these straight-stemmed, widely-spaced pines and firs, for the ground was fairly level and carpeted with grass, or rather a kind of scanty moss, which was almost free from brambles and undergrowth. It would have been far otherwise in a semi-tropical forest, where the trees are entangled by parasites and knotted together by creepers. There were no serious obstacles to interfere with free movement in this vast pine wood. There was, it is true, no beaten path to be followed, not even one beaten by animals; but the trees allowed of free passage, although necessitating occasional détours.

Although game was now scarce, Jack and Mr. Wolston, and Ernest, too, were obliged to use their guns during this stage. It was not a matter of carnivorous animals, lions, tigers, panthers or pumas, some of which had been seen near the Promised Land and in the country round about Pearl Bay. But it was a breed as numerous as it was mischievous.

"The beggars!" Jack exclaimed. "One might almost think that the whole lot came to take shelter here after we drove them out of the woods at Wood Grange and Sugar-cane Grove!"

And after having received several fir-cones, hurled by a strong arm, in the chest, he made haste to let fly a couple of shots in reply.

A fusillade had to be kept up for a whole hour, at the risk of exhausting the ammunition carried for the trip. A score of monkeys lay on the ground, seriously or mortally wounded. When they came toppling down from branch to branch, Fawn sprang upon those that had not got strength left to escape, and finished them off by throttling them.

"If it were cocoa-nuts the rascals were bombarding us with," Jack demarked, "it would not be half bad."

"By Jove!" Mr. Wolston answered, "I prefer fir-cones to cocoa-nuts. They are not so hard."

"That is so; but there is no nourishment in them," Jack replied. "Whereas the cocoa-nut is meat and drink too."

"Well," said Ernest, "it is better to have these monkeys in the interior of the island than to have them in the neighbourhood of our farms. We have had quite enough to do already to protect ourselves from their damage, and to destroy them with traps and lines. If these will stay in their pinewood and never come back to the Promised Land, that is all we ask of them."

"And we ask them politely, too!" Jack added, backing his courtesy up with a final shot.

When the engagement was over they resumed their march, and the only difficulty lay in keeping a steady course towards the range.

For the canopy of pines spread away before them, dense and impenetrable, without a single break, without a single glimpse of where the declining sun now stood. There was not a clearing; not so much as a fallen tree. Mr. Wolston could congratulate himself on having brought neither waggon nor mount with him. The team of buffaloes, and Jack's onager, would have found it impossible to get through some places where the pines grew so close that they were almost entangled in one another, and it might have become necessary to turn back.

About seven in the evening they reached the southern boundary of the pine forest. The upward slope of the ground was so steep that the forest spread in tiers over the lower ramifications of the range, and the mountain summits came into view just as the sun was sinking behind the lesser chains which cut the western horizon.

There was a vast accumulation here of fragments of rock that had fallen from the mountain top. Here, too, a number of streams broke out, the source, perhaps, of the Montrose River, and followed the slope of the ground towards the east.

In spite of their keen desire to reach their goal, Mr. Wolston and the two boys looked about and sought a recess in the rocks, where they could find shelter until the morning. Then, whilst Ernest was busy getting ready their meal, Mr. Wolston and Jack went to the nearest trees to gather armfuls of dry grass, which they spread on the sand inside the little cave. They ate a couple of grouse, and then, being very tired, turned their thoughts to sleep.

But some precautions had to be taken. As day drew to a close animals had been heard howling near at hand, and with the howling an occasional roar was hear, the nature of which it would have been difficult for anyone to fail to realise.

So a fire was lighted at the mouth of the cave, to be kept up all night with the dry wood, of which Mr. Wolston and Jack collected a great heap.

Watch was maintained until sunrise, Ernest taking the first watch of three hours, Jack the second, and Mr. Wolston the third.

Next morning at daybreak all three were astir, and Jack called out in his ringing tones:

"Well, Mr. Wolston, here is the great day at last! In a few hours the dearest wish of your heart will be accomplished! You will have planted your flag on the highest point of New Switzerland!"

"In a few hours? Well, yes, if the climb is not too difficult," Ernest remarked.

"Anyhow," said Mr. Wolston, "whether to-day or to-morrow, we shall probably know what to think about the size of the island."

"Unless it extends right out of sight to the south and west," Jack replied.

"I don't think so," Mr. Wolston answered, "for then it could not have been missed by navigators in this part of the Indian Ocean."

"We shall see, we shall see!" Jack replied.

They made their breakfast of cold venison, carefully saving all that was left, for there would certainly be no game at all upon these barren slopes, which Fawn did not like at all. Outside the cave they slung their guns over their shoulders, for there were no wild animals to be afraid of now. Then, with Jack in front, Ernest following, and Mr. Wolston bringing up the rear, the three began the ascent of the lower slopes.

Ernest computed the height of the range to be eleven or twelve hundred feet. One peak, which rose up almost in front of the pinewood, towered six hundred feet above the ridge line. It was at the summit of this peak that Mr. Wolston desired to plant a flag.

About a hundred yards from the cave the forest belt came to an abrupt end. A few patches of verdure were still to be seen above, grass land with clumps of dwarf trees, aloes, mastics, myrtles, and heaths, attaining a height of six or seven hundred feet, and representing the second belt. But the acclivity was so steep that in some places it exceeded fifty degrees, and they had to tack on the way up.

A circumstance favourable to the ascent was that the mountain side provided a firm foot-hold. There was no reason yet to hold on by the finger nails or have recourse to crawling. The foot got a firm hold on the verdure, broken by roots and jutting points of rock.

So the ascent could be effected without check, zig-zagging so as to reduce the angle of inclination, although it would involve fatigue. Before the summit was reached the climbers would be obliged to halt at least once or twice to get their wind. Ernest and Jack, young and vigorous, in constant training and inured to all physical exercise, might not feel over-fatigued, but Mr. Wolston, at his age, could not afford a like expenditure of strength. But he would be quite satisfied if he and his companions were encamped at the foot of the peak before lunch time; it would only take them an hour or two after that to gain the extreme top.

Over and over again Jack was entreated not to imagine himself a chamois. They continued to mount, and, for his part, Mr. Wolston was determined not to cry halt till he had reached the foot of the peak, where the second belt of the range came to an end. That the most difficult part of the task would then be accomplished was not certain. For if, at that height, the eye could see towards the north and west and east, it certainly would not be able to see anything of the country which lay to the south. To do that they must reach the extreme summit. The country towards the Green Valley was known, between the mouth of the Montrose and the promontory of Pearl Bay. So their most natural and legitimate curiosity would not be satisfied until they had climbed to the top of the peak, or, should the ascent of it prove impracticable, until they had succeeded in working round it.

At last, when the second belt had been crossed, a halt at its extremity became imperative. Rest was necessary after such expenditure of energy. It was noon, and, after luncheon, the ascent of the longest incline of the peak could be begun again. Their stomachs were fairly clamouring for food. Physical effort of such a kind if apt to interfere with the digestion. But the urgency was now to fill their stomachs, without troubling to find out beforehand if they would or would not digest easily a meal whose sole solid dish consisted of the last scraps of the antelope.

An hour later Jack sprang to his feet again, leaped onto the first rocks at the foot of the slope, disregarding Mr. Wolston's warnings, and called out:

"Let him who loves me follow me!"

"Well, let us try to give him that proof of our affection, my dear Ernest," was Mr. Wolston's reply, "and above all, let us try to prevent him from making a fool of himself!"

CHAPTER XIV

JEAN ZERMATT PEAK

THIS peak was merely a prodigious pile of rocks, thrown together anyhow. Nevertheless there were ledges and projections on its face on which the foot could find a firm support. Still retaining the lead, Jack tested these and felt his way, and, following him cautiously, Mr. Wolston and Ernest gradually made their way up.

The surface of this third belt of the mountain was barren and desolate. There was practically no vegetation upon it.

Sometimes the surface was as smooth as glass, and a fall would have ended only at the bottom of the peak. Care had to be taken, too, not to displace any of the masses of rock, and so, perhaps, set moving an avalanche which would have rolled right down to the foot of the range.

Granite and limestone were the constituents of this mighty framework of the mountain. There was nothing to indicate a volcanic origin.

The three adventurers got half-way up the peak without mishap. But they could not entirely avoid starting some landslips.

Three or four huge rocks bounded furiously down the steeps to plunge into the depths of the forest below with a roar like thunder, repeated by the many echoes of the mountain.

At this altitude a few birds were still to be seen hovering about, sole representatives of animal life in this third belt, where, however, they did not seek to light. A few pairs of powerful birds of enormous spread of wing, leisurely flapping through the air, occasionally passed over the summit of the peak. Jack was greatly tempted to fire at them, and it would have been a great delight to him to have shot one of these vultures or gigantic condors.

More than once the young sportsman made a movement to raise his gun to his shoulder.

"What for?" Mr. Wolston called out.

"What? What for?' Jack answered. "Why, to——"

And then, without finishing his sentence, he would sling his gun behind him again, and spring forward over the rocks.

Now the upper crest of the slope became even steeper —a regular sugar-loaf. Mr. Wolston began to wonder whether there would be room for three people on the summit. It now became necessary for the traveller ahead to help the next. Jack pulled Ernest up; then Ernest pulled Mr. Wolston up. They had tried in vain to work round the base of the peak. It was only on the north side that the ascent presented difficulties that were not insuperable.

At last, about two o'clock in the afternoon, Jack's ringing voice was heard—the first, no doubt, that had ever resounded from this pinnacle.

"An island! It really is an island!"

A final effort by Mr. Wolston and Ernest brought them to the summit. There, on a narrow space not much more than twelve feet square exhausted, almost incapable of speaking, they lay down flat to recover breath.

Although the sea surrounded New Switzerland on all sides, it did so at unequal distances from the mountain. Widely displayed towards the south, much more restricted towards the east and west, and reduced to a mere bluish rim up in the north, the sea lay glittering under the rays of the sun, now a few degrees below its highest point of altitude.

It was now evident that the range did not occupy the central portion of the island. On the contrary, it rose in the south and followed an almost regular curve, drawn from east to west.

From this point, fifteen hundred feet above sea level, the range of vision was about forty or forty-five miles to the horizon. But New Switzerland did not extend in any direction as far as that.

"I calculate that our island must be a hundred and fifty to a hundred and seventy miles in circumference. That represents a considerable area, larger than the canton of Lucerne," said Ernest.

"What would its extent be, approximately?" Mr. Wolston asked.

"As far as I can estimate it, taking the configuration, which is a kind of oval drawn from east to west, into account, it might measure a thousand square miles," Ernest replied; "say half the size of Sicily."

"There are a good many famous islands that aren't so big," said Jack.

"Very true," Ernest answered; "and one of them, if my memory serves me, is one of the principal islands in the Mediterranean; it is of supreme importance to England, but it is only twenty-two miles long by ten miles broad."

"What is that?"

"Malta."

"Malta?" Mr. Wolston exclaimed, all his patriotism inflamed by the name. "Well, why should not New Switzerland become the Malta of the Indian Ocean?"

To which Jack replied in an aside with the very natural remark that old Switzerland would have done well to keep it for herself, and to establish a Swiss colony there.

The sky was clear, without the faintest haze in the atmosphere. There was not a trace of dampness in the air, and the land stood out in clear relief.

As the descent of the mountain would only take about a third of the time required for the ascent, Mr. Wolston and the two brothers had several hours at their disposal before the time came for them to get back to the pine wood. So they passed the telescope round from hand to hand, and took a careful survey of the vast country which lay spread out below them.

Ernest, with notebook and pencil, traced the outlines of this oval, through which the nineteenth parallel of the Southern Hemisphere ran for about fifty-five miles, and the hundred and fourteenth meridian east for about forty-seven.

In a northerly direction, at a distance of something like twenty-five miles as the crow flies, a good deal could be distinguished.

Beyond the coast line, a narrow edging of sea washed the portion comprised between False Hope Point and the promontory which enclosed Pearl Bay to the westward.

"It's unmistakable," said Jack; "I need no telescope to recognise the Promised Land and the coast as far as Deliverance Bay."

"Quite so," Mr. Wolston agreed; "and at the far end of that opposite angle is Cape East, shutting in Unicorn Bay."

"Unfortunately," Jack went on, "even with this splendid telescope of Ernest's, we can't see any of the country near Jackal River."

"That is because it is hidden by the wall of rocks which bounds it on the south," Ernest replied. "You cannot see the summit of the range from Rock Castle or Falconhurst, and so you cannot see Rock Castle or Falconhurst from the summit of the range. That's logic, I suppose."

"Logic, indeed, most wise philosopher!" Jack answered. "But that ought to be equally true of False Hope Point, and yet there it is, that cape running out to the north, and since we can see it——"

"Although it may be true that you can see this peak from False Hope Point, and even from Prospect Hill," Ernest replied, "the first condition for seeing anything is that you should look for it. The probability is that we have never looked carefully enough."

"The general conclusion," Mr. Wolston added, "is that the range, properly speaking, can only be seen from above the Green Valley."

"That is the position, sir," said Ernest, "and it is those heights that hide Rock Castle from us now."

"I am sorry," Jack went on, "for I am sure we could have made out all our people. If it had occurred to them to go to Prospect Hill, I wager that we should have been able to recognise them—with the telescope, of course. For they are over there, talking about us, counting the hours, and saying: 'They would have got to the foot of the mountain yesterday, and to-day they will be at the top.' And they are wondering how big New Switzerland is, and if it makes a good show in the Indian Ocean."

"Well said, my boy!" laughed Mr. Wolston. "I fancy I hear them."

"And I fancy I see them," Jack declared. "Never mind! I am still sorry that the rocks hide Jackal River from us, and our house at Rock Castle too."

"No good being sorry," Ernest remarked, "when you've got to put up with it."

"It is the fault of this peak," Jack complained. "Why isn't it higher? If it rose a few hundred feet higher into the air, our people would see us from over there. They would signal to us. They would hoist a flag on the pigeon house at Rock Castle. We would wag them good morning with ours——"

"Jack's off again!" said Mr. Wolston.

"And I am sure that Ernest would see Hannah!"

"I see her all the time."

"Of course; even without a glass," Jack answered quickly. "Ah! the eyes of the heart are long-sighted!"

All that remained was for the explorers to make an accurate survey of the island, noting its general outline and its geologic formation.

On the east, to the rear of Unicorn Bay, the coast showed like a rocky frame enclosing the whole of the desert region which had been previously explored, when the pinnace made her first voyage. Then the cliffs grew lower, and the coast line rose towards the mouth of the Montrose River, where it formed a sharp point to bend back towards the spot where the range rose in the south-east.

Glimpses could be caught of the Montrose, winding like a gleaming thread. The lower reaches of the river ran through a wooded and verdant region; the upper reaches through a barren waste. It was fed by numerous streams from the high levels of the pine wood, and made numerous twists and turns. Beyond the dense forests between the groves and clumps of trees lay a succession of plains and grass lands right to the western extremity of the island, where rose a high hill, marking the other end of the range, twelve or fifteen miles away.

In outline the island was almost exactly the shape of the leaf of a tree.

In the west numerous water-courses gleamed in the sun's rays. To the north and east were only the Montrose and Eastern Rivers.

To sum up, then, New Switzerland, at any rate the five-sixths of it which lay to the north of the range, was a land of wonderful fertility, quite capable of supporting several thousand inhabitants.

As to its situation in the Indian Ocean, it was clear that it belonged to no group of islands. The telescope discovered no sign of land anywhere on the horizon. The nearest coast was seven hundred and fifty miles away, the coast of Australia, or New Holland, as it was called in those days.

But although the island had no satellites lying round its coast, one rocky point rose up from the sea some ten miles to the west of Pearl Bay. Jack levelled his glass upon it.

"The Burning Rock—which isn't burning!" he exclaimed. "And I guarantee that Fritz would not have required any telescope to recognise it!"

Thus New Switzerland, as a whole, was well adapted for the establishment of an important colony. But what the north and east and west had to offer must not be looked for in the south.

Bent round in the form of a bow, the two extremities of the range rested on the coast line, at almost equal distance from the base of the peak which rose in its centre. The portion enclosed within this arc was bounded by a long succession of cliffs, which appeared to be almost perpendicular.

The contrast between the sixth portion of the island and the other five, so generously favoured by nature, was great. The utter desolation of a desert, all the horror of chaos, reigned there. The upper belt of the range extended right to the end of the island, and seemed to be impassable. It was possible, however, that it was connected with the coast line to the south by ravines, gorges, and gullies worn through the steep slopes. The actual shore, sand or rock, where it might be possible to land, was probably a mere narrow strip only uncovered at low tide.

The three were all affected by the melancholy which seemed to be exhaled from this depressing country, and remained silent while their eyes travelled over it. It was Ernest who made the following characteristic remark:

"If after the wreck of the *Landlord* we had been cast upon this coast, our tub boat would have been smashed and we should have had nothing but death to look for—death from starvation!"

"You are quite right, my dear boy," Mr. Wolston answered; "on this shore you could hardly have hoped for a chance. Of course, if you had managed to land a few miles farther north you would have found fertile land and the game country. But I am afraid this awful region has no communication with the interior of the island, and I do not know if it would have been possible to get there through the southern side of the range."

"It isn't very likely," Jack put in, "but as we went round the coast we should certainly have come upon the mouth of the Montrose and the fertile part of the island."

"Yes," said Ernest, "provided our boat could have got up towards the east or the west. But the south coast would not have offered us a bay like Deliverance Bay, where we got ashore without any great trouble."

It most certainly was a happy chance that had cast the shipwrecked survivors of the *Landlord* upon the northern shore of New Switzerland. But for that how could they possibly have escaped the most horrible of deaths, at the foot of this enormous pile of rocks?

The three adventurers decided to remain on the summit of the peak until four o'clock. They took all the bearings necessary to complete the map of New Switzerland—except the southern portion, which must remain incomplete for the present, since they could not see it all. But the work would be completed when the *Unicorn* returned and Lieutenant Littlestone finished his survey of the island.

Ernest tore a leaf out of his pocket book and wrote the following lines:

"The 30th of September, 1917, at 4 p.m., from the summit of——"

There he broke off.

"What shall we call this peak?" he asked.

"Call it the Peak of Sorrow," Jack answered, "because we can't see Rock Castle from it."

"No, call it Jean Zermatt, boys, in honour of your father," Mr. Wolston suggested.

The suggestion was agreed to with delight. Jack pulled a cup out of his game-bag. Mr. Wolston and Ernest followed suit. A few drops of brandy from the flasks were poured into the cups and drunk with three cheers.

Then Ernest got on with his letter.

"——from the summit of Jean Zermatt Peak, we are sending to you, my dear parents, to you, Mrs. Wolston, and to you, my dear Hannah, this note entrusted to our faithful messenger who, more fortunate than we, will soon be back at Rock Castle.

"Our New Switzerland, a solitary island in the Indian Ocean, is about a hundred and fifty or a hundred and seventy miles in circumference. Most of it is immensely fertile, but on the southern side of the range it is barren and appears to be uninhabitable.

"In forty-eight hours, since the return journey will be easier, we may possibly be back with you, and before the end of another three weeks, God willing, we may hope to set eyes again upon our absent ones, for whose return we are so impatient.

"All love to you, dear parents, to Mrs. Wolston, and my dear Hannah, from Mr. Wolston, my brother Jack, and your affectionate son, Ernest."

The pigeon was taken from its little cage. Ernest tied the note to its left foot and let it fly.

The bird rose thirty or forty feet above the summit of the peak, as if to obtain the widest possible view. Then, guided by its marvellous sense of direction, the sixth sense which all animals seem to possess, it flew rapidly away towards the north and soon was out of sight.

All that now remained to be done was to hoist at the top of Jean Zermatt Peak the flag, for which Mr. Wolston's long stick, driven into the ground between the topmost rocks, was to serve as a flagstaff.

When this was accomplished they would only have to make their way down to the foot of the range, get to the cave, fortify themselves with a substantial meal, for which their guns would provide materials, and then enjoy the rest they had earned by such a tiring day.

The start for home would be made at dawn next day. By following the route already discovered, it was not impossible that they might reach Rock Castle in less than forty-eight hours.

So Mr. Wolston and Jack set to work to plant the stick deeply and firmly enough to withstand the winds, which would sure to be violent at so great an altitude.

"The essential thing," Jack remarked, "is that this flag of ours should be flying when the *Unicorn* arrives, so that Lieutenant Littlestone may see it directly the corvette gets in sight of the island. That will stir the hearts of Fritz and Jenny and Frank and your children, Mr. Wolston, and our hearts, too, when we hear the twenty-one guns saluting the flag of New Switzerland!"

It was quite easy to wedge the staff between the rocks and pack it in with little stones.

Just as he was going to fasten the flag to the staff, Mr. Wolston, who was facing eastwards, looked in that direction. He did with such intensity that Jack asked:

"What is the matter, Mr. Wolston?"

"I again thought that I saw——" he answered. And again he raised the telescope to his eye.

"Saw what?" Ernest pressed him.

"Smoke rising from the shore," Mr. Wolston answered, "unless it is a cloud like I saw before, when the pinnace was off the mouth of the Montrose River."

"Well," said Ernest, "is it passing away?"

"No," said Mr. Wolston; "and it must be at the

same spot—at the far end of the range. Can there have been any shipwrecked men, or any savages, camped on that part of the coast for the past few weeks?"

Ernest looked carefully at the indicated spot, taking the glass in his turn, but he could see nothing in that direction.

"Why, Mr. Wolston, that is not where we need look; it's over here, to the south——" And Jack stretched his hand towards the sea beyond the huge cliffs that towered over the shore.

"It's a sail!" Ernest exclaimed.

"Yes, a sail!" Jack repeated.

"There is a ship in sight of the island," Ernest went on, "and she seems to be steering for it."

Mr. Wolston took the telescope and distinctly saw a three-masted vessel moving under full sail six or seven miles out at sea.

Jack shouted, gesticulating wildly.

"It is the *Unicorn!* It can only be the *Unicorn!* She was not due until the middle of October, and here she is at the end of September, a fortnight before her time."

"There is nothing impossible in that," Mr. Wolston replied. "But, nevertheless, before we can be positive we must make quite sure which direction she is going in."

"She is making for New Switzerland," Jack declared. "To-morrow morning she will appear to the west of Deliverance Bay, and we shall be there to greet her! Let us be off, Mr. Wolston; let us travel all night!"

Jack, who was just getting ready to slide down the side of the peak, was checked by a final word from Ernest.

"No," he said, "look carefully, Mr. Wolston. The ship is not steering towards the island."

"That is so," said Mr. Wolston, after watching the movement of the vessel for a few minutes.

"Then she is not the *Unicorn?*" Jack exclaimed.

"No," said Ernest positively.

"Besides," Mr. Wolston added, "the *Unicorn* would come from the north-west, and this ship is going towards the south-east and away from the island."

There could be no mistake on this score; the three-master was travelling east, without taking any notice of New Switzerland.

"All right!" said Jack. "But the *Unicorn* will come soon, and at any rate we shall be there to pay the regulation salute to the corvette of His Majesty King George III!"

The flag was hoisted on the summit of Jean Zermatt Peak and blew out into the breeze, while Jack did it the honours with two shots from his gun.

CHAPTER XV

JACK AND THE ELEPHANTS

IN the evening of that same day M. Zermatt and his wife, Mrs. Wolston and her daughter, were all sitting together in the library after a good day's work.

Of what should they have talked if not of those who had now been away for three days? They felt confident of a happy issue to the expedition into the interior of the island. The weather had been very favourable for it.

"Where ought Mr. Wolston and the boys to be at this moment?" Mme. Zermatt enquired.

"I think they must have reached the summit of the range," M. Zermatt replied. "If nothing occurred to delay them, three days will have sufficed to bring them to its foot, and the fourth would be spent in making the ascent."

"At the cost of much fatigue, and much danger, too, perhaps," said Hannah.

"Not danger, my dear child," M. Zermatt replied. "As for the fatigue, your father is still in the prime of life, and my boys have endured plenty before now."

"Ernest has not all his brothers' endurance," Hannah rejoined.

"Not quite," Mme. Zermatt answered; "and he has always preferred study to physical exercise."

"Come, Betsy," said M. Zermatt, "you must not make out that your son is a weakling! If he has worked with his brains, he has worked quite as hard with his body. My belief is that this expedition will have been no more than a walking tour. If I had not been afraid to leave you three alone at Rock Castle, my dear, I should, in spite of my forty-seven years, have gone on this voyage of discovery."

"Let us wait till to-morrow," said Mrs. Wolston. "Perhaps the pigeon that Ernest took with him will come back in the morning and bring us a letter."

"Why not this evening?" Hannah broke in. "The pigeon could find its loft quite well at night; couldn't it, M. Zermatt?"

"Without a doubt, Hannah. The speed of those birds is so great—thirty miles an hour, some people say—that it could travel the distance from the mountains here in forty or fifty minutes!"

"Suppose I watch until daylight to see if it comes back?" the girl suggested.

"Ah!" exclaimed Mme. Zermatt. "The dear child is dreadfully anxious to have news of her father."

"And of Jack and Ernest too, Mme. Zermatt," Hannah added, kissing her.

"It is a pity that the range is not visible from the top of Rock Castle," Mrs. Wolston remarked. "Perhaps with a telescope we might have discovered whether the flag is flying at the summit of the peak."

"It is a pity, Mrs. Wolston," M. Zermatt agreed.

"That is why, if the pigeon does not return in the course of to-morrow morning, I intend to saddle Lightfoot and go as far as the hermitage at Eberfurt, whence one can see the range."

"An excellent idea," said Mme. Zermatt, "but don't let us begin to make plans prematurely, dear, and since it is now time, let us go to dinner. Why, perhaps the pigeon may come back this evening, before we go to bed, and bring us a little word from Ernest!"

"Well," M. Zermatt answered, "it will not be the first time we shall have corresponded that way. Do you remember, Betsy, a long time ago, when the boys sent us news from Wood Grange and Prospect Hill and Sugar-cane Grove? It was bad news, it is true— of the harm those wretched monkeys and other destructive creatures had done; but it was by pigeon post that we got it. I hope the messenger will bring us better news this time."

"Here it is!" exclaimed Hannah, springing up and rushing to the window.

"Did you see it?" her mother asked.

"No, but I heard it go into the pigeon-house," the girl answered.

Her ear had caught the sound of the little trap-door shutting at the bottom of the pigeon-house above the library.

M. Zermatt hurried out, followed by the three ladies. At the foot of the pigeon-house he placed a ladder against the wall of rock, ran up it quickly, and looked inside.

"It has indeed come back!" he said.

"Oh, catch it, catch it, M. Zermatt!" Hannah exclaimed, all impatience.

When she had the pigeon in her hands she kissed its
little bluish head, and she kissed it again after she had
unfastened the note from its foot. Then the bird was
released and went back into its loft, where a handful of
grain was lying ready for it.

Hannah read out Ernest's letter. The few lines it
contained were satisfactory, announcing the complete
success of the expedition. They held a word of affection for every one, and Hannah had her share.

Full of the glad thought that the return would be
made in the next forty-eight hours, they all went to
their rooms. The message had come; the news was
good! They gave thanks to God, and slept peacefully
until the sun rose.

This next day was fully employed with household
tasks. There was an important piece of work on hand,
which could not have been postponed. A number of
salmon had entered the mouth of Jackal River, up
whose course these fish ascended every year at this
season. The help of the absent three was greatly
missed. Because of their absence, the fishing was not
nearly so productive as it might have been.

During the afternoon all four left their work, crossed
Family Bridge, and took the road towards the hermitage of Eberfurt. Mr. Wolston, Ernest, and Jack
ought to have reached the defile of Cluse, and it would
only take them a couple of hours at most to cover the
distance from the farm to Rock Castle.

But the day wore on, and there was no sign of their

coming, no barking of the dogs that would certainly have scented their masters, no sound of the gun which Jack would not have failed to fire to announce his return.

At six o'clock dinner was ready. It was kept back for the explorers, and, as they did not come, no one cared to sit down to table.

M. and Mme. Zermatt, Mrs. Wolston and Hannah, took a final walk half a mile or more along the road above Jackal River. Turk and Brownie went with them, but remained quiet and dumb, although they would certainly have been noisy and frantic enough if the two brothers had been anywhere near!

The four returned to Rock Castle, not quite easy in mind, but telling one another that the delay could not last much longer. They sat down to table in anxious mood, with ears alert for every sound outside, and none of them had any appetite.

"Come, come, we must be reasonable," M. Zermatt said at length. "If it took three days to get to the foot of the mountain, why should it not take three days to get back?"

"Quite right, M. Zermatt," Hannah answered, "but does not Ernest's letter suggest that forty-eight hours would be enough?"

"I quite agree, my child," Mme. Zermatt added. "But the dear boy is so anxious to see us again that he has promised more than he can perform."

There was no actual reason for serious worry as yet. But that night none of the inmates of Rock Castle enjoyed the same quiet sleep that they had known the night before.

But what, after all, was only anxiety, became trouble and even agony next day, the 3rd of October, when evening fell. The explorers had not put in an appearance. Such a long delay was inexplicable where such strong and tireless walkers were concerned. Some accident must have befallen them. They ought not to have met with any more difficulties when returning than they had met with when going, and they knew the road. Could it mean that they had decided to take another road—a more difficult, a longer one?

"No," said Hannah. "If they had been obliged to take another road, Ernest would not have said that they would be here in forty-eight hours."

An answer to that was difficult to find. Betsy and Mrs. Wolston began to lose hope. Hannah could not restrain her tears, and M. Zermatt knew not what to say to comfort her.

It was then agreed that if the missing party did not come back to Rock Castle next day, all should go to the hermitage at Eberfurt, since they could only come back by the defile of Cluse.

Evening came; night rolled on. There was no news at all. Nothing could now keep at Rock Castle those who were awaiting them there, a prey to mortal anxiety.

In the morning preparations were hurriedly made. The waggon was harnessed, provisions were put into it, and all took their seats. The cattle started, Brownie running ahead. After crossing Jackal River the ve-

hicle went along the woods and fields which bordered
the road to Eberfurt, travelling at its highest possible
speed.

They had gone about two and a half miles and had
reached the culvert over the irrigation canal which ran
into Swan Lake, when M. Zermatt gave the signal to
halt.

Brownie had rushed forward, barking faster and
more furiously than ever.

"There they are!   There they are!" cried Mrs.
Wolston.

And, three hundred yards away, two men appeared,
rounding a clump of trees.

They were Mr. Wolston and Ernest.

Where was Jack?   He could not be far away—a
gun-shot or two behind, no doubt.

Mr. Wolston and Ernest were welcomed with shouts
of joy.   But as they did not come on, everyone rushed
towards them.

"Where is Jack?" Mme. Zermatt asked.

Neither Jack nor his dog Fawn was there.

"We don't know what has become of Jack," said Mr.
Wolston, sadly.

And this is the story he told, a story often broken by
the sobs of all who heard it.

The descent from the summit of the peak to the
foot of the range had been made in two hours.   Jack,
the first to get down, shot some game on the fringe of
the pine-wood.   Supper was eaten in front of the cave,
a fire was left alight outside, and all three retired

within. One kept watch at the entrance while the other two slept soundly.

The night was disturbed only by the distant howling of wild beasts.

From the summit of the peak Ernest had noticed that the forest seemed to be clearer towards the east, and, at his suggestion, the three men went in that direction. It would mean quicker marching, and the distance would only be lengthened by a couple of miles or so.

At eleven o'clock a halt was made. After luncheon the three came on through the thinner forests, where it was easier walking.

About two o'clock they heard heavy trampling and a loud trumpeting noise among the trees.

There could be no mistake whence this proceeded. A herd of elephants was passing through the pinewood.

No, not a herd—only three appeared, two of enormous size, the parents, and behind them a baby elephant.

It had always been Jack's most ardent wish to capture one of these creatures and tame it. The adventurous lad determined to take advantage of this opportunity.

Anticipating an attack, all three put themselves on the defensive, with guns loaded and ready, feeling by no means confident about the issue of a trial of strength with these formidable brutes.

When the elephants reached the end of the clearing, they stopped. Then, catching sight of the three men, they swerved off to the left, without hurrying, and plunged into the depths of the forest.

All danger was over, when Jack, carried away by his irresistible desire, disappeared in the wake of the elephants, followed by his dog Fawn.

"Jack! Jack!" cried Mr. Wolston.

"Come back, Jack! Come back!" cried Ernest.

The reckless young fellow either did not or would not hear.

One more glimpse of him was seen through the thicket. Then he vanished from view.

Full of apprehension, Mr. Wolston and Ernest rushed after him, and in a few minutes reached the clearing.

It was deserted.

Just at this moment the noise of trampling was heard again, close at hand. But no report rang out.

So Jack either had not decided to use his gun yet, or had not been able to.

It would be difficult, however, to overtake him, and it was impossible to pick up his tracks here, where the ground was covered with dead branches and dry leaves.

The tumult gradually died away in the distance. A few branches which had been set a-swaying became still again, and once more the silence of the forest was unbroken.

Mr. Wolston and Ernest beat the fringe of the clearing until evening, wormed their way into the thickest brakes, and shouted to Jack.

Had the unhappy lad fallen a victim to his imprudence? Had he been unable to avoid the elephants' charge? Was he lying motionless, perhaps dead, in some corner of the dark forest?

No cry, no call, reached Mr. Wolston's or Ernest's ears. A few shots, fired at intervals, remained unanswered.

At night-fall, both men, exhausted by fatigue and overwhelmed by anxiety, sank at the foot of the tree, listening intently and trying to catch the faintest sound. They lighted a large fire, hoping that Jack might find his way by its light and join them again, and they did not close their eyes until day.

Throughout these weary hours incessant howling betrayed the proximity of wild beasts. They could not help dreading that if Jack had not been driven to defend himself against the elephants, he still might have fallen in a more dangerous attack by tigers, lions, or pumas.

But he could not be left to his fate. The whole of the following day was spent in seeking his tracks through the pine-wood.

It was labour wasted, Mr. Wolston and Ernest plainly saw the way the elephants had passed, marked as it was by heavy foot-prints, trampled grass, broken branches, and crushed undergrowth. But of Jack himself there was not a sign; not even a sign that he had been wounded, not a drop of blood, not a single mark which might have put them on his track.

There was nothing for it but to go back to Rock Castle, whence they could start again on the search once more in better conditions.

The two traversed the portion of the pine forest

which they had crossed that same evening. They walked all night and all day, and in the morning they arrived at the entrance to the defile of Cluse.

"My boy! My poor boy!" Mme. Zermatt murmured over and over again.

She fell into the arms of Mrs. Wolston and her daughter, who were on their knees beside her.

M. Zermatt and Ernest, plunged in grief, could not utter a word.

"This is what we must do, without losing a minute," Mr. Wolston said at last, resolutely.

M. Zermatt turned to him.

"What?" he asked.

"We are going back to Rock Castle, and we will start out from there again this very day to find Jack's tracks. I have thought of everything, my dear Zermatt, and I entreat you to do what I suggest.

"It was in the part of the forest near the sea-shore that Jack disappeared," he went on. "So thither we must go first, and by the shortest way. To return by the road beyond the defile of Cluse would take too long. Let us go aboard the pinnace. The wind is in the right quarter for rounding Cape East, and after that the breeze from the sea will take us back along the coast. If we start this evening we shall reach the mouth of the Montrose before daybreak. We will go on, and we will put in where the range ends. It was in that direction Jack disappeared as he went through the pine forest. By going there by sea we shall gain two days."

The suggestion was agreed to without demur. There

was no room for hesitation if they wanted to take advantage of the wind which would bring the *Elizabeth* off Cape East in two or three tacks.

So both families got into the waggon again, and the team was driven so fast that an hour and a half later they were at the gates of Rock Castle.

Their first business was to get the pinnace ready to put to sea for a voyage of several days' duration, in which Mme. Zermatt, Mrs. Wolston, and Hannah were all to share.

In the afternoon, after food had been provided for the animals for a week, the pinnace was about to start when it was prevented by an unhappy mischance.

About three o'clock the wind, which had dropped, veered to the east, and was soon blowing a full breeze. The *Elizabeth* could have ventured beyond Cape East, although the sea must be running very high outside. But how was she to get so far as the cape against the violent surge which was rolling in from the sea? It would have been extremely difficult for her merely to leave her anchorage, and to get beyond Shark's Island would have been impossible.

It was heart-breaking. To wait and wait, while the least delay might mean the failure of the search! And if these adverse winds continued, if in the course of the evening or the night the weather conditions did not change, they would get even worse.

"Well," said Mr. Wolston, answering questions which rose in every mind, "what we can't try by sea, we will try by land. The waggon instead of the pinnace! Let us get it ready to go back to Eberfurt."

Preparations were at once made. If the journey was to be by waggon, they would have to make for the south-east, in order to work round the pine forest. The team could not have made their way through it, at any rate, not through the portion which Mr. Wolston and Ernest had explored. Thence they would try to reach the eastern extremity of the forest, that is to say, the point where the *Elizabeth* would put into shore, if a change in the wind allowed her to lift anchor. It would mean a delay of thirty-six hours, but that could not be helped.

Hopes for a change in the weather were disappointed. The wind blew constantly from the north-east and got steadily stronger. By evening huge waves were breaking on the beach at Rock Castle. The night threatened to be a bad one, and, in face of these conditions, the plan of the voyage had to be given up.

Mr. Wolston had all the provisions which had been put on board transferred to the waggon. At the same time final attentions were given to the two buffaloes and the onager, in view of a start at day-break.

Mme. Zermatt was quite broken down, only opening her lips to murmur:

"My boy! Oh, my poor boy!"

Suddenly about eight o'clock, the two dogs, Turk and Brownie, began to show signs of excitement. Mr. Wolston noticed how they ran in front of the verandah across the yard. Brownie was especially restless.

Then distant barking was distinctly heard.

"It's Fawn!" cried Ernest.

Fawn—Jack's dog! Brownie and Turk recognised

him too, for they answered by barking more loudly than ever.

M. and Mme. Zermatt, with Mrs. Wolston and Hannah, rushed out of the verandah.

Jack appeared at the gate and flung himself into his mother's arms.

"Yes, I'm all right!" he cried. "But there may be great danger before us!"

"Danger? What danger?" M. Zermatt asked, hugging him.

"Savages," Jack answered; "savages who have landed on the island!"

CHAPTER XVI

TROUBLE AHEAD

THE two families went back into the dining-room with hearts overflowing with joy, in spite of the disquieting news brought by Jack. Their only thought was that Jack was back again!

Yet could a more serious event have been imagined? Savages were on the coast of New Switzerland! They knew now that the thin vapour seen by Mr. Wolston when the pinnace left the mouth of the Montrose River, and again when he was at the summit of the peak, was the smoke of an encampment pitched on that part of the island.

Jack was faint for want of food. He took his seat at the table with the others, and when he had recovered some of his strength he told the story of his adventures as follows:

"Forgive me, all of you, for the grief and anxiety I have caused you. I let my desire to capture a young elephant run away with me. I did not listen to Mr. Wolston or Ernest when they were calling me back, and it is only by a miracle that I have returned safe and sound! But my recklessness will have this one good result at least—it will enable us to organise a serious defence against these savages if they come as far as the Promised Land.

"Well, I plunged into the very thick of the pine forest after those elephants without any very clear idea, I must admit, of how I should manage to get hold of the smallest one. The father and mother went quietly along, breaking their way through the brushwood, and did not notice that I was following them. Of course I kept out of sight as much as possible, and I went along without its even occurring to me to ask in what direction they were taking me and Fawn, who was as mad as I was, or how I should find my way back! I continued for more than two hours, trying in vain to draw the baby elephant off on a side track.

"As a matter of fact, if I had tried to bring down the father and mother I don't know how many bullets I should have had to use before succeeding, and the only result might have been to infuriate the two brutes and turn them onto me!

"However, I went farther and farther into the heart of the pine forest, keeping no account of time or distance, or of the trouble I should have to join Mr. Wolston and Ernest again, and never thinking—I hope they will not be too angry with me for it—of the trouble I was putting them to if they were hurrying after me.

"I calculate that I must have gone a good five miles to the eastward in this way, and all for nothing. Then a realisation of the position came back to me. Perhaps I was wise after the event; but since the elephants showed no intention of stopping I thought that it would be best I should stop.

"It was about four o'clock. The forest was thinner around me; there were spaces between the trees, and some large clearings. And I think, by the way, that when we want to go to Jean Zermatt Peak it will be best to make straight for the south-east."

"Oh, yes, Ernest's letter told us—you gave it my name," said M. Zermatt.

"It was Mr. Wolston's suggestion that we should do that, papa," Ernest replied.

"Is it not natural, my friend," Mr. Wolston added, "that the highest point in New Switzerland should receive the name of the head of the house?"

"Jean Zermatt Peak, then, let it be," M. Zermatt replied, shaking Mr. Wolston by the hand; "but let Jack go on with his story and tell us about the savages."

"They are not very far off," said Jack.

"Not far off?" Mrs. Wolston exclaimed.

"In my story—in my story, I mean, Mamma dear, for in actual fact they must still be a good twenty-five miles away from Rock Castle."

This answer was somewhat reassuring, and Jack resumed his tale:

"I was in front of a pretty wide clearing in the pine forest then, and I was about to halt, quite determined not to go any farther, when the elephants stopped too. So I held in Fawn, who wanted to fly at them.

"Did it mean that that was the part of the forest where these creatures usually took shelter? There was a stream running between the high grass just

at that spot. My elephants—I felt they were mine!
—began to drink, sucking the water up through their
trunks.

"You will not be surprised to hear that when I saw
them standing still, suspecting nothing, my sporting
instincts got the upper hand of me again. An irresistible desire seized me to get the little one apart by
itself, after I had brought down the other two, even
if I had to spend my last cartridge. Besides, two
bullets might be enough, if they found the right spot,
and is there a hunter who does not believe in lucky
shots? As to how I was to capture the baby elephant
after I had killed its parents, and how I could lead
it to Rock Castle, I did not even give these questions
a thought. I cocked my gun, which was loaded with
ball cartridges. A double report rang out; but if
the elephants were hit they were not much hurt, it
would seem, for they merely shook their ears and
poured a final draught of water down their throats.

"They did not even turn around to see where the
shot came from, and did not bother themselves in
the least about Fawn's barking. Before I could fire
again, they started off once more, so fast this time,
almost as fast as a horse gallops, that I had to give
up all idea of following them.

"Just for a minute I saw their huge bulk among
the trees, above the brushwood, and their trunks
upraised breaking the low branches, and then they
vanished.

"It now became a question of deciding what direction I had better take. The sun was sinking rapidly,

and the pine forest would soon be wrapped in darkness. I knew that I ought to march towards the west, but there was nothing to show me whether that was to the left or the right. I had no pocket compass, and I have not that kind of sense of direction with which Ernest is gifted.

"Still, I thought I might be able to pick up some tracks of my journey, or rather of the elephants'. But the coming of night made it very difficult to do any tracking. Besides, there were any number of heavy footprints, all crossing one another. And what was more, I could hear some trumpeting in the distance, which made it seem pretty certain that it was along the banks of this stream that the herd of elephants assembled every evening.

"I knew that I should not succeed in finding my way back before sunrise, and even Fawn, in spite of his instinct, had no better idea where he was.

"For an hour I wandered about at random, not knowing whether I was getting nearer to the shore or farther away from it. I blamed myself for my recklessness, and the thought of Mr. Wolston and Ernest unable to make up their minds to abandon me and looking in vain for me was very worrying! It would be I who would have delayed their return to Rock Castle, and what would you be thinking about their delay? I thought of all the anxiety you would feel when we did not return within the time mentioned in Ernest's letter. And then there would be fresh toil and hardship for Mr. Wolston and Ernest, and for all that I was to blame."

"Yes, you were to blame, my boy," said M. Zermatt; "even if you did not think of yourself when you left them, you ought to have thought of them —and of us."

"That, of course," Mme. Zermatt answered, kissing her son; "he has been most reckless and imprudent; it might have cost him his life. But since he is here, we will forgive him."

"I come now," Jack went on, "to the part of my adventures where the situation became much worse.

"Up to that time, certainly, I had not run any very great danger. As I had my gun I was safe to be able to get food, even if it took me a week to find the way back to Rock Castle. Merely by following the coast I should have got there sooner or later. As for the wild beasts, which must be plentiful in that part of the island, I hoped if any attacked me to rout them.

"No; what troubled me was the thought of Mr. Wolston and Ernest losing heart as they looked in vain for my tracks. I thought they must have taken their way through this eastern part of the forest, which was not so dense as the rest. In the case, it was possible that they were not far from the spot where I had just stopped. The worst of it was that night was close at hand. So I thought it would be best to camp where I was, and light a fire. Mr. Wolston and Ernest might see it, and its lights would help to keep off the animals that were howling in the neighbourhood.

"But before lighting it I shouted several times, turning in every direction.

"There was no answer.

"There was the last resource of firing a few shots, and I did so twice.

"I heard no answering report.

"But I thought I could hear, on the right hand, a sort of sliding noise among the grass. I listened and was on the point of calling out when it suddenly occurred to me that it could not be Mr. Wolston or my brother coming from that side. They would have called to me, and we should have been in each other's arms before that.

"So it must mean that there were animals coming up, or perhaps a serpent.

"I had no time to assume the defensive. Four bodies rose up in the darkness—four human beings, not monkeys, as I thought at first! They sprang upon me, jabbering in a language which I could not understand. It was only too evident that I was dealing with savages!

"Savages on our island! In a moment I was thrown down, and I felt two knees pressing on my chest. Then they bound my hands and made me get up, took me by the shoulders and pushed me in front of them, and I had to walk at a rapid pace.

"One of the men had taken possession of my gun, another of my game-bag. It did not seem as if they had any design upon my life—not just then, at any rate.

"We went all night like that—in what direction

I could not discover. But I noticed that the forest was gradually getting clearer and clearer. The light of the moon reached right down to the ground, and I felt sure we were approaching the coast.

"I was not thinking much about myself, my dear people! I was thinking of you, and of the danger which the presence of these natives on our island involved! They would only have to go along the coast-line as far as the Montrose River and cross that to reach Cape East, and then come down again to Rock Castle! If they got there before the *Unicorn* got back, you would not be in force enough to beat them off!"

"But did you not say just now, Jack," M. Zermatt asked, "that these savages must be a long way away from the Promised Land?"

"Yes, Papa, twelve or fifteen miles south of the Montrose, and so about twenty-five miles from here."

"Well, in less than a fortnight, and perhaps in less than a week, the *Unicorn* will be lying in Deliverance Bay," M. Zermatt remarked, "and after that we shall have nothing to fear. But go on with your story."

So Jack proceeded:

"It was not until the morning, after a long march, without a single stop to rest, that we reached the cliffs commanding the shore.

"At the foot was an encampment of about a hundred of these ebony rascals—all of them men, half naked, squatting in the caves hollowed out at the bottom of the cliff. They were fishers—at least, so I imagined

—who must have been carried towards our island by the winds from the east, and their canoes were drawn up on the sand. They ran up to me, and looked at me with astonishment and curiosity, as if it were the first time they had seen a white man. But there is nothing surprising in that, since European ships hardly touch this part of the Indian Ocean.

"After they had examined me at very close quarters they resumed their habitual indifference. I was not ill-treated. They gave me a few broiled fish, which I ate hungrily, and I quenched my thirst with water from a stream which came down from the cliff.

"I had a great sense of satisfaction when I saw that my gun, which these savages did not know how to use, and my game-bag had been laid down at the foot of a rock. So I made up my mind to treat these blackamoors to a few shots, if an opportunity presented itself. But the situation was speedily altered by an unexpected event.

"About nine o'clock in the evening, in the outskirts of the forest which ran along the cliffs, there arose suddenly a tremendous uproar which immediately spread dismay among the natives. And you can imagine my surprise when I discovered that the uproar was caused by the arrival of a herd of elephants— thirty of them, at the very least—who were coming slowly along the bank of the stream towards the beach.

"Dismay? It was absolute panic! Evidently this was the first time the natives had found themselves in the presence of these huge animals—beasts with enormously long noses with a kind of hand at the tip!

"And when the elephants lifted their trunks and waved them about and twisted them all together, and all started trumpeting, there was a general stampede. Some scampered off across the rocks, and some tried to shove their canoes into the water, and the elephants looked on at the rout with fatuous amiability.

"I, for my part, merely saw my opportunity, and did not wait for anything more. I did not try to learn what would be the upshot of this meeting between the elephants and the natives, but ran to the cliff, went up the ravine and hurried into cover among the timber, where I found my good old Fawn waiting for me. I need not say that I had secured my gun and game-bag which would be priceless to me.

"I marched all that night and the next day, hunting for food, and only stopping to cook and eat my game, and after twenty-four hours I reached the right bank of the Montrose River, not far from the barrage.

"Then I knew where I was; and I went down to the stream up which papa and I had walked. I had the plains and woods to cross as I went towards the Green Valley, and I got there to-day, in the afternoon. I came through the defile of Cluse, and I cannot tell you, my dear parents, my dear friends, how dreadfully disappointed I should have been if you had started already to look for me along the coast—if I had not found you here at Rock Castle!"

Such was Jack's story.

Who were these natives? Where did they come from? Evidently from the western coast of Australia, the nearest coast, unless, indeed, there was a group of islands somewhere, as unknown as New Switzerland had been until the English corvette arrived. But if these savages were Australians, belonging to a race that is placed lowest in the human scale, it was difficult to explain how they had managed to accomplish a voyage of something like seven hundred and fifty miles in their canoes—unless, perhaps, they had been driven all that distance by bad weather.

And now they had met Jack, and knew that the island was inhabited by men of a race different from their own. What would they do? Would they put to sea in their canoes again, follow up the coast, and end by discovering Deliverance Bay and the dwelling-place of Rock Castle?

It could not be very long, it is true, before the *Unicorn* arrived. Her guns would be heard in another week; a fortnight at latest. And with her anchored within a few cable-lengths, there would be nothing to fear.

So it seemed that it was not a matter of immediate necessity to take precautions to meet an attack by the savages. Moreover, it was quite possible that in the panic caused by the sight of the elephants they had put to sea again. It seemed sufficient that the islanders should keep a watch on the sea opposite Rock Castle.

And so the next day work was begun again, and chiefly the work of completing the chapel.

All took part in this. It was desirable that it should be finished before the *Unicorn* arrived. The four walls had grown already to the height of the roof, and the apse was lighted by a circular bay. Mr. Wolston put in all the timber work, and it was roofed with bamboos which were proof against the heaviest rains. As to the interior of the chapel, Mme. Zermatt, Mrs. Wolston, and Hannah were to decorate it as was proper, and their taste could safely be relied upon.

All this employment continued until the 15th of October, the date fixed for the return of the *Unicorn*. The length of the voyage being taken into consideration, a variation of a week or a fortnight in the date would not be ground for any uneasiness.

The 19th came, and no report of guns had announced the corvette. So Jack mounted his onager and rode to Prospect Hill, and thence to False Hope Point.

He lost his labour. The sea was absolutely deserted as far as the farthest horizon.

He made the same excursion again on the 27th; again without result.

Then, as was not surprising, impatience began to give place to uneasiness.

"Come, come!" said M. Zermatt frequently, wishing to reassure his little company. "A fortnight, even three weeks, is not an alarming delay."

"Besides," Mr. Wolston added, "are we so sure

that the *Unicorn* could have left England at the date agreed upon?"

"But the Admiralty must have been anxious to take possession of the new colony," Mme. Zermatt remarked, rather ingenuously.

And Mr. Wolston smiled at the idea that the British Admiralty could ever be in a hurry to do anything!

But while they watched the sea in the direction of False Hope Point, they did not neglect to watch it, too, in the direction of Cape East. Several times a day the telescopes were levelled in the direction of Elephant Bay, as they called that part of the coast where the savages had camped.

As yet, however, no canoe had been seen. If the natives had not sailed away again, it seemed that they had decided not to leave their encampment. If, unhappily, they appeared beyond Cape East and came towards Deliverance Bay, it might prove possible to stop them by means of the battery on Shark's Island and the guns placed on the heights of Rock Castle. In any event, it was better to have to meet an attack by sea than one by land, and the greatest danger would be if the savages came from the interior of the island, after forcing the defile of Cluse.

As a matter of fact, an invasion by a hundred of these blacks and an assault by them on Rock Castle, in all probability could not be repulsed. It might perhaps be better on Shark's Island, where resistance could be maintained until the English corvette arrived.

And still the *Unicorn* did not arrive, and the end of October was approaching. Every morning M. Zermatt and Ernest and Jack expected to be awakened by the firing of guns. The weather was magnificent. The translucent haze on the horizon melted as the sun rose. Far as sight could travel over the open sea, all eyes sought the *Unicorn*.

On the 7th of November, all joined in an expedition to Prospect Hill. But no sail was passing out beyond the bay. In vain did all eyes scan the horizon to west, east, north! It was from the direction of False Hope Point that they looked for the realisation of their dearest hopes, from the direction of Cape East that disaster might come.

And so all stood in silence upon the summit of the hill, half in hope, half in fear.

END OF "THEIR ISLAND HOME"

[In "The Castaways of the *Flag*," which forms a sequel to this story, you can read how it was the *Unicorn* was delayed, what had happened to her passengers, and how the presence of savages on New Switzerland affected the Zermatts and the Wolstons.]

Lightning Source UK Ltd.
Milton Keynes UK
UKOW04f1440010714

234346UK00001B/16/P